MW00583456

CONSORT OF THORNS

THE WITCH'S CONSORTS #2

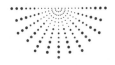

EVA CHASE

INK SPARK PRESS

Consort of Thorns

Book 2 in the Witch's Consorts series

First Digital Edition, 2018

Copyright © 2018 Eva Chase

Cover design: Cover Reveal Designs

Ebook ISBN: 978-1-989096-06-2

Paperback ISBN: 978-1-989096-09-3

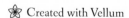 Created with Vellum

CHAPTER ONE

Rose

𝒲e'd locked the door to the small art gallery. Left the shade down over the window. Now the five guys and I were standing in a rough circle under the faint hum of the lights. For the first few seconds, there was no sound except the rumble of a car passing on the road outside.

One of the paintings on the white gallery walls drew my eyes. A new addition. At the upper right, a beam of golden yellow stood out against the swirls of reds and purples that filled the rest of the canvas. Joyous, and yet... The bits of fabric melded into the oil paints made the swirls look slightly erratic. Uneasy. As if they were still deciding whether to move toward the beam's warmth or away.

It was a perfect fit for the atmosphere in the room right now. My gaze came back to my guys. We were standing in a circle, sure, but it was obvious Gabriel was the focus of that circle. Everyone was looking to him.

He'd been gone for years, back for only a couple minutes, but already the old dynamics of our childhood friendships were falling back into place. He'd always been the leader, the one who bound our little group together. Seeing him standing there with that wry smile and a warm glint in his bright blue eyes, it was hard to imagine how we'd come—and held—together the last month without him.

A glow of happiness had lit me up from the moment he'd greeted me outside. But it was clear the other guys' feelings about Gabriel's arrival were a little more... complicated. I could read their hesitance in their stances, feel it like a faint jitter in the spark inside me that fueled my magic. The connection between me and them was so fresh and sharp right now, less than twenty-four hours after we'd bound ourselves together as consorts.

All of us *except* Gabriel, who had no idea what we'd done or been through since he'd been gone.

His dark red hair slanted across his forehead as he looked down at the torn page in his hand. The page I'd torn from my favorite childhood book and given to him the last time I'd seen him, nearly twelve years ago, when I was thirteen and he fourteen.

"It just feels like an ordinary piece of paper now," he said. "But I swear it pulled me here, like something was calling out to me from it." Gabriel raised his head to meet my eyes. "That was you, wasn't it, Rose?"

My voice caught in my throat for a second. The other guys knew all about my magic now, but only as of a couple days ago. Witching folk weren't meant to talk with the unsparked about what we were or what we could do. I'd never discussed it with the guys when we'd known each other as kids.

The four men around me had accepted that revelation, though. It hadn't even been that much of a revelation, with all the murmurs that passed through town about the Hallowell family and our estate. They'd all seen glimpses during our time together all those years ago. Even Gabriel must have had some clue back then. It shouldn't be hard to admit it.

"Yeah," I said. "I didn't know exactly how it would work but... A couple weeks ago, I tried to reach out. I actually thought it *hadn't* worked." I didn't know how to explain why I'd cast the spell. At the time when I'd performed it, in an attempt to call him back to town, our group had felt fragmented, uncertain. I'd thought we needed him to help us tackle the threats I was facing. But we'd found our feet without him, my four consorts and I.

I didn't think the guys who'd sworn their love and loyalty to me last night would appreciate hearing me say that I hadn't been sure they'd be enough.

Thankfully, Gabriel didn't ask. He nodded with his easy smile, not looking at all fazed by the idea that I could have drawn him to me through a scrap of paper. "Well, it did work. It just took me a little while getting here." He glanced around the circle. "And now the gang's all back together. It's been a long time."

"It has," Damon said. He stepped closer to me, his hand closing around mine, his gaze still fixed on Gabriel. His expression wasn't quite a glower, but he clearly had one ready. Which wasn't really a surprise. My lock-picking, leather-jacket-wearing consort might have agreed to bind himself to me alongside three other guys, but he wasn't exactly Mr. Amicable at the best of times.

He'd barely even been friendly to *me* when I'd moved back last month. The gentleness of his fingers clasping mine, despite the possessiveness of the gesture, reminded me of how far we'd come since then.

Gabriel didn't miss the implication of that gesture, of course. His eyebrows lifted. "And some of us are more 'together' than others?" he said, his tone light.

What would he think when he knew the whole truth of it? I wet my lips. "There's a lot more to it than that... A lot's happened in the last few weeks."

"Not that it's any of your business necessarily," Damon put in, his grip on my hand tightening.

Jin's lips twitched with a mischievous smile. "We've all been fairly... busy," my artist said, his gallery's lights glancing off the blue highlights in his black hair as he aimed that smile toward me.

By my other side, Seth shifted close enough to touch my back. Supporting me like he always did, his tall well-muscled frame and his steady composure making him as much a sentinel as a consort. "Rose has *been through* a lot," he said. "Maybe we should stick to other topics for now."

"Right!" Kyler said. Seth's slimmer and more upbeat twin shot a quick but affectionate glance at me and then grinned at Gabriel, his usual enthusiasm dancing in his gray-green eyes even though his posture looked a bit tense. "Where were you getting here from? Where've you been since you left town? It's been, what, four years now?"

Gabriel took it all in—Jin's smile, Seth's touch, Kyler's glance, Damon's hand still wrapped around mine—and a flicker of surprise crossed his face. Only for an instant, there and then returning to his usual relaxed expression, but I caught it anyway. He eased back half a step, as if he'd sensed he might be more of an intruder in our group than he ever should have been. My heart wrenched.

I gave Damon's fingers a squeeze and let go. "Before we get into that," I said, crossing the middle of our shifting circle, "I don't think I've said hello properly yet."

I opened my arms, and Gabriel accepted my embrace. He hugged me back a little more carefully than I would have liked, but I could understand that. Hugging him now was a lot different than hugging the much younger Gabriel who'd tried to comfort me when I'd realized our time was running out all those years ago. Well, he smelled the same as in my memories, somehow sweet and dark like forest moss at the same time, but he'd grown a few inches and put on a fair bit of muscle. There was no mistaking that I was embracing a man, not a boy.

"I'm glad you're here, even if it took a little while," I said, stepping back. "It didn't feel totally right being back on the estate without you here."

Gabriel's smile went a little crooked. "What really wasn't right was *you* not being here. It's good to see you survived all that time shut away in the city, Sprout."

The childhood nickname and the tenderness with which he said it made my pulse flutter. That nickname had stuck as soon as I'd told him my real name, back when he'd first drawn me into the group of boys who'd roamed my family's estate while their parents worked for mine. *Found her sprouting up outside the manor,* he'd told the others with a grin. And just like that, I'd been one of them.

Until six years later, when my new stepmother had discovered how much time I'd been spending with a bunch of unsparked boys and had convinced my father to move us all to Portland to keep me away from them. And left even more chaos in her wake. I'd only found out after we'd moved back that all the guys' parents had been let go from the staff right after.

Gabriel's dad had been the most unforgiveable of those firings. The Lordes had looked after our garage all the way back to when it'd been a stable. Three generations of service thrown away because I'd gone rambling through the woods with his son. And from what the guys had told me, it had hit Mr. Lorde hard. He'd fallen into a depression and then committed suicide.

Was it any wonder Gabriel had wanted to get away from this place? And now I'd pulled him back here without even asking what *he* wanted.

But I couldn't help wishing he'd been here from the start. Everything would have been so much simpler than it was now.

"I heard about your dad," I said, my throat tight. "I'm so sorry. I had no idea about the lay-offs or any of it."

Gabriel shrugged with a rough chuckle, but his gaze darted away from me for a second. "Of course you didn't. I never thought you did. None of that is your fault, Rose. You know that, right?"

He looked at me again, so directly and insistently then that I knew he meant it.

"It was still wrong," I said.

"Well, it's done now, and we all made what we could of the hand we were dealt." He nodded to Kyler. "Since you asked about where I've been—I made it all the way to Argentina. Backpacked around South America for a while. Then came back up and spent a few months here and there, trying places on for size. I was in California just before I came back here."

"Argentina!" Jin said, interest sparking in his dark brown eyes. He was the only other of the guys who'd spent much time out of town. His dad worked as a back-up bassist for various bands and had taken Jin along on at least one world tour, where he'd picked up the inspiration for a few of the paintings hanging on the gallery walls around us. "I haven't been down that way yet. I hear the atmosphere is amazing."

"It got pretty wild," Gabriel said, any tension that had come into his stance when I'd mentioned his dad melting away. "You'd have been blown away by the public art there. Some of those murals—the whole side of a building —I wish I was more of a photographer so I could show you, not that it's the same as standing right there in front of the painting." He glanced around. "Some of the work in here is yours, isn't it? With stuff like that, you'd fit right in down there."

He pointed at the painting I'd been eyeing earlier, and Jin beamed. Trust Gabriel to be able to identify the other guy's style, even years after they'd last spoken.

"Hey," Ky said, snapping his fingers. "Isn't it

Argentina where the political parties have their own beers?"

Gabriel laughed. "Trust you to remember the most random facts. I tried a couple of those. Can't say they're the best I've ever had, but I'd hate to see what our politicians would come up with here."

Damon let out a snort. "God, can you imagine?" he said. He raked a hand through his jagged coffee-brown hair, his stance still wary as he gave Gabriel a more thoughtful appraisal. "How'd you make ends meet, wandering around like that?"

"Oh, you know, a little of this, a little of that," Gabriel said. "There's always some dive looking for an extra server or a mechanic place that's happy to throw me a few bucks if I lend a hand. It wasn't the high life, but I wasn't tied down anywhere."

"There's something to be said for that," Damon said. He looked a little awed despite himself.

"I'd take the security of knowing I've got someplace to come home to, no matter what," Seth said mildly.

Gabriel tipped his head. "It can get a little tiring, always being on the go. I can't say anywhere ever felt like home—not the way this town does."

He paused, and Seth's mouth slanted in sympathy. And just like that, in the space of a few minutes, Gabriel had drawn us all back in again, as if we couldn't ever possibly fit together properly without him in our midst.

Except we had. Last night... Heat rose in my face at the memory. My magic danced in my chest.

How did he fit in with us now, when the other guys

and I were bound, hearts and bodies, in a way completely separate from him?

"Are you going to stay, then?" I asked. "In town?"

Gabriel brought his attention back to me. A shadow passed through his eyes. "I was waiting to see what I'd find here before I made any decisions. From what Seth said, it sounds like your homecoming hasn't been all that smooth. You called out to me; I'm here. If you need me."

The last four words held a question. *Did* I need him?

I had four consorts, and through them I had my magic. Last night, after the five of us had sealed those bonds, I'd confronted my stepmother about the plot she'd formed with my supposed fiancé to allow him to control my magic. To turn me into all but a slave, wracked with pain unless I followed their demands.

I'd sent her off, forbidden from saying anything about what had happened there. Her, I no longer had to worry about. But that confrontation should have ended with me bringing both her and Derek to my father, so we could see them brought to justice by the Witching Assembly. The problem was, when I'd threatened to do it, Celestine had laughed and told me my father had arranged the whole plot himself.

Maybe she'd been lying. Maybe she'd just wanted to make me doubt him. But she'd seemed so sure... and so *scared* of him finding out she'd failed.

He'd be back from his business trip today. Soon. And who knew what would happen when he found her gone? I wanted to think I had nothing left to worry about, but I wasn't sure.

After everything I'd been through to keep my

freedom, I *needed* to be sure. And if it turned out that my own father was a threat to that freedom too, then yes, I was going to need all the help I could get. Dad didn't have magic of his own, but he had powerful friends. If he was capable of treating me, his only daughter, like that, I had no idea what else he might be capable of or how far he'd go to ensure my silence.

"I don't know yet," I said. "But I... I might." I turned to the other guys. My consorts. The thought sent a wash of pleased warmth through my chest despite the bad news I'd come with. I'd hoped to spend an hour or two just enjoying their company—in all sorts of ways—before we came to this part of our reunion. But here we were.

"Gabriel needs to know at least some of what's happened," I said. He'd come. He'd proven he was here for me. The least I could do was trust him. "I can't ask him to stay and help while keeping him in the dark. And... there's more that I haven't had a chance to tell the rest of you yet either."

Seth drew his spine even straighter as if he thought he'd have to defend me right this instant. "What happened?" he said, frowning.

"Well, I guess I'd better start at the beginning." I took a deep breath and looked at Gabriel. "I could call out to you because I'm a witch. But to properly kindle my magic, I needed a consort before I turned twenty-five..."

CHAPTER TWO

Rose

"This Gabriel fellow seems like a charming addition to your group of suitors," Philomena said as we ambled along the gravel shoulder of the road between the town and the Hallowell estate. She twirled her little umbrella, which only shaded part of her face from the glaring sun. But then, even in her long-sleeved dress with its multiple layers of skirts, Phil never got hot. That was one benefit to being imaginary.

Me, I was sweating in my thin sundress. But it was only partly because of the heat. Telling Gabriel pretty much every secret I had and telling the other guys that my ordeal might not be over yet hadn't been the most relaxing experience of my life. At least Gabriel hadn't seemed too shocked. And I'd known my consorts would stand by me. The hard part was knowing how little they could do when even I wasn't sure how to deal with my father.

He'd be home any minute now. That was why I'd headed back. At least I had my best friend for company. Another benefit to her being an imaginary construct—the spunky heroine from my favorite book, a playfully steamy historical romance—was that she could turn up whenever and wherever I needed her.

And sometimes when I really didn't, too. I'd gotten so in the habit of picturing her during those lonely years in Portland that nowadays Philomena seemed to come and go by her own will. So it was a good thing I usually enjoyed her company.

"I don't know if you can call the other guys 'suitors' when they've already dedicated themselves to me," I pointed out, kicking at a bit of gravel. It rattled across the road. "The consorting ceremony is more binding than any marriage you've ever agreed to."

"Point taken," Phil said. She nudged me with her elbow. "Are you planning on doing any consorting with this new one?"

She smirked at me, and I resisted the urge to stick out my tongue at her. I was going to be twenty-five in two months. I should probably get in the habit of acting like it.

"I don't know," I said. "I didn't even know for sure I could take more than one consort at the same time until we completed the ceremony last night. I suppose... if that worked, it should be possible to add another one."

"Mmhm?"

I shot her a firm look. "Speaking on a theoretical level. Gabriel's only just gotten back. I've got to get to know him again. He hardly knows *me* anymore. And after all the history between our families now..."

Gabriel had said he didn't blame me, and he'd sounded like he meant it, but the tragedy that had started with his father's firing had obviously affected him a lot. He'd gone wandering all across two continents just to get away from this place. And now he was stuck crashing on Jin's couch while he waited for me to figure out if I'd called him here for any good reason...

I should have been able to offer him better than that.

"Who knows if either of us would even want to?" I finished. "Or if the other guys would be okay with it? They're my first priority."

"Hmm. Yes. Four husbands is rather a lot in itself." Phil snuck a peek at me with her eyelids lowered coyly. "Although I'm sure it makes consummating that marriage so much more fun."

Damn, now I was blushing again. "Don't start about that. I need to be composed right now. I don't even know how I'm going to talk to my father."

Philomena's cheer faded. "Yes. That is quite the conundrum. I certainly wouldn't have put it past your stepmother to have been lying to save her skin, you know. I've never seen any reason to complain about your father other than his choice in second wife."

"Neither have I," I said. "But he *did* choose her. And the wording in her contract did allow for him to call the shots as much as her. Why would she have included that if she was doing it behind his back?"

"To displace blame if the contract were found?" Phil

suggested. "She could clearly think plenty of steps ahead of the present."

"I know. I've got no idea what to think." I rubbed my arms, suddenly chilled despite the heat. Even the sweet scent of fresh-grown grass and wildflowers drifting over the fields wasn't enough to settle my nerves. "He's always been there for me. Even when he made us move to the city, I could tell it was because he felt it was best for me. He felt like *he'd* failed me. I'm his only child."

And if what my stepmother had said was true, then he'd been willing to chain my magic up so I could only use it with the permission of the consort they had chosen. So I'd be in agony if I tried to use it for myself. And the consort they'd chosen, my supposed fiancé Derek, had cheated on me with one of the girls from the cleaning staff and spoken about me with such disdain... Not that he was aware I knew about that yet. I'd only gotten ahead of their scheme by keeping my cards close.

How could Dad want such a horrible future for me?

Celestine had been able to explain away that too. *He does love you, in his own way.* She'd said he hadn't wanted to be a party to the actual binding of my magic, but that he'd felt he needed to see it done because of how much power I would wield once my spark was kindled.

I looked down at my hands. The flame of my spark, still so brightly lit by my four consorts in spite of all the magic I'd expended last night confronting my stepmother, tingled through my chest. I *had* drawn a lot of power through these hands, from this body. But why should Dad be afraid of that? It wasn't as if I'd ever shown any inclination to hurt people.

Celestine's words had poisoned all my thoughts about him. I needed to set her insinuations aside and make my own judgments from what I could see with my own eyes. In the meantime, no one except for my guys could know about the magic I already held. Most—or maybe all—of the witching people I knew wouldn't even have believed I could have kindled my spark with the devotion of any unsparked man, let alone four of them.

It was a beautiful little secret for now.

"Can't you simply confront him like you did your stepmother?" Philomena asked. "If he shows some maliciousness, you can treat him to the same response."

"If he really has been acting against me, he could pretend to be horrified and then call in a witching friend to subdue me somehow," I said. "And even if he wasn't a good enough actor for that, it's not going to escape the Assembly's notice if he disappears from public life and work too. They'll come investigate me. What I did to Celestine wasn't legal. Without proof of Dad's treachery... it could be me who ends up facing retribution. I need proof, and I need to get it without tipping my hand to him, unless I decide I can trust him."

My pulse thumped faster as I came into view of the estate's stone wall and caught sight of a car parked just beyond the tall wrought-iron gate. Porters were hustling from it to the big old manor house, one of them carrying Dad's suitcase and another a large packing box. Dad had a habit of buying up local delicacies whenever he went on a business trip for our cooking staff to experiment with. "Bringing a little of the world back home to my family," he liked to say.

When I pushed past the gate, my heart flipped right over. He was standing there by the other side of the car, bending over to retrieve something from the back seat. I took a couple steps toward him, and then my legs locked.

Dad straightened up and saw me immediately. His usual warm smile split his face. Nothing about him had changed. He had the same silver-flecked chestnut hair, the same gentle hazel eyes, the same square jaw as when he'd left.

But when he'd left I'd been sure of who he was, and now I didn't know how to be sure of much of anything. Even if he hadn't been a party to my stepmother's scheming, he might not be enthusiastic about my choice in consorts. After all, he'd had some hand in dismissing their parents so callously. I had to tread carefully, for my guys' sakes as much as mine.

I made myself walk forward to meet him. "Dad!"

"My lamb, there you are." He opened his arms for a hug, and I had to return it. I wrapped my arms around him just for a second. The familiar, soothing smell of his lemony aftershave washed over me, and my throat choked up. Suddenly I felt very old and very young all at the same time.

The solid corner of something in his hand bumped my back. I glanced down as I pulled away. "What's that?"

Dad held up the case, well-worn wood with tarnished silver sealing the edges. "An artifact I picked up in my touring around Cairo. More of a curiosity than anything practical, but valuable enough that I didn't want to leave it to the staff to handle."

He popped the clasp and opened the lid. Inside the

case lay an object I could only describe as a wand, as long as my forearm and half as thick. It was made of a wood so dark I could barely make out the grain, polished to a soft shine. An intricate gold-plated design circled its body in rings all up its length, and gemstones gleamed where they were embedded in the spaces between: brilliant green emeralds and deep blue lapis lazuli.

Despite myself, my breath caught with awe. "Wow. That's beautiful." And it had at least once been very powerful. The gold designs included witching glyphs for strength, energy, amplification, and aim. I curled my fingers where Dad couldn't see, sending a testing feeler of my own power toward the wand. No answering magic responded.

"Long since sapped of any spells it used to hold," Dad said, confirming what I'd just sensed. "Too dangerous to keep in the house otherwise, I'd imagine. But it makes a remarkable souvenir as it is, don't you think?"

"Definitely."

He closed the case, tucked it under his arm, and glanced around. "Is your stepmother out?"

Right. He'd have expected her to come out to meet him if she'd been here. My chest clenched for a second before I recovered my tongue. "I'm not sure. I haven't seen her since last night."

"Lyle," Dad called to the porter who'd just re-emerged from the house. "Is Lady Hallowell around?"

The scrawny guy halted. "I can go ask after her, sir."

"Please do," Dad said. He closed the car door, and one of our security guards crossed the yard to meet us.

"Lady Hallowell hasn't been on the premises today,

Mr. Hallowell," he said. "I'm the one who checked the security cam over the gate this morning. Her Jag pulled out around one in the morning. I assumed she had a trip, an early morning flight to catch."

Dad blinked, his forehead furrowing. He fished his phone out of his pocket, presumably to check to see if Celestine had left him any message about an unexpected trip. Of course, he didn't find any. The spell I'd placed on her prevented her from communicating to or about him or me in any way.

He tapped to dial her number and raised the phone to his ear with a frown. I wavered, watching him. If what Celestine had said was true, he'd been counting on her to see through my consorting, with all the additional twists she'd added. But how could I tell the difference between distress over losing his accomplice and the distress any man would show on discovering his wife and consort had vanished?

She didn't answer. He lowered his hand, his face so shadowed with confusion the sight sent an ache through my chest.

I hadn't wanted to handle Celestine's crimes this way. I'd wanted to bring her and Derek to Dad, to reveal everything to him. But that would only have worked if he wasn't a party to those crimes.

"You didn't expect her to leave?" I said, playing ignorant still. "She didn't mention anything about catching a flight to me."

Dad shook his head. He started toward the house. "It's very strange. Perhaps Meredith will know? What's she busy with today?"

The ache deepened. Spark help me, he didn't even know that much. Normally our estate manager *would* have been busy with more projects than I could count, but Celestine had fired Meredith, the low-standing witch who'd looked after our property and my family since my father was a child, practically the moment he'd left. Because she'd seen me turning to the other woman for support, I had to think.

I could tell Dad the truth about that. "She's gone too. Celestine let her go the day after you left. She said Meredith wasn't a good fit for the family anymore. I tried to talk to her, but it was already done—Meredith had left... Celestine didn't want to discuss it further."

Dad halted at the base of the broad front steps and stared at me. "Why on earth would she do that? Did Meredith overstep somehow?"

I clasped my hands in front of me. He did look honestly distressed about Meredith, at least. "I don't know. Not that I saw. I mean, they never got along *that* well, but it all seemed the same as usual."

The furrow on Dad's brow deepened. He pulled out his phone again, striding on into the house. Then he stopped. My former fiancé—who as far as he or Dad knew was still my fiancé—was ambling down the hall to meet us.

Derek paused as he took in my father's expression. Concern crossed his own face—a face I might have called softly handsome before I'd known what a lying snake of a man he was.

"It's good to have you back, Maxim," he said. "Is everything all right?"

He could probably guess. He'd been asking *me* where my stepmother had disappeared to just a few hours ago. Worried about how his co-conspirator's disappearance might affect him, no doubt. I hoped he'd done plenty of squirming.

He wasn't talking to Dad as if my father were a fellow conspirator too, but then, I was standing here.

"I've been informed that Celestine left the estate late last night," Dad said, glancing around the hall as if it might offer some clue. "I don't suppose she mentioned to you where she might have been going?"

Derek held his stance steady, but a little of the color left his face. Oh, yes, let him be imagining how deep a shithole he might have gotten himself stuck in.

"I'm afraid not," he said.

Dad rubbed a hand over his face. "All right," he said. "I'm sure it's nothing serious. I'll sort it out."

No, you won't, I thought, my fingers twisting tighter around each other. No one would ever know why Celestine had left until I let them.

The thought brought a jab of uneasiness—and then a rising tickle of confidence. For the first time, I was the only one in this house with magic. Even if the two men in front of me didn't know it, I held the power here now.

CHAPTER THREE

Damon

*I*t's kind of pathetic how easily you can fall back into old habits. A few days spent hanging out with the old group, and I found myself wandering from Jin's house back through town next to the twins, crossing the town square with our shoes smacking the cobblestones, the mid-afternoon sun searing our heads. You'd almost have thought we were back to being friends. As if I wasn't just tolerating their presence in Rose's life because I had to.

Because Lord knew if she'd be better off with me keeping her all to myself, I sure as hell would have.

Everything with Rose was good, though. The high from last night, the intensity of that crazy ceremony, was still racing through my nerves, as if I had some kind of magic in me too. Maybe I did—a little of hers. I'd felt it when she'd sworn herself to me, when I'd sworn my love back to her.

I loved her. I loved Rose Hallowell. And she loved me. I could put up with an awful lot, knowing that.

Even Mr. Brainiac's inane rambling.

"I should have asked Gabriel if he ever checked out Whaley House," Kyler was saying to his brother. "That's in California—San Diego. From what I've heard it's supposed to be the most haunted place in the country."

"Since when have you been researching hauntings?" Seth said, sounding about as bemused as that humorless guy ever got.

"Oh, I don't know, something caught my interest a few years back and I did a little reading." Kyler shook his head dismissively, his light brown curls jostling together. Almost a year older than me, but sometimes he still sounded like that overeager kid he'd been all those years ago when we had actually been friends. "It could come in handy. If magic and witches are real, who's to say ghosts aren't?"

"Hey," Seth said, abruptly serious again. "You shouldn't talk about that out here." His gaze scanned the square. On a weekday at this time, there was no one around except a few tourists snapping pics of the big fountain in the middle. Kyler hadn't even been that loud. Trust Seth to worry anyway.

They weren't really talking to me, were they? We'd fallen in together as we'd left, but maybe they were only tolerating my presence too. It wasn't as if we had a whole lot in common these days. *Their* parents had gotten through just fine after Rose's stepmother had kicked them to the curb. They hadn't had to watch their mom get beaten down just trying to support them.

My dad? Fuck if I knew where he'd been for the last thirteen years. He started hooking up with some chick from the kitchen staff, ran off with her, and not a peep from him since. Lucky him. He missed getting fired by about ten months.

Kyler lowered his voice even more. "It's amazing that Rose managed to call to him all the way out in California, though, isn't it?"

I made a scoffing sound. "Yeah, real great work on his part, showing up after we'd already handled the problem."

Seth frowned at me. "She'll have an even bigger problem if she can't trust her dad either."

"So what? We'll deal with it like we helped her with her stepmom. *We're* her consorts. I don't think being well-traveled has anything on that." Even if those travels had possibly struck me with a tiny twinge of envy.

Kyler dug his hands into the pockets of his khakis. "You know if he'd been here from the start, he'd be a consort too."

Of course I did. Of course he would have been. But the way Kyler said it, like an unshakeable statement of fact, set my teeth on edge. "Well, he wasn't here, was he? And we were. That's what's important. He can't just ride in on that fucking motorcycle"—of course, of course Gabriel also had to have the sweetest bike I'd ever seen —"and take over everything."

"I don't know," Kyler said. "I think what's important is what Rose decides she wants."

I bit back a grimace. "I think what Rose wants is not to have to worry about any assholes trying to steal control over her magic." My gaze caught on a stout figure hurrying past the shops around the edge of the square. "Speaking of assholes..."

The other guys followed my glance. The barrel-chested man with the egg-shaped head and thinning white hair I'd indicated wasn't anyone we'd have paid much attention to a month ago. He'd have just been Mr. Cortland, that old dude who lived on the outskirts of town. But he was one of Rose's witching people. He'd been helping her stepmother figure out how to bend the consorting spell into a vicious trap. We'd broken into his house to get proof while he was out of town. Apparently he was back.

Kyler's gaze twitched away. "Rose said he'd know we were digging into his things."

More than digging in. When we'd tried to run off with the notebook he'd been recording his awful research in, the damned thing had burst into flames on the doorstep.

"Not us specifically," Seth said, but he'd pulled his eyes away too. "Just *someone*."

"I hope he's scared," I muttered. Mr. Cortland ducked into the fruit market. I cocked my head, considering. "I wonder what he knows about Rose's dad and how much he was calling the shots?"

"We didn't find anything about that in his house," Seth said.

"So maybe we need to mess with *him*."

Seth stopped in his tracks. "Are you crazy?"

I glared at him. "No. I'm just saying—what's he going to do? From what Rose said, he doesn't have any magic. Scare him a little more, maybe he'll cough something up."

"Rose *also* said that she needs to keep pretending everything is normal, or she could be in even more trouble. If her dad is in on it and he finds out she's onto him before she has a way to turn him in—"

"Calm down," I said, holding up my hands. "I'm not going to tell him anything. I was only thinking about what he could tell us."

"I agree with Seth," Kyler put in. "Unless Rose says she thinks it's a good idea, we should leave him alone."

I rolled my eyes, but I should have known better than to think these dopes were going to appreciate my suggestion. Great for them that they'd had a life where they'd always been able to play it safe. Sometimes to get things done, to save yourself or the people you cared about, you had to get your hands dirty.

"Damon?" Seth said, a warning in his voice.

I waved him off. "I heard you, I heard you. Forget I said anything."

He still looked concerned, but he started walking again.

After a couple blocks, we had to go different ways. Kyler raised his hand to me, and I shrugged back. "Don't do anything stupid," Seth said. I didn't bother responding to that at all.

I ambled on another block, just in case they came back after me for some reason. Then I veered down a side street and jogged back to the square.

Maybe the other guys were too afraid to play hardball

on Rose's behalf, but that was fine. That was why she
had me.

My determination wavered when I reached the fruit
market and couldn't see Cortland anywhere. Where the
hell had that asshole gotten to? I meandered across the
square like I was just stretching my legs.

There he was. Coming out of the cheese shop,
heading for the bakery. He must be stocking up his
kitchen after that holiday.

Time for me to do a little stocking up too. Seth and
his patronizing worries. I wasn't even going to talk to the
guy. How could he ever connect a random bit of theft
to Rose?

I didn't follow him into the bakery. Too small a space,
too likely he'd notice me. But after the bakery, I trailed
after him to the general grocery store, where I'd figured
he'd head next. The supermarket was small-town-sized
but still had a few aisles to disappear around and usually
at least a handful of shoppers any time of day.

The old light panels buzzed overhead as I stepped in.
The freezers along the one wall were old too—you could
smell the Freon leaking. It made my nose itch.

I sidled past Cortland when he stopped to
contemplate the cereal boxes. My hand darted out and
eased his phone from his back pocket in one quick,
practiced movement. 17-year-old me had gotten me and
Mom through more than one financial squeeze with that
trick. I shoved it up my sleeve and ambled right back out,
grinning with my victory.

CHAPTER FOUR

Rose

I hesitated outside the door to Dad's office a little longer than would have looked normal to anyone who happened to come by. Thankfully, the only person who appeared was Philomena, with a fan she twitched by her face.

"Off to confront the old man?" she said.

"Might as well get it over with. Either I find proof he's guilty and turn him in, or I prove it to myself that he's not and turn *to* him. Here's hoping it's the latter."

I raised my hand and knocked.

"Come in," Dad said right away, but he sounded a bit weary. I eased the door open and stepped inside, closing it behind me. Phil didn't follow.

Spark take me, it was hard to keep caution at the front of my mind faced with a scene like this. Dad was sitting at his big mahogany desk in a familiar pose, his elbows propped on the gleaming surface. The mingled scents of polished wood and black licorice candy hung in the air. It could have been any night, any time in the past when I hadn't had all these worries nagging at me, except for the graver than usual look on his face when he turned to me.

He had his jar of those licorice candies sitting on the corner of the desk next to him. He always liked to chew on them when he was thinking through a problem—and he'd had a lot to think about today. He'd come down for dinner a couple hours ago, but he'd eaten quickly without saying much.

"Hey," I said. "Still no news?"

He shook his head. "I haven't heard anything from Celestine. I checked in with your stepsisters and her parents, and she hasn't been in touch with them either."

Celestine would still have a reserve of magic from her time with Dad. They'd been consorted long enough that she could sever the bond with minimal discomfort if she needed to feed her spark through intimacy with other partners. She could hide for a long time. It would be better for her to hide while my magic prevented her from explaining anything about why she'd left Dad.

Especially if she really was as scared of him as she'd seemed to be last night.

"I'm sorry," I said, but that last thought made my stomach clench. My gaze drifted to Dad's printer with its sheaf of paper—the same paper the contract between Celestine and Derek had been written on. She'd claimed she and my former fiancé had agreed to manipulate my magic right here in this office. On Dad's request.

I should search the office the next moment I had a chance. It didn't seem likely Dad would have left evidence just lying around, but I had to try, at least.

"She was acting a little strangely after you left," I ventured. "The way she fired Meredith so suddenly. She kept to herself almost the whole time—I thought maybe she was preparing something for the wedding or the ceremony..."

I kept my tone innocent, but I watched Dad's expression carefully. If he knew what Celestine had been supposed to be preparing for my consort ceremony, he'd have to show *some* reaction at the thought that I might suspect, wouldn't he?

His eyebrows drew together. "Did she say anything that sounded strange?" he asked.

That was a perfectly reasonable question even if he was just trying to figure out what had happened to his wife. Could I push a little further?

"Well, the thing about Meredith not being a good fit for the household. That didn't make much sense." I paused as if trying to remember. There might be another way to prod without giving away anything I knew. "I saw her going in and out of her private magicking room a few times. Maybe she left something in there that would give you an idea where she went. We could open it up and look through her things."

Which would be the last thing he'd want me to help with if he thought she might have left anything incriminating in there.

Dad just nodded as if he thought my suggestion was a good idea. A little of the tension in me relaxed.

"I talked to Meredith as well," he said. "She couldn't shed any light on the situation, but sadly she made it clear she didn't feel comfortable returning, either. I don't know..." He sighed. "I'll have to bring in a new manager, someone who can manage the magical wards so we can get access. If your stepmother hasn't returned by then."

The small hopeful note in his voice made guilt pinch my stomach. But if he *didn't* know what Celestine had been doing, he was so much better off without her. I just wished I could already be sure enough to tell him that.

Dad pushed back his leather chair and turned it to face me, his attention and his hazel eyes settling more completely on me. "You came to talk to me. Was there something else on your mind, Rose?"

Maybe this wasn't the best time to bring up this subject. But it was both another test of sorts, and a necessary progression. Even in the best possible case, I was going to need to ease Dad into the idea of my unsparked childhood friends being back in my life.

"Nothing as serious as Celestine being missing," I said. "I just... When I was in town today, I ran into Gabriel Lorde."

The corner of Dad's mouth twitched. "Yes? How is he these days?"

"Well... If you ask him he'll say he's fine, but—I know you, or Celestine, let go of his dad right after we left the estate. The gossip around town is that Mr. Lorde committed suicide."

Dad's mouth twitched again, this time definitely downward. I had the feeling he'd already known that—known it and had regrets.

"If that's the case, it's very unfortunate," he said, his tone subdued.

"Yes. Especially—" I reined in my temper before it could slip out. Whatever else he had or hadn't done since, I was still angry with Dad about how he'd treated my guys' parents. Even if Celestine had orchestrated the firings, he could have made it up to them somehow. "He didn't deserve to be fired. You always said how glad you were to have him on staff, how well he took care of the more temperamental cars... He didn't do anything wrong. None of us, really, did anything wrong."

I met Dad's gaze steadily. He sighed again and rubbed his jaw. "No," he said. "You didn't. You know why we moved, and I still think that was for the best, but... Decisions were made back then that might have been too hasty and weren't easily taken back. I can admit that."

He wasn't saying who had made all those decisions, whether some of them had been Celestine's. Was he still trying to protect her from my dislike? The Spark knew that ship had sailed ages ago.

But we could have that conversation another time. Right now I was more concerned with what he did next.

"Then maybe you can admit that we owe Gabriel a hand up?" I said. "I think he needs it. From what he said, he's been traveling around a lot, and now he's just crashing on a friend's couch. He still sees this town as home, but it's not like there are tons of jobs in a place this small."

To my surprise, Dad followed my train of thought immediately. He gave me an evaluating look, but his voice was calm. "You're suggesting I offer him work."

I spread my hands. "I thought maybe he could take a look at the old Cadillac you've always been saying you'd like to get running again. He learned a lot from his dad, you know. *If* he wants to work for us again. I didn't say anything about that to him without talking to you first, of course."

"I'm glad to hear that," Dad said. I still couldn't quite read his tone. I tucked my hands behind my back, my fingers poised to form a quick magicking. Just an impression of positive feeling to relax him if he started to look worried about my personal investment in Gabriel. It was a spell I'd been taught for use if someone was injured or with a child having a tantrum, but it could work for a case like this too. Because I wasn't done yet.

"I noticed the current garage manager isn't using the apartment up top," I barreled on. "Matt goes back to his house in town at the end of the day. It might be good to have a driver on the premises overnight—we didn't need that in the city, but out here in the country…"

Dad let out a bark of a sound. I tensed up before I realized it was a laugh. "You've thought of everything, haven't you, lamb?" he said, an amused gleam coming into his eyes. "Are you sure he'll appreciate the offer? I remember what he was like as a boy. I got the impression he had a fair bit of pride."

He was considering it. He didn't sound concerned at all. Maybe I was the one who needed that calming spell.

I let out a slow breath and smiled without having to force it. "It can't hurt to ask. And to make all the necessary apologies at the same time?"

Dad's good humor dimmed. "Yes," he said. "There's that. All right. You find out how I can best reach out to him, and he and I will have a talk. I have been wanting to get that damned Cadillac running again."

I couldn't have asked for that to go better. "I will," I said. "Thank you."

I turned to go, but Dad's voice stopped me.

"Rose."

I glanced back. "Yes?"

He gave me a smile that looked a little sad. "I don't think I need to remind you of this, but I'd feel remiss if I didn't. You know it's better if you and Gabriel don't renew your friendship. Strictly professional is always the best policy with the unsparked. It simply makes our lives —and theirs—so much less complicated."

My pulse hiccupped. So he still felt that way even now, did he?

When I was twenty-five, when I could claim this estate as mine with more authority than Dad, he couldn't stop me from associating with whoever I liked. But for now, I didn't want to challenge him too overtly. He could retract the job offer, fire Gabriel if he thought we were acting too close later on. I had a couple of months to change his mind, and if he wasn't seeing things differently by my birthday, it wouldn't matter anymore.

I bobbed my head, keeping my expression as mild as I could. "I know, Dad."

My jaw tightened as I stepped out of the office. One small victory, but I still had so much farther to go. If he'd had any idea just how complicated and intertwined with unsparked guys my life had already become...

The last guy I wanted intertwined in my life chose that moment to enter the hall. Derek glanced me over and ambled closer.

"Worried about your stepmother?" he said.

Ha. I just wouldn't answer that question. "No one knows where she is," I said.

He touched my side, with a sly smile that made my skin crawl. "While there isn't anything we can do... perhaps we could find some way to distract you."

My spine stiffened. Oh, no. I might not be ready to tell Dad what I knew about my former fiancé, but there was no reason I had to play along when Dad wasn't watching.

I pulled away from Derek's touch, letting my tone go frigid. "No, thank you. I'd prefer to turn to my books for that."

Derek blinked. He opened his mouth, but I was already striding into my bedroom.

My heart thumped as I closed the door behind me. I didn't really want to be in here. Not with all these people I couldn't really talk to, couldn't really trust.

Swallowing thickly, I pulled the prepaid phone Kyler had gotten for me a few weeks ago out from its hiding spot behind the loose baseboard on one of my built-in bookcases. For a moment, I just sat there in the armchair I usually used for reading, gazing at it blankly.

"Are you not sure what to say?" Philomena asked, leaning over the chair.

"Not sure who to say it to." But the moment I said that, I knew exactly who I needed.

CHAPTER FIVE

Rose

The hall was dark when I slipped across it to Dad's office. He'd turned in for the night a couple hours ago. I paused, listening, and then flicked my hand to magically unlock the door.

There were other places I'd rather be, other things I'd rather be doing right now, but I had to take this chance while I had it.

I moved across the hardwood floor with soft footsteps. The drawers on the desk offered me nothing but the usual business papers. A file about the deal in Cairo sat beside Dad's laptop on the desk. I popped open the computer and considered the password screen.

I could probably get past that with my magic. But I wasn't adept enough with computers to believe I could put everything back to normal so he wouldn't realize someone had been snooping. I'd need to wait until I could get Kyler on that task.

I moved to the bookshelves, testing the spines, looking for errant pieces of paper that might offer some clue. My fingers skimmed over the silver-edged box that held the wand Dad had brought back from Egypt. I paused just long enough to open it and test the artifact more thoroughly with my magic. Not a wisp of power answered my tug. Nothing ominous there.

The filing cabinet in the corner was locked, but I dealt with that as quickly as I had the door. None of the papers I sifted through looked like anything related to the family, though.

I stopped in the middle of the room in the dim moonlight that streamed through the window, breathing in the wood polish and licorice smell. My feet hadn't found a single wobbly floor board.

If Dad was hiding some proof of treachery, it wasn't in here. I didn't know whether to be happy about that or concerned. Either he didn't have anything to hide... or he was too good at it.

No way for me to know which right now.

It was time for me to leave anyway. I had an appointment to keep.

I slipped out of the office, locking the door again behind me, and waved magic around me to allow me to blend into the shadows as I descended the broad staircase to the arched front door. Cool night air wafted over me as I ducked outside.

It was hard to believe it was just last night I'd snuck from the manor into the woods on our property like I was

now. Then I'd been uncertain and afraid but
determined. Now I strode on with purpose, pulling
magic around me with a sweep of my arms, confident
that it would shield me from any watching eyes. In the
space of a day, I'd earned that confidence—in myself and
my consorts. Including the one I was going to meet
this time.

I saw his tall, broad form silhouetted in the moonlight
on the small stone bridge where I'd met all of them the
night before. Seth turned at the rasp of my feet through
the brush, but the forest was too dark for me to make out
his expression. I hopped across the stepping stones in the
burbling stream and walked up the path to meet him.

"Hey," I said, a smile stretching across my face.

"Hey," Seth said back. He reached for me and tugged
me to him.

I loved how easy it was to slip into his embrace. How
right it felt leaning against his solid chest, soaking up the
smell of his skin like sun-warmed bronze. The heat of his
body tingled over me, a far more effective covering than
the light jacket I'd pulled over my dress. My spark
danced with joy inside me.

"Thank you for coming," I said, keeping my head
tipped against his shoulder.

"Of course." He slid his hand up and down my back.
"Just me?"

"I didn't want to make a big thing about it. I just...
Everything was so chaotic this morning, with Gabriel
showing up, and trying to explain to him what was going
on." I hugged him tighter. "It doesn't feel right being
apart from my consorts this much. I had to see at least one

of you again. And you always make me feel like whatever's happening, we'll get through it."

Seth hummed in agreement, but he eased me back enough to look me in the face. His gray-green eyes searched mine in the dimness. "Did something else happen? With your father—or with Derek?"

I shook my head. "That's all the same. I talked to my dad and he seems to be acting normally, but it's already a weird situation with Celestine gone, so... I don't know. It's so hard to judge. I feel wound up, having to walk on eggshells around him too."

"No wonder," Seth said, stroking his thumb over my cheek. "You thought he was going to help you stop your stepmother, not be part of her plot. Have you come up with a plan for going forward?"

I nodded. "I'm just going to have to push harder. Throw evidence of what Celestine was planning in his face without showing I'm aware of it and see how he reacts. It'll be easier to do that once the new estate manager arrives and we're going through Celestine's rooms. And I'm going to see how long my supposed fiancé will stick around if I'm giving him the cold shoulder. If Derek is willing to leave, and Dad is willing to let him, that'll prove something."

And if they weren't, I'd have to hope I could uncover some concrete evidence I could take to the Assembly before Dad realized I was onto him. And then I supposed they'd take Dad away, imprison him? I'd never known anyone who'd conspired to enslave their own child's magic to be sure what would happen to him.

I sucked my lower lip under my teeth, resisting the

urge to outright gnaw on it. For now, here in the shelter of the forest, I wanted to set that aside and focus on my consort.

I reached up to touch Seth's face, tracing my fingers along his broad jaw and up to the short waves of his tawny hair. "How have you been feeling? No regrets?"

My gut tensed as I asked the question. Seth had been the last of the guys to decide he wanted to go through with the consort ceremony. What if the doubts he'd seemed to set aside had come back now that everything was so much more complicated?

"Not a single one," Seth said, so steady my worries washed away. He leaned against the stone railing of the bridge and collected me against him again. "You know how I feel? Like this is where I was always meant to be."

"It feels that way to me too," I murmured.

"And part of that is protecting you any way I can. If there's anything else I can do to make things easier for you..."

It meant so much just to hear him offer. The Spark only knew what he and the other guys were making of this crazy witching world I'd only just started to introduce them to. The world even I hadn't realized was quite so crazy. Maybe he was still okay now, but soon they'd all be wishing they'd never agreed to tangle themselves up in my life.

My throat constricted at that thought. "What you're already doing is more than I'd ever want to ask. Most of this—it's my world. I'm the one who has to navigate it."

"As long as you know we'll be right there with you," Seth said.

His hand came to my cheek again. He caressed my skin from cheekbone to jaw, and then he tipped up my chin to kiss me. I kissed him back, softly and then with growing hunger. Gabriel's interruption had also put a stop to any more intimate activities my consorts and I might have gotten up to today.

I turned in his arms to kiss him more deeply, clasping my hands behind his neck. Seth's fingers slid into my hair. Giddy tingles ran through my body as his mouth moved sure and hot against mine.

Even when we stopped for a moment, I kept my head tucked close to his. "There is something else, actually," I murmured. "I really don't think you got to have enough of the fun last night. It would mean a lot to me to make that up to you."

Seth chuckled roughly. "Believe me, I enjoyed every minute of last night. You don't owe me anything."

I looked at him with an arch of my eyebrows. "Are you trying to say you *don't* want to have sex?"

His expression was normally so cool and collected, but the heat that flared in his eyes then was enough to melt me. We hadn't yet. Hadn't done more than make out, even though it had felt as if I'd opened myself up to all the guys last night.

"I definitely didn't mean that," he said. Then he glanced through the trees. "Are we far enough from the house that you're not worried about someone wandering out this way?"

We were a lot closer than we'd been last night. And being interrupted would definitely ruin the mood.

I took a step back, raising my hands. "I can make sure

even if they do, they won't even know we're here," I said with sly smile.

Now Seth's eyebrows jumped up. "I guess I shouldn't be surprised. Witch, magic..."

He still sounded a little wary. Seth had always been the most careful of our group, the most worried about what could go wrong. But this time, I was taking care of us.

"Just watch," I said.

I stepped away with him, swiveling on my feet and swaying with arms extended, drawing magic through the air with the movements of my body. Calling up a barrier all through the forest to repel anyone who might take a midnight stroll out this way. Hiding our presence and shutting us off from outside sight and hearing.

As I moved through the form, Seth's gaze followed me, full of nothing but awe and desire now. My own desire flooded me. The moment I'd completed the shell of privacy around us, I caught his hand and pulled him to me.

Seth was no witch. He couldn't see or feel the barrier I'd drawn. But he didn't hesitate now. He believed in me, in supernatural powers he'd known barely anything about a month ago, unwaveringly.

His mouth collided with mine, taut with wanting. I hummed eagerly as I kissed him back. He stripped off my jacket with a careful but insistent jerk. Then he was palming my breast, rolling the heel of his hand against my nipple, making me whimper. And I could. I could do whatever I wanted here, just a short distance from my own home. Anyone who'd ever tried to keep this man away from me could be damned.

I slid my hands up under his shirt, reveling in the solid muscle beneath that hot skin. Seth's tongue parted my lips to tangle with mine. He gripped my waist and hefted me up onto the top of the stone railing with one smooth movement.

My legs splayed around his waist. As I hooked them tighter, kissing him harder, his hand traveled down to cup my sex. I whimpered into his mouth. My panties were already damp with need. Seth groaned.

"Next time," he muttered in a voice so desperate it turned me on even more. "Next time we can take things slow."

"I'm not complaining about this time," I said, and lost my voice to a moan as he stroked me between my legs. Every particle in my body was calling out to take my consort in every way I hadn't yet. I needed this man inside me.

I fumbled with the zipper of his jeans and grasped the hard length of his cock through his boxers. Damn, he was big. Bigger than either of the guys I'd been with this way before. A tremor of mingled apprehension and excitement shot through me. I stroked him, familiarizing myself with the feel and size of him, and Seth groaned again.

He yanked at my panties, easing away just far enough to send them slipping down my legs. As I tugged his jeans and boxers down, he hitched up my dress. Then he was catching me by the thighs, bracing me against him as I balanced on the stones, the head of his cock teasing over my core.

"Rose," he said, like a prayer. His body tensed for a second. "I don't have—"

"We don't need anything, remember?" I said, rocking toward him. "My spark keeps me safe unless I tell it I'm ready."

"Thank God for that," he said in a strained voice, and aligned his cock with my slick entrance.

He eased into me, inch by thick, glorious inch. No, he wasn't too big at all. He was just perfect to fill me, to send bliss tingling through every nerve.

A sigh escaped me. My spark flared to welcome him, the passion between us igniting the power inside me even brighter than before.

Seth held me in place as he sank into me, withdrew, and plunged farther into me. A wave of pleasure rolled up from my core. I moaned, grasping at his shoulders, seeking out his lips. We kissed roughly, our bodies shaking with each thrust of Seth's hips, with the pulse of bliss spreading through us.

Seth trailed his mouth across my cheek and nipped my earlobe. His breath stuttered. He drove himself even deeper, and I gasped as he hit the most sensitive spot inside me. Pleasure shot through my veins. I cried out, so loud I was briefly afraid Seth would stop.

He only drove into me more eagerly. "I'm sure of your magic," he said. "I'm sure of you." His lips grazed the crook of my jaw. "You're everything I could have wanted, Rose."

With those words and another pump of his cock, I

started to shatter. Bliss radiated over my body and my spark sizzled like a firework. I came with another cry, pressing myself toward him to take him into me as deeply as I possibly could. Seth's breath stuttered. With a jerk of his hips, he came with me.

He leaned over me, sliding in and out with a few last gentle strokes. I touched his cheek and brought his mouth to mine. We kissed so long and so intently my head started to spin, but I wouldn't have asked to be anywhere else, with anyone else.

I'd come a long way from the woman I'd been when I'd come back home a month ago. I'd gained a lot. And I wasn't letting any of it go. Least of all this man and the other three I loved.

CHAPTER SIX

Gabriel

There weren't a whole lot of things that scared me in life anymore. So the sinking in my gut as I rode my Triumph up to the gate of the Hallowell estate had to be something else. Trepidation? Sure, that was possible. Maybe indecision over whether I was making the smartest move I could have or the stupidest—because it had to be one or the other. The feeling was nothing worse than that.

The intercom was mounted in the exact same spot it had been the last time I'd been out this way, years ago. I parked the bike where I could to push the call button, pulled off my helmet, and waited out the faint whir of the moving camera mounted on the post overhead. The wind licked over my hair, damp enough with humidity that it actually felt like a lick. Leaning back against my bar bag, the sum total of my possessions at the moment, I shot a smile at the camera.

Whoever was keeping an eye on it today opened the gate. I rode on up the drive to the garage that had been my home for the first fourteen years of my life.

They'd repainted it. The old deep green was covered over with a dark maroon. Otherwise it looked pretty much the same: a low building with a slanted room broken by three dormers, long enough to house the family's primary cars and Mr. Hallowell's small collection of older classics. I could picture the row of hoods in my mind's eye as clearly as if all those doors had been open.

As I stepped off the bike, the side door that led up to the overtop apartment opened and Rose stepped out. She smiled at me, a little proud and a little shy. The wind made her long black hair dance around her pale shoulders. She was wearing a casual tank top and jeans, but I couldn't imagine her looking any more gorgeous to me if she'd been decked out in an Oscars-caliber gown. My heart just about flipped over, seeing her.

If there was anything I was still scared of, it was this woman. I could admit that. I hadn't been able to resist her call. Hadn't been able to resist her suggestion that I take this job—working my way up to the position I should have inherited from my father, if things had turned out the way they should have.

Which also meant, if I'd never beckoned a lonely little girl over to play with me and the other boys. If I'd grown up just watching the girl of the house from afar as she transformed into the woman she was today, without ever knowing what it was like to find the right words to make her laugh, to accept a hug from those slim but strong arms. If I'd stood back and let her marry some asshole "witching" guy who'd have turned her life into hell.

No, what really scared me was that I wasn't sure I regretted anything, despite what had happened because of my decision all that time ago.

"Hey," Rose said. "We just finished cleaning things up upstairs." She swiped her hand past her cheek, a smudge of dust on her wrist suggesting she had literally been part of that *we*. "Do you need help carrying anything?"

"I've just got the one bag," I said, smiling back at her. It would have taken a concentrated effort *not* to smile at Rose Hallowell. I hefted the bar bag off the bike and followed her up the stairs.

I couldn't let her be more than a distant friend to me now, not in any way I showed. I had to remember that. It was better for both of us.

The second I came through the upper door into the apartment, my knees jarred. A wobble filled my chest, potent enough that I set down my bag before my arm wobbled too.

Fuck. I hadn't even thought about the fact that no one would have lived here while Rose's family was out in Portland. No one had lived here since Dad and I had left.

The living room looked exactly the same: a big square with hazy light trickling past the moss-green curtains over the windows on either side of the angled ceiling, black-

and-green striped sofa in the corner, birch-wood tables and bookcase scattered around it. A thick gray rug covered the floorboards between the sofa and the two matching armchairs. Someone must have replaced the batteries in the round clock that hung on the wall, but the second hand still clicked faintly when it passed the six at the bottom.

All furnishings had belonged to the Hallowells. We hadn't even been able to take the dishes, the ones we'd been using for as long as I could remember.

The place even smelled the same: like the clover from the little lawn beside the drive and a hint of gasoline and engine grease seeping through the floor.

It was too easy to picture Dad sitting on that sofa with diagrams spread all over the coffee table, beckoning me over to show me some improvement he wanted to make to this engine or that exhaust system. Too easy to imagine the scent of his coffee—dark roast, preferably Colombian—wafting from the kitchen as he hummed an off-key tune and threw together a meal.

"Gabriel?" Rose said tentatively.

I swallowed the lump in my throat and jerked my head around to meet her gaze, recovering my smile. "Sorry," I said. "It's just been a long time."

"Yeah. I didn't really think about..." Her gaze darted around the room. She'd never been up here before that I could remember. The similarities couldn't have struck her. "If you want to change things up, switch out the furniture, it really wouldn't be any trouble."

"It's okay," I said. "Most of the memories here were good." We wouldn't talk about the memories after.

"Well, if you change your mind, you know where to find me. I think my dad will be coming out to officially welcome you and introduce you to the other garage staff in a few minutes. He just got caught up in a call about some big deal he's helping finalize." She grimaced.

Right. I hadn't really expected to get first priority with the old man. I knew me being here, getting this place and this job, was all Rose. Worrying about me, trying to set things right, even when she had so much to worry about for herself already.

"Things have been okay with him so far?" I asked.

"I think so. It's so hard to tell." She paused, her gaze turning searching. "Are you completely okay with *this*, Gabriel? If being back feels too weird, or whatever..."

She'd already reassured me over and over that she only wanted me to take the job and the apartment if I really wanted it. That she didn't mean to pressure me at all. As if she should be the one taking responsibility for my history in this place.

She'd opened herself up to me so much from the moment I'd come back, trusted me with so much of herself. I'd known there was something magical about the girl I'd known back then, but I'd never realized quite how literal that was.

The thought tugged at my heart. I forced myself to ignore the sensation. I had to be worthy of that trust.

"Hey," I said. "I told you it's fine. It's perfect, really. I can help keep a closer eye on things for you, keep myself out of trouble, *and* avoid imposing on Jin's hospitality any longer. Thank you."

"Okay. I promise to stop asking." She gave me a quick grin. "I guess I'd better let you unpack. I shouldn't be sticking around the garage too long anyway. But if you ever want to talk, shoot me a text, and I'll conjure a little stealth."

Then she was gone, slipping out the door. The room felt dimmer in an instant.

I hauled my bar bag over to the bedrooms—almost veering into my childhood room before remembering I should take the master. To my relief, the bed was made up with a new duvet and sheet set, breaking that feeling of stepping back through time.

I sat down on it, but the history of the apartment still weighed on me. I didn't want to hang around in here. Might as well figure out a more permanent spot to park my bike and take a look at the current state of the cars. I couldn't ask for a better distraction than that.

The first thing I saw after I found a suitable nook for the Triumph was a kid who didn't look much older than eighteen hunched beneath the open hood of a deep blue Mercedes CLS. His grumbling gave me the impression he wasn't all that happy with how the work was going. I came up beside him and cocked my head.

"You want a hand?"

Ten minutes later, I was wrist-deep in engine grease and feeling not too shabby at all about my recent life decisions. Then a guy about my age, dark blond hair swept back from his high forehead, came strolling over around the side of the garage. He propped himself against the side of the garage next to me. He was a decent height and broad-shouldered, but I could tell at a glance, just from the way he held himself, that he'd never been in a fight in his life.

"You must be Gabriel Lorde," he said. "Welcome back to the household."

Said the guy who had been part of it for only about a hundredth of the time I had before. I didn't have to ask to know this was Derek. The dick who somehow thought he deserved Rose. And not just her but control over the most important part of her life too.

"Thanks," I said.

"I'm Derek," he said, straightening up again as if he'd thought better of the whole leaning thing. "Derek Conwyn, Rose's fiancé."

So you think. "Glad to meet you," I said smoothly, and held up my black-streaked hands. "I'd offer a shake, but..."

He nodded dismissively. His gaze slid to the car. "Got right to work, did you?"

"Tyler was having a little trouble with the tune-up. I figured now that I'm here, why wait?"

"Right." He gave me an even look. "Just so you know, this one's mine."

I had the feeling he wasn't just talking about the car, and that he thought *he* was being pretty smooth the way he was handling this conversation. Damn, if Derek turned out to be the only problem Rose had left, he wasn't going to be a hard one.

As much as I'd have liked to reply with an innocent, "Then I'll be sure to take very good care of her," I was here to help Rose, not make things worse. So I patted the side of the car and settled on a bland but warm, "Everything's looking good."

Derek's eyes narrowed slightly as if he were trying to figure out whether I'd missed his double entendre or was making one of my own so subtly insulting he couldn't quite figure out what I meant. Of course this guy would assume he couldn't take anything anyone said at face value.

"Glad to hear it," he said.

"If you're ever interested in upgrading the transmission, just let me know," I added, keeping the same mildly friendly tone. "Never hurts to have a little extra kick, right? I've never worked on a CLS before, but I've done a few like it."

"I'll think about it," Derek said. Now he just looked confused. He definitely hadn't expected generosity. "Well, I hope you settle in here."

He hustled off, taking his unsettled expression with him. I rolled my eyes and went back to the engine.

I'd just finished with the car and was washing my hands when the real man of the estate made his appearance.

"Gabriel!" Mr. Hallowell's baritone rang down the garage's inner hall. He ambled over as I swiped my hands on the towel by the mechanics' sink. "Or should I call you Mr. Lorde now?"

I'd known I wasn't happy about how Rose's dad had kicked mine to the curb all those years ago, but I wasn't prepared for the rush of anger that shot through me at those words. I had to pause and swallow before I could say in a steady voice, "Gabriel will do. Mr. Lorde was my dad."

"Of course," Mr. Hallowell said, his voice dropping respectfully.

That only made me want to punch him more. I slung my hands in my pockets instead. "I hope you don't mind —I've already started getting acquainted with the staff and the cars."

"That just makes my job easier," Mr. Hallowell said. "You always were a gregarious one, weren't you? By all means, make yourself at home."

Was that a jab at my friendship with Rose? Her dad was a hell of a lot harder to read than her supposed fiancé.

"It's not hard to do," I said. "It was my home for longer than I've been away."

"Well, we're glad to have you back on staff," he said, with a slight emphasis on the word *staff*. "It was good timing that Rose ran into you when she did."

I nodded. "Good to see she's doing well," I said vaguely, as if it didn't actually matter to me that much either way. That was what he wanted to hear, I was pretty sure—any indication he could get that I had no interest at all in his daughter beyond the job she'd hooked me up with.

"Yes," he said. "She is. Are you finding everything here without a hitch? Did you need any direction?"

"So far so good," I said. "I remember the maintenance routines. Just holler for me if there's anything special you need taken care of, and I'll be right there."

I gave him my best happy employee smile. Mr.

Hallowell smiled back, but I couldn't tell how much he meant it. What the hell was going on behind those muddy hazel eyes?

If *this* guy was planning to turn Rose into some kind of slave, how the hell was I going to help her stop him?

CHAPTER SEVEN

Rose

The town museum wasn't much compared to some of the huge ones I'd visited on our occasional family vacations. Once a house, donated to the town's historical society by its original owners, the main floor had been opened up into one large room with the most interesting old photos, newspaper clippings, and local artifacts. One or two volunteers, usually pretty old themselves, would always be puttering around offering their opinions on whatever you happened to be looking at.

Down in the basement, where the historical society kept their archives, I could work mostly undisturbed. But calling that dim, dusty-smelling room with its haphazard stacks of unlabeled boxes an "archive" was pushing it. I was trying to be generous, but it was hard not to think it more closely resembled a trash heap.

And not just because of how it looked.

"Have you discovered anything in that one?" Philomena asked, leaning over my shoulder. I was sitting on a hard plastic chair at the room's sole table in the middle of the room. The table was so small there was only really room enough for one of the boxes and a little space in front of it where I could paw through the contents I'd lifted out. This was much to the apparent consternation of the skinny gray-haired man who'd joined me down here about ten minutes ago. He huffed as he peered into one of the boxes by the wall. But hey, I'd gotten here first.

"Not so far," I said to Phil—in my head, because if I started talking to my imaginary best friend out loud, I'd really be in trouble. "I don't even know why they held on to some of this stuff."

I rubbed my gritty fingers together, my nose wrinkling. The last stack of papers I'd taken out had included not one but ten copies of a sale announcement from a hat shop, a school notebook that contained nothing but childish handwriting practice of various simple words, and a random piece of old leather so aged it had gotten tiny crumbs all over everything beneath it.

Phil gave a shudder, her voluminous skirts rustling. "Yes, I'm quite glad I'm incapable of literally digging my hands in—as much as I'd love to offer my aid. What are we looking *for*, exactly?"

"Any reference to the Hallowells." I stood up to dig another armful of material out of the box. "Our estate has been here as long as the town's been around. Maybe one of my long-ago relatives had some kind of, er, relations with one of the unsparked townspeople. Or was reported as having multiple lovers. Or something. If I can give my father —and the Assembly—some proof it was done before, it'll be easier to convince them it's okay that I'm doing it now."

But so far I had nothing. I wasn't even one tiny step closer to making sure witching society accepted my consorts. There *had* to be something. I couldn't let them down.

The room's other occupant brushed past the table with a mutter under his breath and a jerk of his hand over his chest. The sign of a cross. Oh, so he was one of those. My jaw tightened.

Philomena frowned at him as he prodded the boxes behind me. "What on earth was *that* about?"

I'd only started picturing her in my life while we'd lived in Portland. She hadn't had much time to see the varying reactions our family got in the place where we were best known.

"There are always rumors floating around in town about what the Hallowells might get up to on our estate," I said, turning my attention back to the papers. "Most people dismiss the rumors or find them amusing. A few would rather we weren't around at all."

"Hmm," Philomena said, her eyes glinting. "And a few are very, very glad to be around you."

Footsteps were just thumping down the stairs. I looked up to see Jin ambling in, followed by the twins and then Damon. A smile leapt to my face. This had seemed like a good meeting spot for a talk, since I needed to go through the archives anyway. I'd used trips to the town museum as an excuse to come into town a few times in the last month already. This time I'd actually been truthful.

The old guy who was definitely not my fan took one look at the new arrivals and grumbled to himself. Thankfully, he must have decided he'd come back some time when he could have the place to himself. With a scowl at my consorts, he marched past them and headed up to the main floor.

I got up, and immediately my guys were all around me, arms encircling me, heads bent close to mine. I breathed in their mingled scents and felt centered for the first time in days.

Seth caught my lips with his, the firm pressure of his kiss reminding me of our encounter outside my house a couple nights ago with a flare of my spark. Then Jin was there, his fingertips tracing down the side of my neck as we took our fill of each other's mouths. Kyler kissed my shoulder and then claimed my lips, swift and eager, when I broke from Jin.

Damon hung back just slightly, his hand hooking around one of mine, until the other guys had eased away. Then he tugged me to him and kissed me hard, as if he were making some kind of point.

The only point I cared about was having my consorts here with me.

But as much as my spark flickered giddily, wanting more, this wasn't exactly the place for it. They were still counting on me to figure things out so we didn't have to hide our affection away.

Kyler poked at the box still open on the table. "Have you come across anything you can use?"

"Not so far," I said, suppressing a sigh. I motioned to a couple of clippings I'd set aside. "There's a photo and a short article about a big wedding celebration for my great-great-grandmother." She'd let the staff join in the party with their families, so at least that showed friendliness toward the unsparked. "And a spooky story some kid wrote for a contest that used the Hallowell estate. All made up, ghosts and that sort of thing, but I might incorporate it into my modern witching history I'll get back to working on some day. There's been nothing that directly helps our case."

"Your people must keep records," Jin said, cocking his head.

I nodded. "When I'm sure I'm not in danger at home, I could go out to Seattle to the main witching archives... or even to talk to this witch in New York who's researched the more questionable parts of our history, although they've already dismissed her as a crackpot. But I can't explain away running off on some research project while I'm still supposedly getting married in a few weeks."

That crackpot witch *had* come across a few scraps of evidence, though. She'd claimed someone at the Assembly had disliked her bringing it up so much that she'd been fired. But they hadn't completely stopped her from talking about it. If I came to the Assembly showing I'd not just found a precedent but actually *done* what shouldn't be possible...

Well, I didn't really know what would happen. But it

was going to have to happen, one way or another, so I'd better be prepared. As soon as I knew how to handle my dad, that was the next step.

"I guess we'd better get down to work, then," Seth said, taking in the stacks of boxes. "At least five of us will get through the rest faster than you on your own."

* * *

A couple hours later, we were all a little dusty and a little rumpled, every box had been sifted through, and I still didn't have any proof that any Hallowell had ever consorted beyond the current witching rules.

After setting the lid on the last box, I sagged against the table with a long exhale.

Kyler rubbed my shoulder. "Hey, it was kind of a long shot anyway, right? I'll see if I can find anything online to do with witches—I'll have a much wider reach there."

"Most of that is fiction," I reminded him.

He grinned. "Well, I've got a pretty good idea of what the real thing looks like now, so I can make a decent effort of sorting through it. I'll pass anything I find that looks possibly legit on to you the next time I see you so you can check."

So optimistic, even when I was struggling to prove he had a right to be my consort at all. Spark help me, I hoped their actual welcome into my community wouldn't be half as hard as I was worrying it'd be.

"And the rest of us will do whatever we can," Seth said.

"How's Gabriel settling in up at the house?" Jin

asked, and I felt my consorts' attention suddenly sharpen, waiting for my answer. A tingle passed over my skin. It wasn't just because they were so concerned about their old friend, I didn't think.

But there wasn't much to tell them. "It seemed like it was a little hard for him, coming back to the apartment," I said. "We haven't had the chance to talk much yet. I didn't want to, I don't know, crowd him or anything."

Jin laughed. "I don't think he'll feel crowded, Briar Rose."

"Well, come on," Damon broke in. "We'd better leave so Rose can get home."

The guys came back to me for quick good-bye kisses, and then they headed up one by one. I'd give them five minutes' head start and then go up myself, as if I hadn't been part of their group at all.

Despite his comment to the others, Damon lingered. He waited until the last of the other guys had vanished up the stairs and shut the door again.

"I got you something," he said, reaching to his pocket.

Something he didn't want the others knowing about?

He showed me a phone. I blinked at it, not sure what to make of it, until he said, "I lifted it off Cortland."

My gaze jerked up to Damon's face. He gave me a cocky grin, but my heart had hitched. "You stole it from him? Damon, what if he'd caught you?"

"He didn't, did he?" He pressed the button to turn it on. "I know a guy who can get past the passcodes on these things in two seconds flat. I didn't see anything obviously incriminating, but you know what we're dealing with better than I do."

I hesitated, staring at it. Master Cortland, one of my former magic tutors, had only been involved in Celestine's plot peripherally. She'd gone to him for advice on how to twist the magic of the consort ceremony to her purpose. I knew he'd looked into the subject rather than reporting her for criminal magic, so obviously I couldn't trust him, but beyond that, I had no idea how much he'd participated. Or how much he might care now that she was gone.

The answer to that first question came to me quickly enough. Damon scanned through the call history as I watched. Master Cortland had tried to call my stepmother several times two mornings ago. The morning after I'd sent her on her way, after she'd meant to complete the ceremony.

He'd wanted to know if she'd succeeded, I guessed. Or maybe he hadn't even known, just been disturbed when he must have arrived home and discovered someone had messed with his notes. Either way, he'd clearly been worried when she hadn't answered.

"What about farther back?" I said. It'd been a few weeks ago that I'd overheard the two of them talking about the "binding" part of the spell. Who had he reached out to since then?

Damon kept skimming. There was a wide range of numbers, some local, some scattered across the country. A few with the area code I recognized as Seattle. So he'd been chatting with people who worked for the Assembly, maybe, while helping with illegal magic under their noses. I gritted my teeth. I'd make sure they found out about his involvement as well.

I didn't recognize any of the numbers, though, and the rest of the phone's offerings were pretty spartan. Master Cortland, like much of the witching community even in my generation, wasn't all that keen on modern technology. It didn't surprise me that he wouldn't have risked adding any sensitive information to the phone.

I grabbed a scrap of paper and jotted down the numbers he'd called shortly after his conversation with Celestine, in case one of them led me somewhere. I could try to search them out—and if I got nowhere, Ky's hacking skills couldn't be beat. Then I gave Damon a pointed look.

"You need to get rid of this. Leave it on the street so he'll think he just dropped it or something."

He tucked it back into his pocket with a nod toward my paper. "Are those going to lead anywhere?"

"I don't know yet." I let out my breath. "I know you just wanted to help, Damon, but you really shouldn't be taking risks like that. Master Cortland has a lot at stake if his association with my stepmother comes out. The new estate manager will be coming tomorrow. I'll be able to see through my plan to test my dad's loyalties then. We won't have to wait much longer."

Damon shrugged. He stepped closer, his dark blue eyes holding mine. "I can take care of myself, angel. And I want to take care of you." His voice dipped as he leaned in. "In every possible way."

Call me weak, but I couldn't resist him. Not when he looked at me, talked to me, like that. My fingers curled into his shirt as he kissed me. He parted my lips with the press of his, and his tongue stroked over mine. I yanked him right up against me, my spark searing with desire.

With a hungry sound, Damon grasped my waist and sat me on the edge of the table with one smooth movement. He followed, capturing my mouth again as he pushed between my splaying legs. A whimper crept from my throat as the bulge inside his jeans grazed my core. I kissed him back, hard. His hand crept up under the thin fabric of my shirt, heat washing over my skin in its wake, and—

The basement stairs creaked.

We jerked apart with a stutter of breath. I only had time to gesture a hasty spell in the air before a hand closed on the knob of the archive room door.

The figure on the other side paused. Then they headed back up, struck by the sense that they'd forgotten something.

My gaze met Damon's. Both of our breaths were coming a little ragged. Longing coiled in my belly and ran with an ache down to my core, but I knew better than to take too many risks myself.

"I'd better go," I said. "But... later?"

A smile curled his lips. "Later, for sure."

"And be careful," I called after him as I motioned him to the door.

"If I have to be," he replied, and ducked out.

I sent up a brief prayer to the Spark that blessed all witching kind. *Please, by all that is lit and warm, let him mean that.*

CHAPTER EIGHT

Rose

Gabriel knew I was coming. No one could have noticed me leaving the house in the deepening evening, not with the magic I'd cast around me. So there was no reason to feel nervous climbing the stairs to the garage-top apartment.

No reason except I still wasn't totally sure how to talk to this grown-up and stunningly handsome version of the boy I'd once caught salamanders with.

Outside his door, I summoned the energy of my spark and drew it around the apartment with a few sweeps of my arms to mute the sounds of our conversation to anyone outside. Then I knocked.

"Come on in," Gabriel said from the other side. "It's not locked."

I found him flipping through the row of old CDs he and his dad had left behind on a shelf. It'd been a hot day and the heat lingered in the apartment, so Gabriel was only wearing an undershirt with his jeans. He might not have been as brawny as Seth, but there was ample musculature on display as he pulled one case off the shelf and turned toward me. Suddenly I was feeling a little hot too.

"We only took our favorites," he said, looking up from the CD. "I forgot about some of these albums."

"Anything worth listening to now?" I asked.

He chuckled. "From my contributions, only if you're into very dated pop-punk and hip hop. My dad had some new country stuff that might not be bad. Is it better if we have something playing to cover up our voices?"

"My magic will take care of that," I said. "But if you want to put something on..."

"Maybe later." He slid the case back into the shelf and flashed his easy grin at me. "I'm supposed to be listening to you."

The heat I'd felt earlier gathered in my cheeks. "I think it's more the other way around," I pointed out, moving to the couch.

"Right." He ducked into the kitchen. "Do you want anything to drink?"

Already the perfect host, even though he'd hardly have had time to stock his fridge. I didn't think he'd like it if I acted like he was some kind of charity case I couldn't bear to take anything from, though. "What have you got?"

"So far just beer and lemonade."

Getting even a little buzzed around him didn't sound like the wisest idea right now. "Lemonade would be great. Thank you."

He came back out with a bottle of beer for himself and a glass bright with lemonade. I accepted the drink and tipped back a gulp of the sweet-and-sour liquid.

Gabriel sat down at the opposite end of the couch. He leaned one of those well-muscled arms across the back cushion, stretching his feet out toward the coffee table, looking totally at home. Which I guessed he had a right to.

"I'm not sure I have much to report yet," he said. "I guess you know your dad and Derek went out for a drive today."

I nodded. "They were going to check out a property Derek thought might fit what one of the investors Dad works with is looking for. Derek's kind of... half architect, half real estate agent." In a community as small as ours, if you wanted to mainly work for witching folk, you had to be pretty flexible. "Did you overhear anything?"

"Just some general business talk," Gabriel said. "They didn't mention you or your stepmother while they were by the garage. They seemed friendly enough, though."

I made a face. "The two options are that they're plotting illegal magic together or that Dad still thinks Derek's his future son-in-law. Either way, there's no reason for them not to be friendly."

"Yeah. I'll continue keeping an eye out. And it's not as if I'm confined to the garage. I can always take a little stroll through the gardens on my time off, maybe conveniently when they're out there, if you text me a heads up." His grin turned sly.

"Thank you," I said.

"It's not a problem." The grin faded. For a second, his

bright blue eyes were completely serious. "I came back here because I was worried about you, Rose. It seems like I had good reason to be. I wish I'd already found out something you could use."

"You only got here a couple days ago," I said. My throat tightened. I took another gulp of lemonade. "And I asked my dad about giving you this job to help *you* more than to help me."

This time his smile was softer. "I know that, Rose."

That look, that smile, made my heart flutter in a way it hadn't earlier. I groped for a change of subject. "I didn't come out tonight just to get a report on what you've seen either. How are you doing? It looked like you were getting along okay with the other staff." I'd seen him laughing with Matt, who managed the garage and served as our main driver, when I'd headed out to town this afternoon. "I guess you get along with just about everyone, though, don't you?"

He laughed. "I do meet the occasional person who just won't warm up to me."

"Oh, yeah? I'd like to see that just to know it's possible." I gave him a playful nudge with my foot. "But I guess you met all kinds of people with all that roaming around you did. Do you still keep in touch with anyone you met in all those places?"

Gabriel shrugged. "Not really. I'm not the best pen pal. More of a face-to-face guy, you know. But the ones I got along with, they know they could hit me up if they were passing through town."

I wanted to ask if he'd hit it off with any women, but that felt too personal somehow. Maybe because I'd have been asking with more than just innocent curiosity. "Is there somewhere you'd want to go back to? When everything has settled down for me? I know it must be hard, being back here again."

Gabriel was already shaking his head. "No," he said, lightly but definitively. "There are places I'd still like to see, for sure. Things I'd like to experience that I haven't gotten to yet. But I'd be happier sticking to shorter travels with somewhere definite to come back to in between. I think I was always missing things about this place—the estate, and the town—while I was on the road. Missing just having a home base that felt like it was mine. I guess this isn't really mine, so—"

"It *is*," I broke in. "As long as I'm here on the estate, as long as you want a home here, you've got it."

He paused, gazing back at me, as if he hadn't expected to get that much vehemence in response. Then the corners of his lips quirked up. "And how could I leave for very long when you're here now? If you'd been here back then, I don't think I'd ever have taken off."

The fluttering came back, stronger this time. I wet my lips and made myself focus on my glass for a moment. "Keep flirting like that and you'll put Jin out of a job."

Gabriel laughed again. "That's not flirting," he said. "That's just telling it like it is. I'm not asking for anything from you, Sprout. But even before I left here, I was missing you. You're part of what makes this place home."

He said it so straightforward and honest an ache formed in my chest. I swallowed my lemonade, but the sensation didn't leave. I made myself look up at him again. "It didn't feel right without you here, either."

Our gazes stayed locked for a long moment. Gabriel cocked his head. "Good thing I came, then."

"Yeah."

He turned his head—casually, but I thought his shoulders had tensed a bit. "So you and the other guys... That whole ceremony you did—it's pretty serious, isn't it."

The ache turned sharp. I didn't know how to tell him that I wished he'd been there then without it coming out all wrong somehow. Pressuring him or presuming too much.

"We're basically married," I said. "In the witching sense of the word. Which is a little more serious than the regular sense, since we're sort of tied together now."

"Four husbands." He glanced back at me and raised an eyebrow. "You never did back down from a challenge, did you?"

I had to smile back. "It's not like that. I... I love all of them. I couldn't have just picked one."

I wanted to say, "I love all of *you*," but I couldn't really, not yet. Not with Gabriel just back. I'd meant what I'd said to Philomena about us needing to get to know each other again. We were only just getting started.

But it already felt like it would be so easy to fall back into loving him.

"So how is that all going to work once you've gotten the 'marriage' all approved or whatever?" he asked. "They'll all move in, and..."

"And I guess we'll have to get a really big bed," I said without thinking, and my face flushed hot. Gabriel choked on a laugh, but something in his eyes made me feel even hotter and more pained at the same time.

Before I could figure out how to recover, an engine growled outside. The electric gate hummed open. I frowned and got to my feet, catching myself from pulling back the curtain.

Gabriel went instead. He peered outside. "Dark sedan. Looks like a Lincoln. You weren't expecting company?"

"No." But someone had been, or the gate wouldn't have opened so fast.

"I'll have to go down and park the car."

"Right. Of course. I'll wait here."

I stood near the open window as he went down. Voices filtered in from outside. Dad had come out to meet our guest.

"Matilda," he said in his warm, even voice. "I'm glad you were able to move up your schedule."

"It sounded like you were in dire straits, Mr. Hallowell," a dry female voice responded. "Frank will be coming along tomorrow as planned."

Matilda. My body froze. Matilda Gainsley. The new estate manager Dad had hired. She wasn't supposed to be arriving until tomorrow morning.

I should have been glad. With her here I could go forward with my plan to surreptitiously present Dad with evidence of Celestine's treachery, to see how he'd respond. But now she was between me and where I was supposed to be.

Luggage thumped out of the trunk. The engine started again as Gabriel must have brought the car around to the empty spot that had used to belong to Meredith's pale green Chevrolet. The voices faded as my father escorted Mrs. Gainsley to the house.

Gabriel came hurrying up the steps a minute later. He took one look at me and frowned. "What's wrong?"

"That's the new estate manager," I said. "She's a witch. I don't know... If I use magic to slip back into the house, she might notice." I hadn't gotten much practice at hiding it. I'd never done any major magicking in front of a fellow witch yet.

If it'd only been myself I had to worry about, I might have marched right over there without magic and let them think whatever they wanted about my visit here. But it wasn't just me. Dad still controlled the estate. In a lot of ways, he controlled Gabriel's fate. If I brought magic to bear against him over a matter like that, *I* could be the one who ended up imprisoned by the Assembly.

Gabriel rubbed his jaw. "You could stay here until— Oh, damn. Your dad will want to introduce you, won't he?"

I nodded, calming my breath. I was a witch. I was alight with magic. There had to be a way.

My mind leapt back to an urgent trip I'd made a few days ago, to listen in on a conversation between Celestine and Derek. I'd pulled my magic around me and let it transport me right from one room to the next.

From the garage to the house wasn't that far. I thought I could do it. Dad might be calling for me to come down even now.

My gaze darted to Gabriel. "This is going to look strange," I said. "But I have to go right now."

"Rose?" he said. I was already moving. I swiveled on my feet, faster and faster, picturing the comforting glow of my reading lamp, the rows of built-in bookcases, the cozy four-poster bed. My spark blazed up through every nerve. Then I whipped my arms around my body.

My skin went cold. The world went black. With a snap, I was lurching on my feet across the hardwood floor of my bedroom.

I'd been right. "Rose?" Dad's voice carried up the stairs, through my locked door, sounding puzzled.

"Coming!" I hollered back and combed my fingers through my hair, finding my balance. I could do this. I'd already done it. I was here. No witch could tell I had magic when I *wasn't* using it.

I hurried out and down the stairs. Dad and Derek were already standing in the foyer. And so was Matilda Gainsley.

She was a short, knobby-chinned woman with a bun of pale orange hair. Her dark eyes considered me as I descended. Moldy cinders, I already didn't like her, if only because I had the feeling she didn't miss much.

And also because she wasn't Meredith, who should have been here. I swallowed hard.

"Hello," I said. "Sorry, sometimes I get wrapped up in a book and just tune everything else out. You must be Mrs. Gainsley. It's a pleasure to meet you."

"The pleasure is all mine, Miss Hallowell," Mrs. Gainsley said. She clasped her hand, as dry as her voice, around mine just for a second.

"Well," Dad said, "let me show you to your rooms.

CONSORT OF THORNS 75

You should get some rest after that trip. We can get started going over your duties in the morning."

"I'll be up bright and early," Mrs. Gainsley said. "I always am." The smile she gave me looked a little bit sharp.

I trailed after them as they headed up, and Derek came along behind me. He stopped beside me when I reached my door. Dad pointed out the estate manager's office to Mrs. Gainsley and then directed her down the rightward branch in the hall toward the adjoining sitting room and bedroom that served as the private quarters for the resident estate manager and her consort.

"Well, maybe things can start to get back to normal," Derek said in a hesitant voice. "As normal as they can be with your stepmother missing."

How had he been feeling about that—not knowing where his accomplice had run off to? I'd have taken more pleasure from his uncertainty if he hadn't turned to me right then. Turned to me and leaned his hand against the door frame so close it brushed the side of my arm.

"Rose," he said, leaning his head closer too. *That* was the same tone he'd used on Polly, the girl from the cleaning staff I'd heard him fooling around with and insulting me to. Apparently my previous coldness hadn't quite put him off.

How dare he think he had any right to get intimate with me after everything he'd done to me and planned to?

I pressed my hand against his chest and pushed. "Not right now. Back off."

Derek's eyes darkened. He didn't move, only dipped his head even more. His nose grazed mine, and my stomach flipped, threatening to eject the lemonade I'd been drinking all over his nice linen shirt.

"I think it's about time we started acting more like two people about to be married," he said, with an edge in his voice that sounded almost like a threat.

My fingernails dug into my palm. Every inch of my skin screamed to shove him away with a burst of magic. But I couldn't reveal that much to him. The Spark knew I couldn't trust *him* with the knowledge that I'd somehow come into my magic.

"If you're going to act like this, I'm thinking we shouldn't get married," I said, letting acid creep into my own tone, and pushed harder with just my arms.

To my relief, the comment and the shove was enough to dislodge Derek. For the moment. He took a step back and looked at me narrowly for a second before he relaxed his expression.

"I'm sorry if I overstepped," he said. "I wouldn't want anything to interfere with our consorting. Not with your birthday coming so soon."

He said it calmly enough, but that was definitely a threat. He thought I still needed him to kindle my spark.

I couldn't reveal to him that I didn't.

"Of course not," I said. I gripped the doorknob and ducked away into my bedroom. As soon as the door was closed behind me, I sagged against it, clutching my queasy stomach.

I needed him out of here, out of my life. But how could I convince him to leave if he didn't care how willing I was?

CHAPTER NINE

Seth

When I'd texted Damon asking if I could stop by his place to talk, I hadn't expected him to suggest the Bluebell Café as an alternate meeting spot. It didn't seem to fit his current image. But when I came out to the back patio with its picnic tables under bright gingham umbrellas, lilting piano following me through the screen door, he was sitting there already halfway through a slice of peach pie, looking satisfied if not exactly relaxed. When did Damon ever look really relaxed?

I started to think this conversation might go better than I'd hoped. My mistake.

"Hey," I said, sitting down across from him as he dug into the rest of the pie. "Thanks for coming."

He shrugged and shot me a wary glance. "Your mom

still makes the best pies," he said, as if he needed to explain why he was eating.

A flash of memory hit me: We must have been only eight or nine years old, the five of us guys and Rose, sitting on the gritty floor of the estate's old hunting cabin that was one of our favorite haunts, laughing and scooping mouthfuls of still-warm apple pie out of the pan with our hands. My mom had passed her creation off to me and Kyler from the manor's kitchen with a grin. *I made something extra for you kids.*

I'd realized when we'd brought it out there to meet them that we should have brought plates and forks too, but Damon had said, *Aw, it'll be cold by then. What do you think hands are for?* And plowed right in. We'd been a mess afterward, but nothing a splash in the pond couldn't fix.

I could almost taste the apple sweetness and the cinnamon from back then. Suddenly I had a craving for a slice from the café. But I wasn't here to get a snack. I was here to make sure Damon didn't get us into any messes we *couldn't* easily clean up.

"So what did you want to talk about anyway?" Damon asked, spearing a piece of the crust with his fork. "Need an extra hand with something you wouldn't go to your brainiac brother for?" He smirked at me.

"No," I said. "Actually, I thought maybe I could help you out. I was talking with one of the contractors Dad brings on for some of the projects—Mr. Lewis, the electrician. He said he'd be open to taking on an assistant as an apprentice. Paid, of course."

Damon lowered his fork. "You're trying to hook me up with a job." His tone was unreadable.

"Well, yeah."

"I work, you know," he said, starting to bristle, and that was my first clue this wasn't going to go well at all. "I pay the bills I need to. I don't need you or anyone else pulling favors for me. Why did you think I'd want to be an electrician's assistant?"

"It's a good job," I said. "In a few years you could be fully qualified. Electricians make a lot of money, you know. And it's not like people are going to stop using electricity any time soon."

"I didn't ask for a list of selling points," Damon said. "Why are you trying to get me a job at all? I'm fine."

God, how would Gabriel have handled him? He'd always managed to somehow cool Damon down without turning him sulky. I didn't have even that kind of magic. I wavered and settled on honesty. Honesty and one thing I knew for sure Damon cared about.

"I know you are," I said. "I'm not worried about you. I don't think you need charity. I'm thinking about *Rose*. We're all tied to her now. The kind of 'work' you're doing, the way you make your money... the people you work for... The deeper you get with them, the more you're bringing them into her life too." And Lord knew she had enough on her plate without having to cope with small-time gangsters casing her and her estate.

Damon scowled at me. "I've been dealing with these guys for years. I think I can manage to keep them away from Rose."

"So you didn't go to one of them to crack Mr.

Cortland's phone?"

His eyes twitched. Uh-huh. "How do you know anything about that?" he demanded.

"She passed some phone numbers on to Kyler yesterday for him to look up," I said. "She told him where she'd gotten them. We're all in this together now. You can't just—"

He couldn't just steal people's fucking phones and draw Rose even more into the line of fire, I wanted to say, but I thought better of it at the last second. Damon was already fuming. You could practically see smoke rising off that spiky hair.

Okay, it was probably time to call this. Attempt number one at bringing Damon back to the non-criminal life: total failure.

He shoved his plate away and stood up. "No one is going to take care of Rose better than I will," he said darkly. "So take your pity and your job offer and shove it up your ass."

He stalked off down the alley, not even bothering to walk back through the café.

When he'd passed out of sight, I leaned my head into my hands and groaned. Great work, Seth. Way to make your case.

How much was it my fault and how much Damon just being impossibly stubborn, anyway?

The problem was, that didn't matter. He was still a problem. I'd wanted to do *something* to make Rose's life a little easier, a little safer... Otherwise there was nothing to do but wait.

And now that was still all I had to do. Also, I might

just have made her life a little worse, if Damon went and did something even more stupid because he was pissed off at me.

I headed back through town, but the restless urge wouldn't leave me. *My* work for the day was already finished, pointless as installing a new sink to replace Ms. Lindel's perfectly good old one had seemed anyway. I wanted to see Rose, but I couldn't just stroll over there whenever I liked until it was safe for her to reveal that she'd taken us as her consorts. Damn it.

I ended up rambling down one of the back roads that circumvented the Hallowell property. I could see the stone wall, the trees of the wood shading it, the distant peaks of the manor beyond. It was a warm day, but the breeze ruffled my clothes briskly enough that I started to wish I'd brought a jacket. Not enough to turn back, though. Maybe I'd spot something out here that she could use. It might be a long-shot, but I wouldn't be doing her any good sitting around at home.

The land around the road here was mostly vacant fields, but up ahead an old farmhouse loomed. My gaze returned to it between glances at the Hallowell estate. The bones of it looked solid enough, the frame straight and the roof stable. Part of the porch had collapsed, though, and the eaves trough was sagging. A few of the windows were broken, splinters of glass glinting against the plywood behind them in the light from the sinking sun.

A forlorn-looking For Sale sign swung on its post out front. I could see why no one had snatched this place up yet. It didn't just need a hell of a lot of repairs—it was out in the middle of nowhere, almost an hour's walk outside of town, with the closest neighbors being the Hallowells. They weren't the kind of neighbors most people around here could imagine popping by for a quick hello or to ask to borrow a cup of sugar.

It'd be just a five-minute walk from the farmhouse's dilapidated porch to the Hallowell estate's stone wall. Maybe fifteen minutes from there to the manor, if I was judging the distances right.

A gleam of an idea started to jitter in my head. I turned away from the estate as I came up on the farmhouse and ambled over for a closer look.

Some teens from town or somewhere else nearby must have gotten into it. Amateurish spray paint tags colored the worn clapboard slats. I couldn't tell what color the slats were meant to be under the layer of gray grime coating them.

The awning was standing straight enough. Based on the size of the place, I'd guess it had at least four bedrooms. It didn't look pretty, but looks could be fixed.

I folded my arms over my chest, considering the building. My heartbeat kicked up a notch. Was I crazy to even think about this?

Even if I was, at least I'd be keeping busy.

It wasn't as if I could make any decisions yet. I walked back to the For Sale sign, pulling out my phone, and dialed the number listed there.

"Silverton Realty," a bright voice answered. "How can I help you?"

"Hi," I said. "What's the current list price on the farmhouse out on Hallowell Lane?"

CHAPTER TEN

Rose

I breathed into my spark and exhaled slowly, sweeping my right foot out and behind me. My back arched as I reached my arms toward the bedroom wall. In the yellow glow of the lamp, my limbs cast long shadows on the floor. The wind warbled, rustling the heavy curtains covering my window. Magic radiated through all of my movements, even though I was keeping it contained inside my body for now.

I dipped my hands low and straightened up. With a quick swivel, I was facing my bed again. The bed where I'd supposedly come up here to sleep in. But I'd already felt as if Mrs. Gainsley had been watching me curiously a few times today. Maybe I was giving off some sort of lit-spark vibe without even trying.

My audience, Philomena, sat on the edge of the bed

at rapt attention. "It really is quite magical to watch," she said, and gave me a little clap as well.

I laughed. "That's a fairly basic form. If I'd released the magic, I'd just have cooled off the room a little."

"Well, why don't you release it, then? If there's a better show to be had, I'm all for seeing it."

I gave her an amused look. "I'm trying to work on my control. To make sure when I *do* need to use my magic, I won't expend much extra that another witch could notice."

"A witch like that new estate manager of yours?" Phil said. "Hmm. Yes, I'm not sure I quite like the look of her."

"It's not about how she looks. She could be a completely lovely person, and I still wouldn't want her to know I've kindled my spark already."

"I take your point." Phil bounced on the mattress. "Perhaps I could give you some tips. I happen to have *excellent* self-control. Why, there was that time I was just *dying* to tear off Lord Haverton's cravat, but I managed to keep my hands to myself. For the five minutes until the maid left the room. Not to mention the Duchess of Canterbury's luncheon, when—"

The window rattled with a knock. I jumped and turned. Had that just been a branch in the wind?

The knock came again, soft and steady, almost playful. My pulse settled, and a smile crossed my lips. I didn't throw caution to the wind, but as I walked over to tug back the curtain, I was pretty sure of what I'd see outside.

I was right. Kyler grinned back at me from the other side of the glass. He was perched in the oak tree outside like he'd done the first night I'd been back, when he'd come to confirm I'd returned home.

The wind tossed his tawny curls as if it meant to chuck him right back on the ground, and his knuckles whitened where he was gripping the branch. I shoved the pane higher and yanked out the screen. My consort scrambled in, accepting my helping hand.

I peered outside for a moment. No security guards nearby. I yanked the curtain shut again and turned to Kyler.

He was still holding my hand. Without a word, he pulled me to him, dropping his mouth to mine. The kiss was so sure and full of desire I melted into it. We'd come a long way from the first awkward peck I'd pressed to his lips a few weeks ago. And I hadn't been able to see any of my consorts since yesterday in the town museum.

I hadn't used enough magic to be hungry on my spark's behalf, but I was hungry in all sorts of other ways. If we'd been able to behave as proper consorts did, I wouldn't have left their sides for more than a few minutes in this first week after the ceremony.

On the other side of the room, Philomena cleared her throat. "I think that cooling spell might be in order now. I'd better, ah, find another way to occupy myself."

I kissed Ky again, reveling in the heat of his lean body, in his smell: lightly musky with a hint of mint. His arms came around me, but after the kiss he eased back a few inches, still grinning.

"I'm thinking I should get in the habit of stopping by more often."

The thought of how much risk he'd taken to stop by

at all chilled a little of my desire. "You should have let me know you were coming. I could have given you some cover."

"I didn't need it," he said. "I was careful. Security hasn't changed their patrols much since my dad was on duty here."

The guys had snuck into the estate dozens of times before, but I had trouble feeling completely reassured. So much was at stake now that we had so much more to hide.

Stepping back from Ky, I cast a quick silencing spell over the room that would let sound in but not out. Nothing another witch should be able to sense from outside my door—which was locked, but not securely enough to feel quite safe.

A spell on the door itself, Mrs. Gainsley might pick up on if she came by. I hesitated, and then dragged my reading chair over to block it from opening.

"Okay," I said, brushing my hands together. "Now I feel better. *Are* you just stopping by, or is something else going on?" My heart gave a sudden lurch. "The other guys are all okay, aren't they?"

"Yes, yes, don't worry," Kyler said, holding up his hands. "There was some information I wanted to get from you, and I wasn't sure if doing it by phone would be secure enough."

I stepped closer to lean my head against his shoulder, and he slid his arm around my waist. "Well, now I'm intrigued. What kind of information?"

He chuckled. "Nothing all that exciting to you. I was just thinking—you know you said the other day that you wished you could go to Seattle to check out the witch-related records there?"

"Yeah. But I—"

"I know," he said gently. "You can't explain away the trip. But no one will think anything of some techy dude heading over to the city for a few days. I figured I could hang around, see if I can crack whatever security that Assembly of yours has on their internal network... Maybe I can dig up some records for you that even you couldn't get to."

He offered me one of his brilliant smiles, so pleased with himself that my heart squeezed. Both with gratitude and with nerves. "Are you sure? If they realize that you're poking around in their business... The Assembly takes their secrecy pretty seriously." Would they hurt him? Wipe his memory?

Kyler waved off my concern. "I've managed to get into international banks and government databases," he said. "No one's caught me yet. It's not as if I even need to be in the building. They'll never notice me, and I won't leave a trace. Maybe I can ferret out a little more info about the people those phone numbers belonged to—and about your Master Cortland too. My preliminary digging hasn't turned up anything suspicious."

Hope was already overtaking my worries. Kyler did know what he was doing when it came to computers, better than anyone I'd ever known—and witching folk didn't tend to be all that tech savvy in the first place. Who knew how much he might be able to discover out there? I'd put my plan into action with Dad tomorrow, he'd scour the Assembly's digital archives, and in just a couple days we might have all the answers we needed.

"All right," I said. "So I guess you need to know exactly where the Assembly building *is*. I assume you have to be close for all this special server hacking?"

He laughed. "That would help." He dipped his head a little closer to mine. "But just so we're clear, that's not the only thing I came for."

My breath caught at the promise in his voice and the mischievous glint in his gray-green eyes. "No?"

"If I'm going to be away from here for a while, I definitely need to get in all the Rose time I can beforehand," he murmured, nuzzling my cheek.

"I see," I said. "And how were you thinking we'd use that time?"

"Oh, I'm just full of ideas."

"Like always," I teased, and then he was kissing me again, and I couldn't think about anything but the tender slide of his lips against mine.

My bed was just a few steps away. I sat down on the edge, and Kyler bent over me, his hands traveling up under the thin cotton top of my pajamas. His thumbs stroked over the peaks of my bare breasts, and I whimpered against his mouth.

He kissed me harder, teasing my nipples with careful strokes of his fingers until they were so stiff it was almost painful. Pleasure radiated through my chest. I wanted to pay him back with some of that exquisite torture.

As our kisses grew sloppier, I reached to cup the bulge of his erection through his chinos. Ky made a rough sound in his throat, his tongue sweeping over my lips. He rocked into my touch. I eased my palm up and down over the hard length of him. I'd taken him into my mouth before, but never anywhere else. Right now there wasn't anything I could imagine wanting more than to meet him core to core.

I scooted back on the bed, pulling at Kyler's shirt to bring him with me. He climbed after me, and I tugged the shirt right off him. The planes of his slender body were smooth and delightfully firm, his muscles twitching when I grazed the heel of my hand over his nipples.

He wrenched my pajama top off me and leaned in for another kiss. The heat of his chest against my breasts sent the glow of my spark rippling all through my body. But when I reached for the button of his pants, he hesitated, gazing down at me.

"I've only done this once before," he admitted. "And that was years ago, at some stupid college party, and I was drunk enough from trying to work up the courage to make a move that I hardly even remember it. So... it might take some practice before I catch up with the other guys."

He said the last bit with a wry grin. A giggle slipped out of me. "Plenty of practice. Sounds good to me. It's not like I'm any kind of expert." I arched an eyebrow at him. "I'm surprised you're not. Is sex the only thing you've never bothered to research?"

He guffawed and lowered his head to nip my ear. "Oh, believe me, I've researched that subject plenty. So I may not have the *experience* to back it up, but I do know, for example, the most likely ways to make you moan without even needing to touch you here, or here."

His fingers grazed my breasts and my clit with a

shiver of bliss. Then he rested his hand on my side. He pressed his lips to the underside of my jaw, kissing his way down the side of my neck with soft flicks of his tongue. His fingers traced an airy line from my ribs down to my hip bone, over and over, as his mouth continued its journey. Quivers of pleasure ran through my skin. By the time he'd reached my collarbone to nibble a sensitive spot just above it, I was trembling with need. That moan he'd been looking for spilled out of me.

"Okay," I said, groping for his pants again. "Enough experimenting. I want you inside me, now."

A flush spread up Ky's neck to his face. His eyes gleamed with eagerness. He helped me yank his chinos down and then kicked them aside. I lay back as he eased down my pajama pants with a teasing graze of his fingers. He kissed a trail down my belly in their wake. One hand dipped between my thighs. He groaned as he felt how wet I was. I rocked against his hand, needing more.

"Kyler..."

I was on the verge of begging, but he didn't make me. He climbed back over me, guiding his cock to my entrance with one hand. Both our breaths hitched as he eased the head over my clit and down. I arched my hips up, and he slid into my opening as easily as if we'd been made to fit together, filling me all the way.

For the first moment, he bent his head to my shoulder, a shudder running through his chest. "Rose," he said. "You have no idea. God." He kissed me, wildly, and then he started to move.

He took his time finding his rhythm, but every thrust, tentative and then more sure, sent me spiraling higher. As he met me faster, harder, our bodies melded together even more tightly. Bliss jittered all through my nerves. I kissed him roughly, my hands sliding over his shoulders, his chest, wanting to touch every inch of him.

"I think," Kyler murmured, his voice getting ragged, "if I just..."

He angled his hips so the base of his cock bumped my clit with each stroke. A sharper bolt of bliss shot through me. I'd like to find whatever website taught him to do that and give them a gold medal.

I bucked to meet his thrusts, intensifying the contact. Sending the pleasure racing through me even higher with the searing rush of my spark. My body started to shake. A cry caught in my throat. "Ky!" I said, and he rolled his hips one more time. My orgasm crashed over me, sparkling behind my eyes.

"Oh fuck oh fuck," Kyler groaned, but there was no complaint in those words. His hips jerked, and he came inside me in a hot rush.

We rocked to a halt together, both of us panting. Our skin was slick with sweat everywhere it touched. I loved the feeling of it. I pulled him down beside me on the bed, aligning my body as closely against his as I could.

Ky hummed happily. He tucked my head under his chin and held me tight, and for just a moment, I imagined he could stay here with me for the rest of the night.

What a lovely dream that would be. How much longer until I could make it a reality, and not just with him but with all my consorts?

CHAPTER ELEVEN

Rose

"So what are we looking for again?" Philomena asked.

I hung back beside her as Mrs. Gainsley moved her body through a magical form to release the seal on what had once been Celestine's private magicking room. Once I could announce my kindled spark, it would be mine.

"We're not going in to *look*," I told her silently. "Well, not really. We're going in to make sure Dad finds something."

The air vibrated with released magic I wasn't supposed to be able to feel. My father, watching at my other side, didn't react at all. A faint chill tickled over my skin. Then, with a sigh, the door swung open.

"Is it okay if I help you search?" I asked Dad as the estate manager stepped back to let us by.

"By all means," he said, without any sign he was

worried about what I might find inside. "Just let me know if you come across any official-looking documents. Anything related to her business operations may be confidential. Better to let me handle those."

Like a box full of magical contracts? Was he trying to ensure I didn't stumble on the one signing my magic over to Derek or just taking a normal professional precaution?

Argh. I couldn't keep relying on speculation. I'd conjure up some "proof" for him, subtle enough that he'd believe Celestine might have held on to it but blatant enough that he'd have to realize she'd been up to something shady, and his reaction would tell me everything I needed to know.

"Okay," I said to Phil as she breezed along with us into the windowless room. "Look for a good place for a stray paper to just happen to be lying out. Somewhere he'll believe Celestine could have hidden it—or missed it —but where he'll see it while he's searching."

"Aye, aye, my lady," Phil said with a wink.

The sound of our footsteps seemed to dull amid the windowless walls. Dad and I crossed the polished wooden floor to the room's sole piece of furniture: a large cabinet at the back. I wasn't supposed to have any idea what it contained, but the truth was I'd searched most of it last week. With the magic I wasn't supposed to have either.

Dad opened the cabinet doors and gave the shelves a quick glance. I did a similar mental inventory, though for different purposes. It wouldn't make any sense for a note to be mixed in with supplies like feathers or gems, or to be sitting out far too obviously on a shelf. The contracts box wouldn't work, because it contained only official documents...

A deeper chill sliced through me. The contracts. I'd taken the one relating to my consorting out. Now that I didn't have to worry about Celestine tracking it down to retrieve it, I'd secreted it away in the pages of one of my novels—a gothic romance featuring a vain and ruthless stepmother as the villain, which seemed appropriate. But if Dad were expecting to find it, if he looked through that box and found it missing...

Common sense broke through the rising haze of panic. It was okay. If he didn't find it there, he'd just assume Celestine had hidden it somewhere else. That would be the obvious explanation, not that I'd managed to find it and hide it using my theoretically non-existent magical powers.

Dad grabbed the first couple boxes off the top shelf. I knelt down and tugged out one from the lowest, which I hadn't made it to in my explorations before. I didn't look at the box of contracts waiting for us, now at eye level, but my skin prickled with my awareness of it.

"It's too bad I can't just put the contract back," I said to Phil as I pawed through a heap of incense packets. "You couldn't ask for better proof than that. But it's also the only proof *I* have. I can't risk Dad keeping it if he really is in on the scheme."

Philomena cocked her head. "Can't you just conjure a new one? Stick it right on the top, so he'll see it the second he opens the box..."

I shook my head, just slightly. "There's a certain quality to magical contracts. You can *feel* the binding magic in the signatures. I couldn't conjure something that intricate and specific, at least not until I have a lot more practice using my powers. Even without any magical ability, Dad would know it wasn't right."

I pushed the incense box back onto the shelf and reached for a bag that proved to be full of glyph tokens, some on smoothed stone, others carved into what looked like chunks of bone. Those weren't standard, but some witches felt the former life essence gave the tokens an extra kick of power. I restrained a shudder as I shoved that bag back.

"What about those books?" Phil said with a tip of her chin. Dad had just opened up a box of old journals and private witching texts stamped with family names. Private archives and spell notes. I'd dismissed them when I'd made my earlier search because they hadn't looked recently used, but Dad was considering them.

"I'll have to go through these later," he said. "I doubt they'll say much if anything about your stepmother's recent activities, but if nothing else offers guidance..." He ran his hand through his dark hair and turned back to the shelves.

I exchanged a glance with Philomena. That could be perfect. While he was distracted with the rest of his investigation, I could quickly conjure a slip of paper tucked inside the first notebook. He'd see it as soon as he started paging through them. I could even leave it poking out a little to draw his attention.

I'd already come up with the wording I'd use... Notes about binding and the consort ceremony, the date when mine was supposed to happen, a mention of some of the resources Master Cortland had been looking up. Any witching man would recognize the morbid significance of the symbols. I'd spent a good deal of the day yesterday poring over the few papers I had with Celestine's actual handwriting on them and practicing conjuring an accurate facsimile.

The false evidence only needed to convince him long enough for him to act. Or not act, as the case might be. My stomach twisted at the thought.

The outcome didn't matter right now. What mattered was getting there—getting an answer, even if it was hard to accept. I just had to perform the magicking without him noticing...

A rustling sounded near the door. My head snapped around. Mrs. Gainsley had come into the doorway. She was watching the proceedings.

Shit. I couldn't magick anything with her watching.

I yanked out the last box at the bottom of the cabinet as I stewed. How to send her off, for long enough that I could finish the magicking...? I wet my lips and looked up again.

"Matilda," I said. My tongue stumbled over her first name. She'd told us all to call her by it as we always had with Meredith, but it felt strange to me being just as familiar with her, a relative stranger, as I'd been with the woman who'd practically raised me alongside my father. "Would you mind—I was thinking it might be useful to have any records of purchases Celestine asked Meredith to make on her behalf, so we know what supplies in here are most recent. Could you check the office for those?"

"Yes, of course, Rosalind," she said. My hackles rose

despite myself. Celestine had always insisted on calling me by my full name too.

The estate manager slipped away. I eased the lid off the box in front of me, watching for the right moment. My gaze fell on a stack of file folders inside.

Celestine had been keeping some other sort of records in here. I hadn't made it to this box last time. The contract had been such a damning find I hadn't seen the need to keep going.

At the same moment, Dad hefted the box of contracts. He peered inside, and his eyes sharpened. He rested them against the shelf, looking at each intently as he paged through them.

Now—this was my moment.. I turned away from him and faked a cough, rotating my arm and then dancing my fingers through delicate movements, hidden close to my chest. My spark jittered inside me. Power flowed into my hand. Just one little piece of paper, a few lines of handwriting, the image in my head made real... *There.*

The paper trembled into being just under the cover of the first notebook in the box he'd set aside earlier, a corner jutting out exactly as I'd intended. A wash of relief swept through me as the energy inside me ebbed.

It was done. As soon as he looked at those books, I'd know whether my father was the loving if sometimes distracted man I'd always thought he was... or my worst enemy.

"What are those, then?" Philomena asked, kneeling beside the box I was supposed to be looking through.

I turned back to it. "Let's find out."

The first couple file folders held magazine clippings

of dresses and make-up—nothing that made a whole lot of sense to me. It was hard to imagine my stepmother lowering herself to even looking through unsparked fashion magazines, let alone drawing ideas from them. But then, it wasn't as if there were any regular publications on witching fashion. Maybe she'd been driven by desperation.

The corner of my mouth twitched with amusement—and stiffened when I opened the next folder. A photograph of Derek stared back at me. My pulse hitched.

She had a file on my theoretical fiancé. I probably shouldn't be surprised. She must have done plenty of research to determine he was the best candidate. There might be some interesting material in there for my own use. Was it just this folder, or had she filed away more than one with information on him...?

My fingers stilled with the next folder half-open. Another young man smiled up at me from another photo —not Derek. I didn't even know this guy. Who the hell was he?

Another potential candidate?

"What have you got there, Rose?" Dad asked. Damn, I'd been staring long enough that he'd noticed my hesitation.

My instincts pulled me in two directions at once. I forced out an answer.

"Nothing. Just some magazine clippings. I'll keep looking, though."

I made myself move on to the next folder—another witching man, one I recognized from a trip we'd taken a few years ago to Edinburgh—how many of them were there? I dug deeper.

Five. Five likely candidates my stepmother had gathered. The folders under those were more clippings, these ones of various foreign locals. Travel planning? I didn't know why she'd kept that in here, but I didn't really care about my stepmother's eccentric habits right now.

I needed the chance to go through these files undisturbed. To know which other witching men looking to consort I might need to inform the Assembly about. Had she *approached* any of the others? Had any of them done something to make her think they'd be willing to commit a lifelong crime on this scale?

Matilda's footsteps tapped toward us down the hall. Moldy cinders. I gritted my teeth, focused on the spark inside me, and made a hasty gesture with my hand as if swiping a bug off the top of the stack.

The five folders vanished—and hopefully had reappeared under my pillow in my bedroom.

"Dad," I said, raising my head and fishing out one of the travel folders. "Some of these clippings are of different places around the world. Maybe they'd give you some idea of where she might have gone?"

"Thank you," Dad said. "Let me take a look."

Matilda reappeared at the doorway. She was holding a small record book and a handful of receipts. "I've gathered everything relating to magical purchases," she said. "But it doesn't look as if any of the ones your former estate manager had date from after your arrival here."

"I guess they probably won't be that useful then," I

said, sitting back on my heels. "But thank you for looking." I glanced up at Dad. "I think I've covered the bottom shelves. Are there any boxes or bags up there you haven't gone through yet?"

Dad shook his head, still flipping through the file of travel clippings I'd shown him. "They're mostly standard supplies, exactly what you'd expect. I appreciate your help, lamb. And maybe something we've found here will help me find some answers. But I think we're done here."

He set down the box of files on top of the box of books and hefted them both. I followed him out into the hall. Derek was just heading from his room to the stairs. He paused at the sight of us. His gaze seemed to stick on the boxes in Dad's hands as Dad strode into his office. Derek's jaw tightened.

Oh, he didn't like the thought of what Dad might have found in Celestine's things at all, did he? That ought to be a good sign. A sign that he didn't believe Dad would approve of her scheme.

Please, Spark above, let it be a good sign.

CHAPTER TWELVE

Kyler

When I'd told Rose I could blend into the Seattle scene no problem, even I hadn't realized it'd be this ridiculously easy. I was perched at a bar-height table beside the broad front windows of a downtown coffee shop, my laptop open in front of me and the big gray building that housed her "Witching Assembly" across the street. The room around me was filled with the clatter of fingers tapping frenetically on keyboards and tablet screens.

I swear anyone who *wasn't* hard at work on a computer of some sort would have stuck out like a sore thumb.

I took a drink of my coffee—bitter black and still so hot it almost burned my tongue, just the way I liked it— and got down to work. I'd picked the table in the back corner, so no one could wander over and happen to look over my shoulder as I pried into the security around the Assembly's local network.

Hacking was a lot like carving a sculpture out of a hunk of marble. At least, what I imagined that would be like, from that time I'd spent a few nights reading about ancient Greek artistic techniques. Jin probably would have had a better idea.

But anyway, you started with what looked like a big, blank, impenetrable block, and you felt along it with your chisel until you found the right point to chip away so that it cracked along just the right lines. And then you kept chipping and cracking it open until you discovered the form waiting underneath.

Thankfully, I was a lot happier working with carefully placed bits of code than a literal chisel. And no doubt a lot faster too. In a matter of minutes I'd stripped away the outer layers of security and was diving into the standard interface of the Assembly's private databases.

This was only the outer layer, though. I skimmed past daily agendas and contact lists and meeting minutes, all stuff any employee would have had access to. Just to be thorough, I did a quick search for "consort," which led me to the Consorting Advisership department behind a security wall I could already tell was pretty flimsy. Otherwise in the main network there were just a few mentions in general records of the Advisership's activities and schedule, announcements of recently joined consorts...

Would my name, and the other guys', be up there next to Rose's some day? The idea made me feel giddy and a little itchy at the same time. I wasn't totally sure I wanted the bureaucrats inside that industrial-looking building cataloguing our relationship. It was ours, not theirs.

I left the outer rim of the network behind and dug into the Consorting Advisership's locked section. Chip, chip, chip, crack! Nothing to it.

The wall crumbled away, leaving me staring at a vast array of data—completed consort ceremonies, new applications, interviews conducted, follow-up communications sent, and on and on.

A sick sort of curiosity prickled at me. I found myself typing out Rose's name, even though I knew I wasn't going to enjoy seeing the information that was associated with her in here right now.

Several files came up—all of them for her and that Derek asshole, of course. The initial declaration of intent to consort. Her stepmother's filing that she would conduct the ceremony. Notes from an interview when the advisers had come to the estate last month. *The couple meets the criteria for a solid and stable partnership. No concerns noted.*

Solid and stable my ass. These people had magic—you'd think they'd be able to pry hard enough to discover one of the people in that partnership was planning on turning the other into a slave.

Anger rippled through my chest, but I had to tune that out. I was working to get Rose out of that mess right now. Which meant I had to get down to the real work.

Studying a few of the standard forms, I figured out a way to quickly search for any that might have involved more than two partners. That effort turned up zero

results. Determining whether there was any standard
record of a witch taking someone outside the witching
world as a consort was trickier, but after coming at the
subject from several angles, I felt I'd covered every
possible base.

The only differently labeled consorting records I
found mentioned a "soul-bound" ceremony. The notes on
them seemed to indicate it was something more intense
than the regular consort ceremonies. They required a
lengthier interview and follow-ups reporting on the
witch's magic, which apparently was more powerful
afterward. But hardly any of those had happened in the
last hundred years.

Why not? The records didn't offer much of a clue. I'd
have to ask Rose when I got back. If there was a way we
could offer her even more strength, I was all for it.

I found no accounts of a witch consorting with more
than one man, or with a non-witching man, any time
since the Advisership had started keeping their records
this way—back to the '30s. I guessed they'd digitized hard
copy records going back that far to account for all witches
still living.

But if any witches still living had done either, Rose
probably would have known about it anyway. I couldn't
reach the paper records they might have in storage from
earlier times from my computer... and the thought of
trying to search through those manually made my head
hurt. But I'd do it if I had to. I'd bet I could clone a
security card to get into the building if it came to that.

I wasn't quite at that point yet, though. A few times
my searches had nudged up against another wall within

the Advisership's archives. I'd like to know what lay on the other side of that.

This wall was a little better built. It took me fifteen minutes to crack through instead of five, but then I was in. It didn't look like the section I'd opened up was part of the Advisership's domain after all, just a subsection adjacent to their operations. The documents I came across first were all marked as security reports by the Assembly's "Justice Division." The people I guessed Rose was hoping to turn asshole Derek and possibly her father over to. What kinds of "justice" had they needed to do when it came to past consort relationships?

I opened up a couple of the files. The first one was an account of domestic violence between a witch and her consort. She'd battered him badly enough that he'd needed medical attention. The witch had been sentenced to two year's imprisonment while she waited out the remaining time before the consort bond could be safely severed. Then she'd been put under a spell that prevented her from touching anyone—to regain her powers through hooking up with them or to hurt them—for ten years after that. Fair enough, but nothing that related to Rose's case.

The second one was a broken consorting. The man had delayed and delayed the ceremony only to outright cancel it at the last moment before his fiancée's twenty-fifth birthday. Too late for her to find someone else. With her spark unkindled, she'd lost her magic. The Assembly's Justice Division had ruled that the man had entered the engagement in bad faith and required he offer his former partner a big payoff in restitution.

My stomach twisted. That could have been the fate that Rose would have faced if she'd had to leave Derek but hadn't been able to turn to us. How could any amount of money compensate for losing the powers you were born to wield?

As I nudged at the code, I caught another barrier, well-disguised even within this closed section of the network. An even deeper sublevel with very limited access granted—unless you happened to know how to finagle your way into that access.

What kind of records would they want to keep super-secret, for only select member's eyes? That was something I definitely needed to know.

And whoever had set up this secure section really didn't want me to know. I prodded and poked at the code, my mouth slanting into a frown. They'd gotten someone who actually knew what they were doing to build this wall for them. I'd get in, no doubt about that, but it was going to take more time and effort than the first two layers.

I set the laptop downloading the files from the less secure section so I could go over them later at my leisure, and then I took a quick break. The walk across the coffee shop and the steam of a fresh cup of coffee helped reset my brain. Then I dove back in.

Test for a weak spot here. Jiggle this potential backdoor there. Nope, nope—ah ha. A little loophole hardly anyone ever thought to plug. I wriggled my way in, and a new but small set of files appeared before me. What did we have here?

Before I could open any up, a movement across the

street caught my eye. Two middle-aged men in what looked like posh law enforcement uniforms had emerged from the Assembly building. They headed straight across the street with an air as if they expected the traffic to dodge *them*.

My skin tightened. They were heading straight toward the coffee shop. There shouldn't be any way anyone could know I'd snuck into their network, but suddenly I had a very, very bad feeling about this.

I knew computers, but I didn't know magic. The witches in the Assembly could be capable of detecting all kinds of things I hadn't considered. Shit.

I had to get out of here, but I couldn't leave without some idea of what I'd just found. My fingers darted over the keyboard, instructing my computer to download all the files in the super-secret section I'd gained access to.

Trying to look as if I'd simply finished the work I'd come here to do, I eased the laptop shut, tucked it into my shoulder bag, and slung that behind me so it wouldn't be obvious. Then I grabbed my latest cup of coffee. If I veered over to the counter first...

I swung past the order pick-up area and then headed toward the door as if I'd just popped in for take-out. The two law-enforcement-looking dudes came in when I was halfway there. My heart thudded, but I glanced over them as if they were just a strange sight, not anything I associated with myself.

Keep breathing evenly. Don't clutch the strap of the bag too tightly. I was on my way out anyway, not fleeing for my life.

Whatever had brought the guys across the street, it

obviously hadn't allowed them to pinpoint the culprit in any more detail. They glanced at me and my cup of coffee and then moved on. I didn't stick around to find out how they were going to try to narrow down their search. The second I was out of view of the windows, I hustled right round the block and hailed the first taxi I saw.

I only popped open my laptop again when I was back in the pastel-colored, slightly sour-smelling motel room. My connection to the Assembly's network would have broken automatically when I'd gotten out of range, but there should have been enough time—

As I stared at the screen, my spirits sank. I'd only managed to download five files from that extra-secret section. They must have slammed down a new wall after they'd detected the intrusion, right after I'd started to download.

The first file, when I tried to open it, proved to be just a corrupted fragment. So did the second. I winced. I might have come out with nothing after all.

I wasn't feeling all that hopeful when I clicked on the third file. My heart leapt when it opened without an error. Then my gaze skimmed down the contents, and my body went rigid.

It was a report a lot like the other Justice documents I'd looked at, but with a series of glyphs along the top that meant nothing to me. The report itself concerned a witch who'd been engaging in "relations" with an "unsparked" man. Some widow off in an isolated nook of Ireland. So that kind of relationship *had* happened before—and not that long ago. The date on the record was from eight years ago.

But that fact wasn't exactly a positive given the rest of the contents. For "stepping outside the boundaries of witching society" and "to maintain order and consistency among the community," the Assembly, or at least a small group among them, had intervened. A gas stove in the witch's house had been meddled with—she'd disappeared with her home in a blaze of fire, no evidence left behind. And the man she'd been seeing had been hit by a car on a lonely road not long after, killed on impact.

At least, that's what the spells had been adjusted to look like. Just a couple of random, unconnected accidents.

I leaned back on the motel bed, my arms abruptly shaky. Nausea coiled around my stomach.

So *that* was how Rose's Assembly dealt with witches who'd done what she had. At least a few of them knew it was possible, and they were determined that no one else should ever know, no matter who they had to hurt along the way.

CHAPTER THIRTEEN

Rose

*I*t was almost eight in the evening. Derek had asked me to join him for a game of cards then —in front of my dad, so I'd felt I had to play along to avoid raising Dad's suspicions—but I didn't feel ready to budge from my room. Not when my anxious texting hadn't given me better news.

Sorry, Jin wrote. *I haven't heard anything from Ky since that group message this morning either.*

Seth and Damon had already reported radio silence. I hadn't been able to get an answer from Kyler despite my several texts throughout the afternoon. All I knew was that early in the morning he'd cheerfully reported he was heading off to "crack some witchy networks" and since then there'd been nothing but silence.

Let me know as soon as any of you do hear anything,

okay? I wrote to all of them in our group message. I couldn't bring the phone with me, since I wasn't supposed to have it at all, but I'd check it again as soon as I was back in my room. And if we still hadn't heard from Ky by morning...

I didn't care what anyone on the estate thought. I'd be making that trip to Seattle myself. I'd drawn Ky into this world, and I had to protect him from it.

Spark help me, I wished there didn't seem to be so many parts of my world my guys *needed* protection from right now.

Of course, Seth said. *You know I'll be watching for any message from him too.*

I'm sure Mr. Brainiac can think his way out of whatever tight spot he's gotten into, Damon put in. *Or maybe he's just too busy hacking away to chat. Let's hold off the panic until tomorrow.*

Before my teeth could even quite set on edge, he sent a message apart from the group conversation, just to me. *Don't worry, angel. If anyone's messed with one of us, they're going to regret it. We'll get him back.*

My lips twitched, halfway between a smile and a grimace.

I shoved the prepaid phone back into its hiding spot. If I didn't get down there, Derek was going to come looking for me. And after the other night, the last place I wanted to meet him was outside my bedroom.

I'd just reached for my doorknob when Dad's voice filtered through from the hall on the other side. "Derek, do you have a moment? I was hoping we could talk."

Apparently my supposed fiancé had already gotten

impatient enough to come up. "All right," he said, sounding a little wary.

What exactly were they going to talk about? Had Dad gone through Celestine's books and found the paper I'd planted there? Maybe he was going to interrogate Derek about how much he knew.

My pulse skittered. I listened for the click of Dad's door shutting. Then I eased open mine and peeked into the hall.

No sign of our witch estate manager. I could get away with a little magic out here.

I slipped down the hall to Dad's office. If I could just hear... No, I wanted to see, too. I couldn't risk any misunderstandings, not with so much on the line.

Dragging in a deep breath, I raised my hands toward the ceiling to summon the energy of my spark high. I stepped forward and back, drew my arms back to my body, and slowly but surely wrapped that magic around me. Let every bit of me look like nothing but air.

A wave of dizziness passed over me. I caught myself against the wall—and stared at it. I couldn't even see myself, not my arm nor the fingers braced against the cool plaster.

I'd done it. Now to get inside. With a whirl and a slash of my arms, I threw myself into the teleportation spell that had served me well in the past.

I was only hopping a few feet this time. The flash of blackness darted past my eyes, and then my feet were jarring against the thick pile of Dad's rug at the back of the room.

Dad was sitting at his desk. He'd left Derek standing

across from him. My former consort-to-be rocked back on his heels, his stance casual but his expression a bit tight as he chuckled at something Dad must have said.

The box of Celestine's books was sitting by the corner of the desk near my former fiancé, the stack of them looking completely undisturbed since Dad had carried them out this morning. The corner of my conjured paper was still sticking out from the top one.

So Dad hadn't found it yet. He'd called Derek in for some other reason. I wanted to hear what *that* was too.

"You don't have to worry," Derek said. "Nothing has changed in that regard. It really couldn't, could it?"

"That's true," Dad said with a faint smile. He leaned back in his chair. "I just like to consider all the factors. You and my daughter still seem somewhat... distant from each other."

What regard? What factors? I itched to shake the answers out of them, but all I could do was watch. Was Derek going to tattle on me, report how I'd pushed him away? Would he want Dad to know that or not?

"From what I saw in Portland, Rose is pretty independent," he said. "It's not a surprise that she's slow to share her trust, is it? But we've been getting to know each other, and I know we're both still committed to the consorting. I'm doing my best to show I'm worthy of the trust she's already placed in me."

Oh, was he? I'd hate to see his worst then. My hands clenched. I didn't just want to shake him now—I wanted to punch that ingratiating smile right off his face.

"I can't argue that Rose has always been a bit of a loner," Dad said. "My fault, mostly, trying to raise her out here. But you knew that about her from the start." He eyed Derek.

Derek spread his hands. "And my comment wasn't a complaint, only an observation. I look forward to continuing to get to know her better, even if it takes some time."

Dad made a humming sound. Was that all this was? He'd noticed my hesitation around Derek and wanted to feel out how Derek felt about the match now? They weren't talking as if they were planning on forcing the issue.

Derek let his hand come to rest on the top of the box of books, and my back stiffened. He'd been eyeing those books earlier. He knew that he'd be in as much trouble as Celestine if their arrangement was discovered by an outside party.

"I do want my daughter to have a worthy partner," Dad said. "And believe me, I'll speak up if I see reason for concern. Just as forewarning." He smiled again, pleasantly enough, but with a glint of steel in his hazel eyes.

Derek chuckled again, less convincingly this time. Dad pushed back his chair and bent to retrieve something from one of the drawers on his desk.

"You'll have a little more alone time in the next day or two," he said over the rustling of papers. "I think I've pinpointed my wife's current location. I'll be traveling out to meet her shortly—my flight leaves in a few hours."

Moldy cinders. He'd tracked down Celestine after all?

I barely had time to panic over that revelation before

Derek's hand crept right down on the stack of books. Dad swiveled to check something on the shelves behind him, and Derek gave the books a quick nudge, looking through the titles, I guessed. I clamped my mouth shut on a squeak of protest when his thumb slid over the protruding corner of paper under the cover of the first.

He glanced at my dad and lifted the cover. His shoulders went rigid.

No.

I jerked my hand, slamming the cover shut with a burst of magic. But Derek had already snatched out the paper I'd conjured. Dad turned at the sound, and my former fiancé shoved the paper into the pocket of his pants.

No, no, no.

"What was that?" Dad said, and Derek started to make some dismissive gesture, and I wrenched at the magic inside me for a way to turn this situation around. My body shuddered with the surge of frantic emotion.

The spell I'd cast to make me invisible was starting to crack. I glanced down and saw a sliver of my hand. My heart lurched. Dad's gaze started to shift from Derek, and I swung my arms around myself. With a flash of black and a hitch of breath, I'd whisked myself back to my bedroom.

My legs wobbled. I knelt on the hard floor, catching my breath. My spark still burned, but an ache spread through my chest around it. I was casting difficult spells, with magic I'd had little opportunity to practice before now. It was wearing me out.

What if Derek had realized magic had compelled the

book shut? Could he connect that moment to me? I couldn't go out there this frazzled.

My mind settled on the last place on the estate where I'd really felt secure. I needed that. Needed to ground myself.

I dropped onto the floor and grabbed my secret phone out of its hiding place. My fingers darted over the keypad. *Is it safe for me to come?*

Gabriel answered a moment later. *All clear.*

Scrambling up, I threw myself into the teleportation form one more time. The ache twanged through my limbs, but darkness snapped around me. And then I was stumbling forward, my shin bumping the coffee table in the garage-top apartment.

Gabriel appeared in the kitchen doorway. He blinked at me for a second. "Rose? I... wasn't expecting you quite that fast."

Maybe I should have given him more warning. I dragged in a shaky breath, swiping my hands across my face. "I'm sorry. I just needed to get out of the house, to get my bearings. And there's nowhere on the estate I feel safe right now except here."

"Hey." He walked up to me and set his hands on my shoulders. "It's not a problem. What happened?" His eyes darkened. "Who made you feel you weren't safe over in the house?"

"It's nothing you need to fix," I said quickly. "There's just so much... I'm feeling a little overwhelmed—not knowing if Kyler's okay, and Derek just found the 'proof' I tried to plant and grabbed it before Dad could see it. And now Dad's leaving for at least a day, because apparently he knows where my stepmother is..."

"Is there any way you can stop him?"

"Not without revealing my magic, and all the consequences that'll come with that." I drew my spine straighter. "It might not even be a bad thing. My spell on her should hold. It doesn't *seem* like he's in on their plan. There's just too much I'm still not sure of."

A flicker of some emotion passed through Gabriel's eyes. "I'm here," he said. "Whatever I can do to keep you safe. You can be sure of that, at least."

His hands were still on my shoulders, the heat of his body flowing from them into me. A pang of desire ran through my chest and down to my core. I closed my eyes against it.

I couldn't have him like that. But there were simpler things I could ask him for.

"Can you just talk to me a little before I go back?" I said. "Anything that has nothing to do with witches or getting married would work."

Gabriel laughed under his breath. "All right," he said. "I can do that. Come sit down, and tell me when you're ready for me to shut up."

I followed him over to the sofa. We sat a short distance apart, but he reached out to curl his fingers around my hand, his gaze bright as it held mine.

"Do you remember that time—we were maybe ten or eleven?—and we found that stray kitten hiding out by the hunting cabin? Kyler ran to read up on how to handle feral cats and Seth snuck us into the kitchen to steal some fish—Damon acted like he was too tough to care about some cute kitten so of course he was the only one it really warmed up to." Gabriel grinned. "Not that we were successful enough to keep it around for more than a few days before it went looking for new adventures. But that experience was actually useful a couple years back when I ended up sharing a hostel room in Costa Rica with a resident cat that might as well have been feral. The thing I realized..."

I sank into the sofa cushions, letting his warm voice wash over me, feeling my nerves settling even more. Knowing I was never going to be ready for him to stop. I wished I could listen to him talk all night.

When we'd finished our second round of euchre, Derek set down the cards. My body tensed. After listening to Gabriel talk about the mountains and the ancient ruins he'd explored, I'd been able to return to the house calm and collected—and not the least bit regretful that I'd made Derek wait a half hour for that card game I'd promised. But now he clearly had something else in mind.

"Why don't we take a little time just to talk," he said, but he immediately scooted his chair closer to mine. A jitter ran through my nerves. Somehow I got the feeling *talking* wasn't exactly what he had in mind.

"Maybe I came on too strong the other night," he said. "We don't have to move quickly. I'm not asking you to let me into your bedroom. But it would be to our benefit to start getting to know each other a *little* better before the consort ceremony, don't you think?"

He set his hand on my knee, sending a shiver of revulsion up my leg. I shifted away and stood up. Dad had already left for his flight. I didn't have to pretend I was still planning on getting consorted to this snake.

"I think we know each other exactly as well as we need to," I said crisply.

"Come on now, Rose," Derek said, getting up too. "What is it you need to feel more comfortable with me?"

I needed him to not have been plotting against me and sleeping with the staff and saying horrible things behind my back. Since I wasn't going to get that, he was shit out of luck. But I couldn't say anything about that.

As I turned over my possible answers in my head, Derek seemed to take my hesitation as giving in. He touched my shoulder. "Wouldn't you like a little taste of your spark?"

Without waiting for an answer, he lowered his head to kiss me.

It was a soft kiss, meant to be gentle, but the brush of his lips made my stomach turn. I jerked my head to the side, and my hand shot up in a burst of anger, with a quick snap of a magicking just out of Derek's view.

His expression twisted, his arm coming around his belly. "I'm sorry," he said. "I think we'll have to briefly postpone any—"

He scrambled around the table and dashed toward the nearest bathroom.

Philomena strolled past him with an amused glance.

"Thank the heavens you got rid of him. What did you do to him?"

"Just made him feel even queasier than he made me," I said. Maybe I'd let him stay that way until he decided to leave here for good.

Phil laughed and clapped her hands. But my small flicker of triumph died when I turned and saw Mrs. Gainsley standing in the room's other doorway. A rush of cold shot through me.

Had she seen me do that magicking? Forcing Derek away from me?

Her expression gave no sign either way. "Miss Hallowell," she said, "since it appears your father will be gone for tomorrow, I wondered if you wanted some say in the kitchen's meal planning."

"Oh," I said. "Yes, sure, that would be nice. I'll go down and talk to them directly in the morning, though. I'm sure you've got enough keeping you busy without that too."

She nodded and turned to go, leaving my skin prickling. I made a quick motion behind my back to dissolve any trace of my spell from Derek's body. As satisfying as the idea of laying him low with some magical illness was, another witch would be able to sense my influence. Might even be able to trace it directly back to me.

I had all the magic I could have wanted in me, but until I could use it openly, I couldn't rely on it to save me.

CHAPTER FOURTEEN

Rose

The second I saw Kyler standing in the middle of Jin's gallery, I threw myself into his arms.

"Hey!" he said, hugging me back. "It's okay. I'm here now. No worse for wear, either."

"I was so worried." I pressed my face into the soft fabric of his cotton tee. He *was* here, lean and solid in my arms. The tension in my chest that hadn't quite ebbed even when I'd gotten his text this morning finally released.

"All's well that ends well?" Jin suggested.

"Nothing has ended yet," Seth said.

Damon was rolling his eyes when I drew back from Ky. "Thank you, Mr. Gloom and Doom. We all needed that reminder."

We'd gathered here in the gallery before, but somehow it felt more ominous today with the shade cutting out most of the spring sunlight from outside and the tang of paint faint but sharp in the air. Maybe because Ky's smile at seeing me had already fallen into a frown.

When even my normally cheerful guy looked a little gloomy, something was really wrong. He hadn't told us anything about what he'd found out in Seattle yet—or why he'd gotten so nervous he'd decided it was safer not to contact any of us until he was back in town.

"Is Gabriel coming?" he asked. "I think he's involved enough that he should hear this too."

I nodded. "He left a little earlier, but he was going to take a round-about route so it wouldn't be obvious he was coming into town at the same time as me. I'm sure—"

A knock on the door came before I had to say he'd be there soon. Jin leapt to let Gabriel in.

Gabriel came to join us in our loose circle—a circle closer and more at ease than the one he'd entered a week ago, but still off-balance with him in our midst.

He didn't seem to let it faze him. He turned to Ky right away, with his familiar easy confidence. "So what did you dig up in Seattle?"

"Yes," I said, refocusing on that urgent concern. "What *happened*?"

Ky grinned crookedly. "Nothing really. Mostly my own paranoia. I think your Assembly must have some kind of magical detection system in their computer network. Right after I got into one of the more secure sections, they kicked me out and sent some guys to take a look in the coffee shop where I was working. But I got out of there fast. I waited to come home until I was sure they hadn't connected the unexpected activity to me. We should be safe."

"You went all the way out to Seattle and came back with nothing?" Damon said, folding his arms over his chest.

"Hey," Gabriel said mildly. "It's not like any of the rest of us would have gotten *anywhere* with that network, let alone far enough in to scare them. That's fucking impressive."

Kyler shot Gabriel a smile and cut a look toward Damon. "And I didn't say I got nothing." But then he hesitated, a shadow crossing his face. My gut knotted.

"What is it, Ky?" I said.

He looked at the floor and then at me. There was so much pain mixed with the affection in his gaze that the knots inside me pulled achingly tight.

"I don't think you're ever going to be able to tell anyone about our consorting, Rose," he said quietly. "Even if there are people who'd be okay with it, the ones who aren't... I only managed to recover one of the most secure records, but it was about a witch who got involved with a guy who wasn't one. Someone in the Justice Division of the Assembly arranged to have them *killed*."

In the wake of that word, silence blared through the room. It took me a few seconds to find my tongue. "Killed?" I repeated. "You mean they just..."

His mouth pulled into a grimace. "They used magic to make it look like it was a couple of separate accidents, her and the guy. But there wasn't even any debate about it, as far as I could tell. Standard procedure, as soon as they found out. Eliminate the problem and the evidence."

He dragged in a shaky breath. "There were two names on the report, signing off. One of them is Eliza Hammersmith, one of the women in the Assembly that Mr. Cortland was talking to."

A sharper chill washed over me. "You think *he's* involved in... in murdering people?"

Ky shook his head. "I don't know. I'm not sure how many people even in the Assembly are in on those kind of... operations, or whatever you want to call them. I had to do a lot of digging just to find those records. Very few people were on the approved list, and that area of the network was set up so you wouldn't know it was there at a glance. But if Cortland suspected you'd started seeing us—any of us—and mentioned it to Ms. Hammersmith, we'd still be in just as much trouble."

My knees wobbled. Seth was at my side in an instant, his hand on my back. Jin came up on my other side, slipping his arm around my waist. They both bowed their heads close as the shock of that information rolled over me.

"Hey," Jin said. "It's just one case. That's all you have, right?" He glanced at Ky, who nodded.

"I've got no idea what the other records in that section were about," he said.

"You'd never heard anything about the Assembly resorting to violence?" Seth asked me.

"No." My voice came out small. "If it was necessary, because a witch was being violent and they had to subdue her in self-defense, but otherwise... We have due process. We have lawyers and trials like anyone else."

Except when a witch dallied with an unsparked man,

apparently. Spark help me, what had I dragged the guys I loved into?

I tried to catch my breath and slow my spinning thoughts. I'd thought no matter what happened with my father, I'd be able to present a case to the Assembly, show that a consorting like this was possible and fruitful... So much for that. So what options did that leave me with?

"You didn't see anything in your searching about my dad, did you?" I asked Ky.

"Just what looked like standard stuff, his witnessing of your engagement, that kind of thing. Nothing that made me think he's involved in anything... murderous. But the way your stepmother was going to manipulate your ceremony isn't something they'd officially report anyway, right?"

"No. But so far, with everything I've seen, it looks like he has no idea what Celestine and Derek were planning. Maybe I can go to him, and he'll have some idea of where to go from here, how to keep the Assembly from finding out."

"Are you sure you're ready to trust him?" Gabriel said. "I know he's your dad, and I know Celestine isn't trustworthy, but he has made... questionable decisions before."

He had, and particularly when it came to my guys and their families. I bit my lip. "I don't know. Maybe when he gets back from trying to talk to Celestine and I see how that's affected him, I'll have a clearer idea. Or I can go back to my original plan." I could conjure another paper like the one Derek had stolen. Push Dad toward it more insistently.

I couldn't risk opening up to him about what I'd done when not just my life but all four of my consorts' were on the line.

"And if it seems like I can't trust him... I'll figure something out. I just need time to think." I glanced around at my guys. "I promise I'll do everything in my power to keep you safe."

My consorts eased closer around me. Seth dipped his head right against mine, his breath warm against my cheek. "You know we'll do the same for you," he said.

Jin kissed my shoulder. "We're in this until the end, Briar Rose, brambles and all."

I held out my hands, taking Kyler's and Damon's. "Right here with you," Ky said firmly.

"Yeah," Damon said. "It'll take an army of witches to get rid of me now."

My thudding pulse slowed with their presence all around me. My gaze drifted from them to the one guy now completely outside our ring of devotion.

Gabriel was watching us, his expression rigid, his normally bright eyes darkened with emotion. When they caught mine, the heat in them seemed to leap from him to me, sweeping through my body from head to toe. My heart skipped a beat. Then he was wrenching his gaze away with a clearing of his throat.

"I'll still be keeping an eye out around the house," he said. "I can try to chum up to Derek more and see what he'll spill. However I can help, I will. It'd probably be better if I get back to the estate well ahead of you, though."

"Gabriel," I started. What was wrong with me that I

ached to call him over to join us, after what I'd just learned?

What was wrong with me that I couldn't find the words to do it, as much as I wanted to?

His jaw worked, but he smiled. "I'll see you at the house," he said, and ducked out the door.

My throat tightened as the lock clicked back into place behind him. Kyler studied my expression.

"He should have been here," he said.

The words echoed my thoughts so well that for a second I could only blink at him. "What?"

He tilted his head toward the door. "Gabriel. He should have been here when you first got back. He should have been part of this. You know he'd have wanted to be." He paused, his gaze searching mine. "And I think you'd have wanted that too."

My hands tightened around his and Damon's.

Jin stroked my side soothingly. "It's all right," he said. "We all know we wouldn't have been a group in the first place without Gabriel. He's one of us, even if in some ways right now he's not. We don't have any right to be jealous."

"Speak for yourself," Damon muttered, but his expression softened when I looked at him. "You deserve all the love in the world, angel," he added. "I'm not going to say I like sharing you, but I wouldn't get in the way, if that's what you want. I'm here, aren't I?"

"I shouldn't want to bring him any more into this mess than he already is," I said. "If I took him as my consort too, then he'd just be in more danger."

"And you'd also have more magic to fight that

danger," Seth said. "Is it *possible* to take another consort after you've already done the ceremony with us...?"

A choked laugh spilled out of me. "I wouldn't know unless I tried. I didn't know it was going to be possible to take all of you as consorts in the first place. But... it feels like it should work. If he and I decided we wanted to. If I was okay with putting him in that kind of danger too. And if you all were okay with it. *You're* my consorts. My loyalty is to you first. You have to know that."

Seth hugged me to him and then leaned in for a kiss. "He's one of us," he said. "Even if not that way yet. I don't have any problem with completely reuniting the group."

"No argument from me either," Jin said. "The more the merrier?" He winked at me.

"I don't think you should need our permission," Ky said. "But if you want to have it first, you've got it from me too."

Damon shrugged, his hand still clasped around mine. "I've told you how I feel, Rose."

"Thank you," I said. Relief rolled over me, washing away the guilt I'd felt over my stirring feelings. One less thing to weigh on my mind. One less uncertainty hanging over me. Whether Gabriel and I came together as something more than friends or not, at least I wouldn't have to feel I was betraying my consorts by simply thinking about it.

No, I had much more to worry about from the guy who *thought* he was going to be my consort but wasn't.

"I think I need to do something about Derek," I said. "He's gotten... pushy. And there's only so much I can do to put him off without having to justify myself to my dad."

Damon bristled. "Pushy how?" he said, his voice dark.

"Just... trying to reinforce his position as my fiancé, I guess," I said. "Wanting us to be more intimate, not really taking no for an answer." I shuddered at the memories. "I can get rid of him in the moment with magic, but I don't like using it when I'm not supposed to have it yet. When someone might see. And just telling him I'm not interested isn't working."

Did he think there was some hope of him getting control of my magic still, or did he just see enough other benefits in continuing the engagement? Just thinking about his possible motivations made me feel slimy by association.

I turned to Jin. "I had an idea that might help. If I showed you one of the witching glyphs, do you think you could incorporate it into an image so it was there, but no one would be able to actually see the lines of it? Hidden inside a more complex picture... or even painted right over might work. Just something small, that I could wear as a necklace. Even if the glyph isn't visible, I could imbue it with enough magic to, er, repulse him."

Jin's dark brown eyes gleamed. I could practically see inspiration sparking behind them. "Absolutely. Just show me what you want me to work in. It'll be a fun challenge. With the extra benefit of knowing it'll get him to back off."

A glimmer had lit in Damon's eyes too. He rubbed his mouth. "A necklace," he scoffed.

"Have you got a better idea?" Seth asked.

"Maybe. We'll see. That asshole clearly has a lot worse coming to him."

"Well, while you figure out what that is, I'll stick to my idea," I said dryly, and then to Jin, "Get me a piece of paper? The glyph for warding should give me the right vibe..."

CHAPTER FIFTEEN

Jin

The old, vine-shrouded towers at the far end of Rose's property had always looked beautiful to me in an aged, majestic sort of way. Now, coming back to them for the first time since the consort ceremony, the sight of them sent a deeper thrill through my chest.

This was where we'd all come together. Where I'd sworn myself to Rose and her to me.

Our lives had gotten even more complicated since then, but I hadn't regretted that decision for a second.

"Maybe we shouldn't have done it," Seth had said to the rest of us yesterday after Rose had headed home. "We knew she wasn't sure how the rest of her community would react, and we still agreed, and now they might kill her for it."

"We didn't know," Kyler had pointed out. "We

couldn't have known. We made the best decision we could with the information we had."

"If we *hadn't* been there for her, she'd be chained to that prick of a fiancé now," Damon had said, his hands shoved deep in his pockets. "If you think Rose would prefer that to dying, you haven't been paying much attention."

"I know," Seth had said to both of them. "I know." He'd shoved his hand back through the close-cropped waves of his hair, looking so grim I'd wanted to shake him.

Rose had magic. She had four consorts' worth of magic—four incredibly devoted consorts. What she needed was us holding her up, not fretting about things we couldn't change anyway.

So I'd shooed them out of the gallery and gotten to work on the project she'd given me.

I brushed my fingers over the little bulge in my hip pocket as I came to a stop by the towers. It had taken me half the night to perfect the pendant I'd made for her, but I didn't think anyone could look at it and decipher the glyph hidden within the lines and colors now. I'd picked vibrant yellows and greens and blues—light and life. That was the kind of energy I wanted to give her.

My gaze fell on the arch between the towers. I couldn't see the log that lay in the clearing beneath it, the log where we'd eased Rose down that night and she'd pulled me to her—

I was half hard just remembering it.

Twigs crackled in the forest behind me. I turned to see Rose herself emerging from the depths of the woods. A leaf had gotten tangled in her black hair. As she joined me, I reached out and plucked it free. Then I bent in to kiss her.

There was something magical, no question, about the way her body instinctively melded into mine. About the thump of her heart that seemed to echo my own pulse. Her fingers slid around the back of my neck, gentle but insistent, and I kissed her harder. That faintly sweet lilac smell drifted off her, mingling with the taste of strawberries in her mouth.

She drew back far too soon. "Did you finish it already?" she asked, worry crinkling the corners of her eyes. My stomach squeezed, seeing that concern. Goddamn it, if I could have blotted that fiancé of hers right out of the picture of her life, I'd have done it in an instant. No one should be allowed to make her this scared —scared enough that she'd felt she needed a permanent shield against him.

"I knew you wanted it as soon as possible," I said. "He hasn't hassled you again, has he?"

She shook her head. "I managed to keep my distance all last night. But he's been watching me like he's figuring out his best strategy for trying again."

"I hope this works to repel him, then," I said, pulling out the pendant. I'd fixed it on a fine gold chain.

Rose's eyes widened when I handed it to her. She traced her thumb over the swirls of color, like bits of filigree bleeding into each other. "Jin," she said. "It's gorgeous."

I had to grin. "I'm glad you think so."

"Not that I'm surprised," she said, grinning back.

There. That was the Rose I wanted to see. The Rose she deserved to be, happy and carefree.

Her cares came back a moment later with a darkening of her expression.

"Your art has always been so important to you," she said. "You mean to keep working on it for the rest of your life, don't you?"

Was she thinking about how short that life might be if we were found out? I grasped her hand, closing her fingers over the pendant. "My heart's in my work almost as much as it's with you," I said. "The way you can call up feelings, thoughts, with the right combination of colors and textures... But there's no reason I shouldn't be able to keep at it."

Her mouth twisted. "I want to think that. I started wondering, last night... if maybe we should all just run away. Find some place to live where no one will know us, where the witching folk will never find me. Does that sound silly?"

Oh, my Briar Rose. "Not at all," I said gently. "But I think you deserve more than that. This estate is yours. You shouldn't have to run away from your home."

"You and the other guys shouldn't have to worry that one careless comment could ruin everything," she said. "I don't want you to have to live the rest of your life being constantly on guard. I doubt you'll create very inspired art feeling like that."

"I don't think it'll come to that," I said. "Besides, your dad managed to find your stepmother how quickly? And she's just one woman. Do you really think we could hide and feel completely secure *anywhere*?"

"No." Her brow furrowed. "That's why I stopped wondering. I just wish I had a better solution already. I guess this is a tiny start." She squeezed the pendant and glanced around. "This is the best place I can think of to cast the spell. I want to imbue it with all the power I can."

"Do you mind if I watch?" I asked.

She hesitated, just for a second. "Of course not," she said, with a little laugh, but maybe those old instincts, the ones that had told her she had to hide what she really was from us when we were kids, still had a hold over her. I hoped she'd be free of that worry soon too.

The warm breeze drifted around us as she stepped into a clear space amid the trees and foliage. Her skirt rustled around her knees. She clasped the pendant in both hands and raised them up toward the sparkling of sunlight showing through the leaves overhead. Then she started to cast her spell.

The best I could describe it was a dance. Precise but graceful movements, flowing from one position into the next, in time with a music I could almost hear just watching her. I could feel it, deep in the center of me where I'd felt the bond between us snapping into place: the tremor of charged magic.

I'd be damned if that didn't turn me on too.

Rose pressed the pendant over her heart and swiveled in one last slow circle. She bowed over, her hands clenching tight around the necklace. Then she straightened up and let out her breath. Her dark green eyes were gleaming like gems and her pale skin practically glowed. I didn't know how anyone could *not* see the power in her.

Maybe all that hiding away was making her forget just how potent she was too. I could help with that.

I moved to her as she clasped the gold chain around her neck. The pendant fell low between her breasts. Low enough that she could tuck it under her shirt, out of sight.

Unless that shirt happened to come off, of course.

I rested my hands on her waist and leaned close, kissing her forehead. "Watching you work your magic is the most breathtaking thing I've ever seen," I said. "You've got so much power in you. I may not be a witch, but I can feel it, see it. We don't need to run. It doesn't matter what anyone thinks about us or about you. It doesn't matter what they try to do. You could take on anyone—your dad, your fiancé, that entire Assembly."

She shivered at my words, but from her smile it was a shiver of pleasure. "You think so?" she said.

"I know so. There's nothing you couldn't do now that you've woken up, Briar Rose. All you have to do is call it up." I kissed her temple, her cheek, the corner of her jaw. Her sigh tingled over my neck. "You know what I'd like right now? To make love to you on a bed."

The gleam in her eyes brightened. "I can arrange that," she said, with exactly the confidence I'd been hoping to spark. She slipped away from me, throwing herself into another spell. Spreading her arms and letting the magic flow from each bend of her elbow, each twist of her wrist.

A long rectangular shape formed in front of us. It solidified into a mattress covered by a silk sheet. Rose stopped, her breath a little rough, her mouth stretched in a triumphant smile.

"I didn't figure we needed a headboard and all that," she said, arching an eyebrow at me.

"Not if it means I need to wait any longer before I do this," I said, and scooped her off her feet.

We tumbled together onto the conjured mattress. Rose's fingers tangled in my hair, and mine teased up under her blouse. We kissed until my breath was ragged too. I stroked my hand up and down her side, closer and closer to the curves tucked away inside her bra.

I brushed my knuckles over one nipple, already pebbled, and she whimpered. Her teeth grazed my lower lip. A bolt of pleasure shot straight through me to my cock.

Oh, I knew what I wanted. I knew just what both of us needed.

As I loosened her bra to caress her skin to skin, Rose slid her hand down my chest to the fly of my jeans. God, yes. My erection throbbed at the light pressure of her touch. No woman had ever turned me on half this much. I didn't know how much it was the bond of magic between us and how much just Rose, but who the hell cared?

She jerked the zipper down and palmed my cock. I groaned, teasing her nipple to a stiffer peak. Her hips swayed toward me, as needy as I was. Yeah, it was time.

I eased my hands down to grip her thighs, tugging her skirt up. As I rolled onto my back, I pulled her with me, guiding her so she straddled me.

Heat flared in Rose's eyes. She arched against my cock, and we both moaned.

"That's right," I murmured. "I'm yours. You take

control, with all that power in you. Whatever feels good, you take."

She made a desperate sound as she freed me from my boxers. I helped her strip off her panties. She hesitated over me, her dark hair falling like a curtain on either side of her face, her cheeks flushed.

"I've never—"

"It doesn't matter," I said gently, touching her hot skin. "You can do anything. Ride me, Rose."

A tremble passed through her, eagerness dancing in her eyes. She stroked my length until I was even harder, my head spinning with need. Then she sank down onto me, admitting me into the hot slick center of her.

I groaned, clutching her thighs harder. A whimper slipped from her lips. She rocked over me, taking me deeper as her skirt pooled over us. "Jin," she said.

"Right here," I managed to say, even as my head spun with bliss. "You feel fucking amazing, Rose. You always do. Oh, yeah, just like that."

She moved, bobbing up and down, bracing her hands against my chest. Her head tipped back, her eyelids fluttering. Pleasure was coursing all through my veins, but I didn't let that completely distract me. My thumb settled over her clit, letting that little nub bump up against it with every pump of her hips.

A gasp escaped her. She pumped faster, pressing against me harder. I thrust up to meet her in time with the rhythm she'd set. Her hands clenched against me, fingernails nicking me with a sweet, sweet pain. I could have let go right then, but she needed her release first. This was for her first. Always for her.

"Feel that spark," I said, imagining a little flame swaying inside her. "Feel the power you've got. So much of it, Rose. I'll give you everything you could need, we all will, and it's yours to wield."

She moaned and ground herself harder against me, chasing her peak. "I can do anything," she said in a tumble of words. "I can do *anything*. This is my life. I've taken my consorts. I'll see us all through this. I won't back down."

She plunged over me, taking me even deeper than before, and her channel clamped around me. Her hips jerked. I groaned, unable to hold myself back any longer. My balls tightened, and I spilled myself inside her in one glorious rush.

Rose dipped down over me, her body shaking but soft and sated. She kissed me tenderly on the mouth. Then she eased back up, holding my gaze.

"I won't let them hurt you," she said fiercely. "Not now or ever." And I swear I could see that spark dancing in the back of her eyes.

CHAPTER SIXTEEN

Rose

The power of my spark hummed through me as I walked up to my father's office door. He'd gotten home while I'd been out at the towers with Jin. The protective weight of the pendant hung against my sternum under my shirt, and the fresh heat of that little interlude tingled under my skin.

I could do this. Get my answers, see this horrible situation through, even if Dad had betrayed me. Even if he still meant to.

I knocked on the door. "Dad?"

No answer. I was about to knock again, louder, when the hall floor creaked. When I looked up, my father was walking toward me. A faint smile touched his lips when he saw me, but his eyes stayed solemn.

"Looking for me?" he said.

"Yeah, I— Matilda said you'd gone up to your office."

He nodded, reaching past me to open the door. "I was just putting Celestine's things back in the magicking room," he said as he ushered me in. "No need to have them cluttering my office now. She hasn't given any indication she wants them returned... I suppose I should have Matilda send the family volumes to her daughters, and you can go through the rest of the supplies and see what you might want for your own use before we get rid of the rest."

The finality in his voice made me pause. My pulse hiccupped. "Did you talk to Celestine then?"

She shouldn't have been able to talk to Dad, not with the spell I'd put on her... But that had been the first magic I'd ever cast of that sort. Maybe I'd gotten it wrong somehow.

Dad was already shaking his head. Thank the Spark. "It's... a very odd situation," he said. "But I was able to gather that she has no intention of returning or remaining a part of the family."

He sounded pained. My gut twisted in spite of how glad I was to have Celestine out of our lives.

"I'm sorry," I said, and I meant it. I was sorry for his loss even if I knew it'd had to happen. If Dad hadn't been a part of her schemes, Celestine had hurt him too. Had made *me* hurt him by acting suspicious, by hiding so much awful truth from him. A prickle of anger ran through me.

Then my gaze settled on Dad's desk, which was much barer than the last time I'd been in here. He'd put away Celestine's things—including the box of books I'd been planning to use to plant that bit of conjured evidence.

Shit. I couldn't just conjure it right there on his desk —he wouldn't believe he'd missed it.

"I know you are, lamb," Dad said. "I suppose it's a good thing I've got plenty to distract myself. The final details of that Cairo deal are coming into place. The witching families involved are wanting to celebrate, but I had to tell them I couldn't be away again so close to your consorting. They even suggested we have a party here, as if you want to be dealing with that." He chuckled.

"Oh," I said, my stomach twisting for a totally different reason.

I meandered over to his bookshelves where the case with the Egyptian wand he'd brought back from his business trip was sitting. I flipped open the lid, looking at the gem-laid magical tool, as if it would give me some inspiration.

So much power it'd once held. So much power it must have been dangerous. That was how Celestine had talked about me, after I'd confronted her. The excuse she'd given for enslaving my magic. I'd be too powerful. I couldn't be allowed to wield that power unrestrained.

But she and Derek could be trusted with it? Ha.

I turned the idea over in my head as I glanced back at Dad. She'd said that power was why he'd orchestrated the plot. Maybe there was a more direct way I could get at his feelings.

"Dad," I said, tentatively. "When the advisers from the Assembly came to talk to Derek and me about our consorting... One of them mentioned to me that they expected my magic to be particularly strong. Because of your bloodline and Mom's."

Dad's expression brightened with a more confident smile. "I've always told you you've got a lot of history to live up to, haven't I?" he said lightly. "Is that what you wanted to talk to me about?"

"I guess I hadn't really taken the idea that seriously before." I drifted back to his desk so I could watch his expression closely. "It's a little— I don't know. A little scary? Thinking about going from having no magic to having so much."

No, it wasn't. It was fucking glorious. But if Dad had his own fears, I wanted to draw them out.

"Oh, lamb," Dad said. He came around the desk and took my hand with a reassuring squeeze. "Why do you think I insisted on all those lessons while you were growing up? I found the best tutors I could for you. They'll have given you all the groundwork you need to work with your spark. After all that practice, from what I've heard, you should find it as natural as breathing."

"Oh," I said with a little laugh, and my spark danced in my chest. Yes, that described it pretty well. I'd sooner give up breathing than that glow of magic inside me.

"Your power will take time to develop, too, as you and Derek build the trust and intimacy between you. It won't hit you all at once. So you'll have time to adjust as your spark expands."

Really? Was that only because I wasn't all that connected to Derek to begin with, or would the same thing be true with my actual consorts? It was hard to imagine the flame inside me burning even brighter, even headier... But maybe it could. A giddy thrill trickled through me.

"So you don't think I have any reason to worry?" I said.

"Not at all," Dad said, warmly but firmly. "I'm looking forward to seeing you come into your powers. You've waited a long time, but you'll show the witching world just what a Hallowell is capable of."

He sounded so happy about it. So proud. Nothing about his expression or his tone suggested the slightest concern about how I might use that power. I tucked my hands behind my back and curled my fingers in a subtle magicking designed to gauge his mood. I didn't have any experience reading the impressions that echoed back over me, but I sensed nothing from him that was hostile.

I knew my father, didn't I? This was exactly the man I'd thought he was, not the terrifying figure Celestine had tried to convince me of. One last jab to throw me off, to wound me while she still could—was that all her claim had been?

I was never going to know for sure that his loyalties were with me until I tested him outright, by laying out what I knew. I was going to have to trust him enough to attempt that sometime. And if this was all an act, if he'd played out some master con on me... Well, I had all that magic at my disposal. What could he do to me? None of his connections mattered if I forced him silent the way I had my stepmother. I'd find some way to navigate around the Assembly too, if it came to that. One step at a time.

Jin was right. I had to remember what I was, what I was already capable of.

"Dad," I said. "There's something else I wanted to talk to you about. I just need to get something from my room first, to show you—I'll be right back."

He looked at me curiously as he let go of my hand. "Of course, Rose. I can wait."

I shot him a quick smile and hurried out of the office. In my bedroom, I ran my fingers over the spines of my massive book collection. There.

The contract between Celestine and Derek that had signed my magic to his control after our consorting lay folded beneath the book's back cover, right where I'd left it. I exhaled in relief and slid it into my pocket. I was just turning back toward the hall when the front door thumped open downstairs.

"Mr. Hallowell!" a frantic voice shouted. "Mrs. Gainsley!"

I darted to the top of the stairs as Dad emerged from his office. The young guy from the garage staff—Tyler— was the one who'd called out. He was standing on the threshold supporting a slumped figure with sandy blond hair.

Supporting Derek. My heart lurched as I recognized my supposed fiancé. His sandy hair was flecked with blood, his face mottled red, and his hand clutched against his side. As I stood there frozen, his arm slipped from Tyler's shoulders and he collapsed onto his knees.

CHAPTER SEVENTEEN

Rose

I might not have been feeling the most friendly toward my former fiancé at the moment, but I wasn't going to leave him to stagger around bleeding in my front hall. I dashed down the steps with Dad right behind me.

"I'm fine, I'm fine," Derek was muttering as he pushed himself upright, gripping the end table, but he so obviously wasn't. His breath was coming with a faint squeak through his bloody nose and he already had a black eye forming. His yellow shirt and gray slacks were mottled with dirt and drops of blood. From the way he held himself, I could tell there were more bruises down his side. He winced as he shifted his weight.

"Get the first aid kit," Dad barked at Tyler. The garage assistant ran off. Derek tipped back against the wall with a thump and a grimace. He could barely open that one eye.

"Sit down," I said, cringing in sympathy. "You shouldn't be pushing yourself. What *happened*?"

Derek stayed where he was. He swiped his hand past his mouth, which only smeared the grit and blood there more.

"I'm not even sure," he said in a raspy voice. This close, I could smell the sweat on him, laced with the faint metallic tang of that blood. "I was driving back here, between towns, and I had to stop for a bunch of guys carrying something across the road. The next thing I know, they're dragging me out of the car and beating the shit out of me. Took my wallet and left me. I managed to drive back... The Spark only knows what the damned car looks like."

Right, because the state of the car was the most important consideration here. I stared at him. What the hell could have provoked an attack like that? "You didn't know who they were at all?"

He shook his head and winced. "Not a clue. Never seen them before. They were unsparked, so it's not like I'd have been doing business with them. They looked like some kind of gang, I guess. Leather jackets, scruffy."

"But they left your car," I said. They hadn't just wanted to steal from him.

They'd mostly wanted to beat him up.

Dad's jaw set. He must have been thinking the same thing. "There are always murmurs passing between the neighbors about us being a little 'odd,'" he said. "Maybe a

few of the unsparked decided they didn't like the idea of
the Hallowells expanding their strange family."

"No one around here has ever *hurt* any of us," I
protested. The worst I'd ever had directed at me was that
jerk's muttering in the museum archive the other day.

Dad caught my eyes. "There's always a first time.
And it isn't the first time, not really. Just the first time
you've been here to see. We can never trust the
unsparked—because this is how they react the moment
they invent any reason not to trust *us*."

He motioned toward Derek and then reached to take
the younger man's arm. Tyler ran up with the first aid kit.
Dad accepted it and started walking Derek to the still-
open front door.

"I think I'd better get you to the hospital to have
you checked out, just to be safe," he said. "Or to the
nearest medic, if she's around." A witch medic, he
meant, but he couldn't say that in front of Tyler. Tyler,
who was unsparked too. Tyler who was looking at the
scene with total bewilderment. *He'd* never have hurt
a fly.

Dad shot one last glance back at me. "Don't leave the
estate. I'll tell the staff not to let anyone unfamiliar in.
These miscreants might not be finished yet."

"But..." I didn't know how to finish that thought.
None of this made any sense to me. Some gang going out
of their way to rough up Derek just for the sake of doing
it? Why would anyone even care that much...

A chill washed over me as the door clicked shut.
Leather jackets. A gang. Hadn't Seth or Kyler said
something about Damon being mixed up with criminals,

doing work for them on the side? He'd hinted at it himself.

That look he'd gotten when I'd talked about how Derek was getting pushy with me. He'd even texted me last night asking if I knew the next time Derek would be out of the house. I'd thought he'd been hoping to make a surprise visit or something, but no. He'd been asking because of this, hadn't he?

My hands balled at my sides. I waited until I heard the car engine rumble away outside. Then I hurried out back and into the forest, making for a spot on the wall I could slip over without anyone being able to tell Dad I'd ignored his direct order.

I was almost twenty-five. I didn't need to follow orders. But I sure as hell could give them.

* * *

Damon didn't answer my knock. I scowled at the scarred green door to his basement apartment and rapped my fist against it again. He might not even be home. I couldn't text him on my regular phone. Was there a payphone somewhere I could—

"Hey, angel." The man himself came sauntering down the narrow walkway beside the house. "I saw you hurrying by back there, didn't think you'd want me shouting after you. To what do I owe the pleasure?"

He paused, taking in my expression, and the satisfaction that had warmed his own faded. His voice sharpened in an instant. "What's the matter? Did that asshole—"

"You're the asshole," I snapped. "What the hell were you thinking?"

Damon blinked, but I saw understanding light in those dark blue eyes. He could put together the pieces. Because he was the one who'd laid them out. His stance tensed. "Not the reaction I was expecting."

"Because clearly you weren't thinking at all," I said.

His eyebrows arched. "Why don't you come in and tell me all about how stupid I am downstairs? This doesn't seem like a public kind of conversation."

I made a face at him, but I held my tongue while he unlocked the door and let me in. I tramped down the steps into the dim, earth-smelling apartment and immediately spun around. Damon stopped at the bottom of the steps, his arms already folded over his chest defensively.

"Those guys you work for, hang out with, whatever," I said. "You sent them to beat up Derek?"

"He was a problem," Damon said. "I figured a move like that was an easy way to convince him maybe he doesn't want to stick around here harassing you after all. You can't say he didn't deserve it, after what he was ready to do to you."

"I don't care whether he deserved it or not," I said. "I don't want you attacking people for me. He'll get what's coming to him the official way when I show the Assembly what he was planning. It didn't have to get... bloody."

"So you're squeamish," Damon said with a shrug. "That's okay. That's why I handled it for you. Now it's done. You don't have to feel guilty. You didn't know."

"It's not okay," I said, slashing my hand through the

air in frustration. "You didn't make anything better. You made it *worse*. I was getting ready to expose him to my dad as a villain, and now he looks like a victim. My dad's thinking we can't trust any of the unsparked—how am I supposed to tell him I'm consorted to four of them now? That one of my consorts arranged to have his friends kick the crap out of one of us? It was already going to be a hard enough sell without that detail."

"So don't tell him about it," Damon said, his voice more heated now. "What do you need your dad for anyway? He's probably in on the whole thing. You don't need any of them. You've got us—you've got me."

"Damon—"

"This is how I operate," he said, taking a step toward me. "This is how I know how to handle things. You knew I didn't color inside the lines the very first time you came to me. So don't act like it's a big surprise."

I stepped right up to meet him, setting my hand on his chest to hold him in place and glaring back at him. "I'm not surprised you'd think of doing something like this. I'm surprised that after everything we've been through, everything you've heard about how *my* people operate, you still thought it was a good idea to go ahead with this, without even talking to me. *Do* I 'have' you, if you're going to run off doing shit that makes you feel better without caring how I'd feel about it?"

Damon's face darkened. His mouth opened. But as he held my gaze, whatever he'd been going to say faltered. "Rose," he said, low and rough. "Of course I did it for you."

My voice softened. "Are you sure?" I said. "What

were you thinking about more—how good it'd feel to know you made Derek suffer, or how I'd react when I found out? Did you really think I'd be celebrating?"

His jaw worked. "He was coming after you. Trying to force himself on you. I couldn't just let him—"

"You wouldn't have been letting him," I broke in. "You would've been letting me take care of the situation. Which I did." I touched Jin's pendant through my shirt. "But now even more people are mixed up in this mess than were before. What did you even tell those guys to set them on Derek?" I paused, a worse thought hitting me. "What do you owe them now?"

"You don't have to worry about that," Damon said, but I thought I saw a little worry creep into his expression. He pushed past me abruptly, stalking to the edge of his bed and sitting down there. His fingers raked through his dark hair. "Whatever comes up, I can handle it. It's on me." He glanced up. "Do you really think... it's going to screw up your chances of getting your dad's help? If he even would have helped."

My gut knotted. "He's not going to be in the most receptive mood to hearing about my consorting, even if I manage to leave out your connection to Derek's attack." I still had the contract burning a hole in my pocket. Would it be better to throw that at Dad the second he got back or to wait until Derek had recovered a little, until any protective instincts Dad might have felt toward his soon-to-be son-in-law had faded some?

"That's not what I was aiming for," Damon said.

"I know." My breath came out of me in a rush. I walked up to him and set my hands on his shoulders. "I know you just wanted to protect me. I know who you are, Damon, and I'm not going to tell you to be some other way. All I'm asking is that you don't go off doing things like that on *my* behalf, all right? Or at least ask me first to make sure it's what I'd actually want?"

His mouth tightened, but he nodded. He rested his hands on my waist, tugging me a little closer. The heat of his touch bled through my thin shirt.

"I don't want to hurt you," he said, looking up at me. "You do have me. Body, mind, heart—soul, if I've got one. I'm just... not very good at this yet."

Emotion tightened my throat. I leaned over, tipping my face close to his. "I can't ask for more than that."

His hand came up to touch my cheek and guide my mouth to his. The kiss was so slow and gentle and not at all like the Damon I knew that it was hard not to see it as an apology, even if he didn't want to say it with words. The tenderness of it left me breathless.

"Is this really what you want?" I murmured when our lips parted. "Hanging out with some gang, helping them do... whatever else it is they do? That's how you want to spend your life?"

I felt him start to bristle again. "I've done what I have to—"

"Hey. I'm not telling you that you can't want that. I just want to know. So I can know you as well as I possibly can."

He was silent for a bit. Then he said, "I don't know. It's hard to think about what I *want* separate from what I need, what I can get... I want you. I want my mom taken care of. But if I could have that without all the crap...

Hell, sometimes I think there's nothing I'd like more than for things to be like they used to be, way back when. Running around in the forest, swimming in the pond, just being. Being happy, being a part of the world."

His face flushed a little as he admitted that. "Yeah," I said quietly. "That was pretty wonderful."

I kissed him again, my lips lingering against his until a groan worked its way from his throat and he pulled me closer. "Rose," he mumbled.

I swallowed thickly. "I can't stay. If my dad gets back before I do, I'll have more explaining to do than I think I'm ready for."

Damon nodded. "You've got no idea how hard it is to keep letting you go, angel," he said, his thumb tracing over my side.

I gave a choked laugh. "I do. I have to keep doing it four times over. But maybe it won't be much longer before we can spend more time being together than being apart."

CHAPTER EIGHTEEN

Gabriel

*W*hen I saw the estate manager head out through the gardens with one of the staff, I ducked in through the manor's front door. My legs stalled for a second in the expansive hall: chandelier twinkling overhead, gold-framed paintings on the walls, sweeping mahogany staircase rising up to the second floor.

It wasn't that the place was grander than some of the temples and mansions I'd toured around during my roaming across this continent and the next. If anything, it felt smaller than I was expecting based on memories I hadn't updated since I'd last poked my head in here as a preteen.

There was just something so stately and snooty about the atmosphere... Like it disapproved of my very existence.

It reminded me of Rose's dad.

Thankfully, he was still off wherever he'd taken that jerk of a fiancé. That was the only reason I was risking venturing in here anyway. In a way I was thumbing my nose at him and whatever he did think of me.

I climbed the stairs, trying not to worry that I might somehow be getting engine grease everywhere. I'd washed my goddamn hands. In the second-floor hall, I paused to get my bearings. I'd never been up here at all, even as a kid. But I knew which window was Rose's bedroom from the outside. Over by the big oak tree. Which meant from inside it should be right—there.

I could tell I'd picked right when I reached the door. A hint of that soft lilac smell that followed her everywhere lingered outside it. I knocked lightly.

There was a rustling as she got up. The door eased open, and then she was right there in front of me, staring at me, her eyes going wide.

"You—" She cut herself off with a strangled sound and grabbed my arm, yanking me into the room. She pushed the door shut with her back braced against it. It connected with the frame with a thud.

"What are you doing here?" she whispered. "No, don't tell me yet. Wait a second."

For the second time in a week, I watched Rose will the magic out of her body. The spell she was casting didn't look as dramatic as that moment when she'd whipped herself right out of my apartment in an instant with a tremor of energy so potent it had raised the hairs on my arms and the back of my neck. The movements of her arms and feet now were slower, more solid. But I still felt a tingle pass through me, seeing her in motion. I wasn't sure how much that sensation was the magic itself and how much my own awe.

Rose was always pretty. When she was working her magic... I'd never seen anything more gorgeous, anywhere I'd traveled in the world. Beauty and strength and passion melded into one.

Awe was definitely the right word for what I felt. We wouldn't get into the other emotions that might be stirring around in my chest—or lower down.

"All right," Rose said with a smile, lowering her hands. "We don't have to worry about being heard now. Being sneaky got a whole lot easier with my spark kindled."

I chuckled. "I'll bet." I finally managed to tear my gaze away from her to take in the room.

So this was Rose's bedroom. Her bed, with a mint green duvet embroidered with a vine pattern along the edges. One wall all full of bookshelves—packed solid with books, of course. And... several novels scattered on the hardwood floor around her armchair. I glanced back to her with an eyebrow raised.

Rose waved off the implied question. She sank down on the floor by the books, folding her legs under her. Her jeans hugged her curves and the spaghetti strap of her black tank top was dangerously close to slipping over the peak of one slim, pale shoulder. I schooled my eyes on her face as I hunkered down next to her.

"You can tell me what you're doing here now," she said—lightly, so I knew it wasn't a way of telling me to leave.

"I heard about your fiancé," I said. Tyler had come running into the garage babbling the whole story. And then we'd spent a couple hours cleaning up the blood that had dribbled on the driver's seat and inner door of Derek's Mercedes. I wasn't sure if him driving back here in that state was impressive or imbecilic. Possibly both?

"He's not my fiancé," Rose said, her back tensing. She frowned at the books. "But yeah. It's not good either way."

"Am I right in guessing Damon had something to do with it?"

Rose's gaze darted up. "Is it that obvious?"

I gave her a half smile. "To someone who knows the guy." Who knew how that guy looked at Rose anytime she was in his view. If I'd heard that Damon had murdered Derek, I didn't think I'd have been surprised.

Hell, I wasn't sure if I'd go that far myself, but I couldn't say I'd have pushed Derek out of the way of a speeding car if the situation presented itself either.

Rose rubbed her face. "He sicced some of the guys in that gang he works with on Derek. Because he thought it would help. But I'm pretty sure everything's just more of a mess now."

"So you... decided to make a mess with your books too?"

A laugh hitched out of her. She clapped her hand over her mouth. But when she lowered it, she was still smiling, if only a little.

"I don't know," she said, nudging the nearest book with her fingertips. From the covers, they were mostly romance novels—bodice-ripper historicals and more modern looking ones—along with a few that looked like various types of fantasy. "I've spent so much time buried in books. Trying to figure out what was missing in my life. Connecting with the characters. Hoping somehow they'd prepare me for being a grown-up and all that comes with it."

Her lips twisted. "I'm twenty-five in six weeks and sometimes I hardly feel like I know anything. None of these helped at all, not really. I've learned more about my community and all the things wrong with it in the last month than all those years before..."

"That's not so strange," I said. "You know what you've been presented with. I had no idea what life was like outside this town until I went to find out just a few years ago. I experienced a hell of a lot of amazing things, sure, but I also ran into all kinds of people and attitudes I'd rather weren't part of my world." And man, what a wake-up call that had been. It must be so much harder for her, when she'd dedicated so much of herself to being a part of her community.

"I think it's a little more excusable in your case," she said. "Your world is a whole lot bigger than my witching one."

"Maybe so. But now you know. You can act on what you know."

"Yeah." She didn't look reassured.

"I've got to tell you," I said, "I always liked to tease you about how much you loved reading, but I bet you did learn an awful lot that way. Different perspectives. Different lives. Kind of like traveling, but without having to leave your room."

"So, the coward's way of traveling."

"Rose." I waited until she looked up at me. "I know you. The last thing you are is a coward." How could she think that even for a second? She'd gone against every rule she'd been taught to protect herself, to follow her heart. She was standing firm with the other guys even when it could be her life at stake. I'd admired her plenty back when we were kids, but now... Now she put me to shame.

"If I'm not a coward, then why do I feel so scared?" she burst out. "I was going to tell him—I was going to tell my dad the whole thing about Celestine and Derek and— But then Derek came in and now my dad is furious about the unsparked. And there's still this little part of me that's not even completely sure he's not worse than both of them. I keep thinking I have a handle on what's happening to me—to us—and then I get thrown for another loop..."

She made a frustrated sound and shoved her hands back into her hair. My chest tightened. I eased closer to her, setting my hand on her shoulder. On that warm, bare skin. Fuck, I couldn't think about her like that right now. She needed me to comfort her.

She already had four other guys for anything more than that.

Scooting across the last few inches between us, she leaned into me. I stroked my thumb over the peak of her shoulder. Her eyes slid closed, but her mouth stayed tight and crooked.

"I should be able to do better than this," she said in a low, ragged voice. "I asked them to be with me, I swore myself to them, and now I can't even figure out how to admit what I've done to my own dad. And every day there's some new horrible thing they're finding out about what they've gotten into, what kind of people they're mixed up with now... How long is it going to be before they wish they'd never agreed to the consorting?"

"Don't think like that," I said. "You can't— Rose, there's no way in the world any of them are ever going to regret that decision."

She looked up at me. "How can you know that?"

Maybe, if I'd taken the time to think about it, I'd have come up with a better answer. One still honest, but a little less raw. A little less likely to get me into trouble. But the pain in her eyes loosened my tongue, and before I knew it, the most baldly true answer I could have offered spilled out.

"Because I know nothing could be as bad as knowing everything they do and *not* being able to be there for you in every possible way."

I clamped my mouth shut, but it was too late. The words were already out. I couldn't even break the spell of Rose's gaze, holding mine in place as she studied my expression. She was so close now, her arm resting against mine, that she might have been able to feel the heady thump of my heart.

"There are people who'd kill you for being here like this with me," Rose said. "And you'd still want to commit yourself to me even more?"

I'd had time to think *now*. "Why don't we just forget I said that," I said. "It's a moot point anyway. What I was getting at is, I know how the *other* guys feel, and it's obvious they'd rather be with you than anywhere else."

"I'm not going to forget it. Did you mean it or not?"

I let out my breath, but I still couldn't look away. "When have I ever been in the habit of lying to you, Sprout?"

Something in her expression changed, like a faint light coming on that I hadn't realized was missing until I saw it now. So hopeful it made my chest ache. Her hand rose to skim the edge of my jaw, and my pulse leapt. When she shifted forward to kiss me, God help me, I leaned right in to meet her.

The brush of her mouth against mine sent a tremor of energy over my skin. I tipped my head, and her lips parted, a hungry, needy sound escaping them. Her body was so vibrant next to mine it might as well have been made of light. Her hand trailed sparks down my side, and my fingers tangled in her hair as I kissed her harder. She shifted against me, suddenly feeling so beautifully fragile—

What the *fuck* was I doing?

I jerked back, my breath ragged. Rose grasped my hand. "It's okay," she said.

"How is it okay? You—the guys—"

"They know," she said quietly. "We talked about it. Nothing definite, of course, since I didn't know how you felt, but... You belong with us. We belong with you. *I* belong with you, as much as I do the rest of them. We don't have to rush into anything, and you don't have to promise me anything, not right now, but if you want—"

"No." I pushed myself to my feet, shaking my head. "I can't do this. I know what I said, but—I can't."

Before I had to explain myself any further, I hurried out of her room. Down the stairs and back to the garage, which was as close to Rose as I actually belonged. I didn't stop until I was in my apartment, the door locked behind me.

I stood in the middle of the living room, my breath raw in my throat, my chest aching. Inhaling and exhaling slowly, I willed my pulse to even out. I'd caught myself. I'd gotten out of there. Maybe not as quickly as I should have, but...

I'd ruined too many goddamn things in my life. I wasn't going to let myself ruin her too.

CHAPTER NINETEEN

Rose

Looking at the consort files I'd grabbed from Celestine's magicking room was awfully depressing. Like a road map laying out all the standard preferences and expectations of witching society.

How much of a fortune did each guy have? How much money did he bring in with his job? How prestigious was said job, with how much room for moving farther up the ladder? What prominent figures did he have in his family? How much magical ability had his female relatives demonstrated?

There were notes upon notes of each of the guys' family histories and current position in the community... and nothing about what sort of a person they were. Had they ever done something to help someone else rather than focusing on building their own fortune? What did they do with their spare time that wasn't for making money or impressing anyone?

Were they actually a worthwhile person for a woman to spend her life with?

"Aiming to add even more husbands to your household?" Philomena said, leaning over my shoulder.

I blinked at her. Phil. She smiled at me, and my heart squeezed. I'd told her, after I'd completed the consorting, that I'd still need her company. But it'd been at least a day since I'd last imagined her into being beside me, hadn't it?

She might have developed a mind of her own, but she was still ultimately a product of mine. And mine was turning to her less and less, even unconsciously, it seemed.

There were too many all-too-real people stealing my attention, in ways both good and bad.

"No," I said quickly, past the pang in my chest. I flipped one file folder closed and opened the one underneath. "These are the possible consorts Celestine was considering for me. The men she thought might agree to her scheme, apparently."

"Hmm." Phil plopped down on the bed across from me. "Then I suppose it's no surprise you don't look all that excited about what these potential suitors might offer."

"No." What *had* I been expecting? Celestine hadn't cared whether I was happy. The only real surprise was that there wasn't more detail on why she'd thought these particular guys would agree to a lifetime of highly illegal magic.

Or maybe she just hadn't wanted that part of the files

to be obvious to anyone who happened across them. I paused and then waved my hand in a gentle circle over the papers, testing the energy of my spark against them.

A tingling tickled over my palm. Ah-ha.

"There's a spell on them," I said. "Let me see if I can..."

I curled my fingers, a little tug, a little twist, and... There.

A scrawl I recognized as Celestine's handwriting shimmered into sight along the margins of the page. She'd magically charged those notes so it took more magic to make them visible. Very clever, but not clever enough.

According to my stepmother, the guy whose file I was looking at—Samson Evandale—had expressed to her in confidence that he felt it was unfair that the witching women held all the magic. She'd also discovered that he'd been covering up a nasty gambling habit. Pride and public image were his pressure points.

I shuddered. So those were the real criteria my stepmother had been looking for. Resentment and weakness.

I shuffled back to Derek's file. He'd been sore about losing his family estate to his younger sister. Wanting to shame his parents with his success. That was why he'd wanted Celestine to gift them all that money theoretically from his investments, I supposed. Lovely. *Ultimately a coward*, Celestine had written. *Does not handle uncertainty well. Always keep him a little off-balance.*

"What a catch my fiancé was," I muttered.

"I fully approve of continuing to keep him off-balance," Philomena piped up. "Steal your stepmother's strategies."

I wrinkled my nose. So far I wasn't sure that had worked out so well for me.

The other guys had similar write-ups. One of them, Killian Sorensen, Celestine had noted as an ideal "emergency back-up" if the original engagement fell through. *Wants to claim property back from his niece inheriting. Needs a consort who can bring pressure to bear soon. No need to keep promises made once he's on the hook.*

Okay, I was pretty sure I needed to wash my brain out after this glimpse inside her way of thinking.

Feeling queasy, I closed the folders and tucked them away in their hiding spot. "I need to figure out how to pitch my actual consorts to my dad," I said. "With a minimum of him freaking out over them being unsparked." My perusal of those files hadn't helped at all. If anything, they'd made me more uncertain myself.

"Do you even *have* to tell him?" Phil asked. "Just get rid of that rake of a fiancé and you can take your time with the rest."

I shook my head. "He knows as well as I do that I need a consort before I turn twenty-five. If he thinks I don't have anyone other than Derek, he'll try to find someone else. There's no getting around it. He's going to have to know. At least about one of them, to start."

Phil pursed her lips. "So who is the most eligible of your no-longer-bachelors?"

I flopped back down on the bed beside her, draping my arm over my forehead. For a second my thoughts slipped to the guy who remained a bachelor—and apparently planned to continue that way, given the way he'd reacted to me this afternoon. Gabriel. The look in his eyes when he'd pulled away from me, almost... horrified. A sharp twinge ran through my gut, remembering.

It was fine if he didn't want me that way. The last thing I wanted was to pull him into this mess unless he was all in. But the way he'd been talking right before, I'd thought we'd been on the exact same wavelength. I'd been so relieved...

But I'd been wrong. So I'd give him his space and let him decide when he was ready to deal with me again. For now, I had the four guys who had committed themselves to me to vouch for.

"I couldn't start by telling Dad about Damon, that's for sure," I said. "Works crazy hours for sketchy people he's not allowed to talk about. Would probably say something snarky to Dad within ten seconds of being in the same room with him. That... is going to take some work."

"The others, then," Phil prompted.

"Let's see." I considered. "Jin might come across fairly well. His dad is an established musician. Jin's making a living with his own art. Contributing to the community by showcasing other local artists in his gallery. Worldly and well-traveled. I've got angles there." If we just forgot about the whole unsparked thing.

"Seth and Kyler... Their dad owns his own business." Not that my dad was likely to be impressed by a hardware store. I tapped my knuckle against my mouth. "Ky's the town tech expert. We'll leave out the hacking stuff. Seth clearly has a strong sense of loyalty, staying with the family business. Um..."

"You're not inspiring much confidence at the moment," Phil said.

I groaned. "I know. I'm just trying to see them through Dad's eyes. What would matter to him—enough to offset the whole 'not witching folk' problem."

They were devoted to me and they loved me. And I loved all of them. They'd protect me. They'd defend this estate if they needed to. They were risking their lives just by being with me.

Not that they had much choice about that now that the ceremony was already done.

I couldn't think about that. They were with me, and I was with them, and I had to defend *them* with everything I had. Which meant convincing Dad that I was better off with them than any witching man he could have offered me. Convincing Dad to help me hide the choice I'd made from the people in the Assembly who'd kill us over it.

Yeah. No pressure. Ha.

"You could always wait a little longer," Phil offered.

"No," I said, sitting up. "I've put it off long enough already. Dad's shown no indication he wants anything but what's best for me. I just have to change his mind and convince him that *this* is what's best. I want Derek out of this house. I want to be able to see the guys without so much sneaking. I just have to... do the best I can to explain all of it."

Time to just get it over with. Derek had gone to his room after breakfast, saying his ribs were hurting him. The witch Dad had managed to summon had sealed the cracks, but he was still bruised up. Dad would be back in his office. I could catch him there, lay it all out like I'd meant to yesterday, and see where we went from there.

As I was heading for my door, my phone rang in my purse. I hesitated. Who'd be calling me? It was my regular phone, and I didn't normally hear from anyone on it outside of the family.

With a grimace, I backtracked and fished the phone out of my purse. I didn't recognize the number.

I raised it to my ear. "Hello?"

"Rosalind," a clear, haughty voice carried through the speaker. My heart lurched with the thought that it was Celestine, defying my magic and my orders. Then I realized it sounded far too young. The next words confirmed my suspicion. "I hope you've got some explanation for what's happened to my mother."

"Hi, Evianna," I said, dropping into my armchair. It was my older stepsister, who I enjoyed talking to only slightly more than I'd enjoyed spending time with her mother. Which was not at all. I felt a lot less guilty playing ignorant with her than I did with my Dad. "I don't know what you're talking about."

"Oh, please. Something clearly sent her running away from your estate without letting any of us know what was wrong. Don't tell me you have no idea why. It's probably your fault."

If she thought that attitude was a good way to get me talking, she had another thing coming. "I honestly don't know," I said, almost enjoying the lie. "I got up the other morning and she was just gone. Maybe it was something between her and my father? Or maybe she was involved in things we didn't know about at all. She didn't bother to tell us. If anyone should know, wouldn't it be *you*?"

"Yes," Evianna said snippily. "That's exactly how I know she must have been forced out, suddenly. Otherwise she would have talked to me first. And it must have been something horrible for her not to talk to me about it *after*. You Hallowells think you're so above most of the rest of us. But believe me, if you're not going to talk, I will find out some other way."

I rolled my eyes at the ceiling. "I don't know what you think I could have done. Your mother was a fully-fledged witch. I haven't even come into my magic yet."

"We both know there are ways of getting around that. Tools you could have acquired. Friends you might have turned to for help."

Except I hadn't. "Why don't you just talk to your mother?" I said. Let Celestine make up some excuse. She'd gotten herself into this mess, really. She'd created it.

Evianna drew in a sharp breath. "I would have *liked* to," she said, sounding suddenly ragged. "If I'd know where she was before..."

My body tensed at her use of the past tense. Wait a second. "What are you talking about?" I said. "Before what?"

"Oh, so you aren't gloating over that already?" She sniffed, a hitch of what sounded like genuine grief creeping into her voice. "She's gone. There wasn't time for a witching medic to get to her. Maybe it wouldn't have made a difference anyway. The way the car... I had to go identify her, you know."

My heart thumped hard. "What car? Evianna, I don't know what you mean."

Except I did. She'd said enough. I just needed her to confirm it.

"She died last night," Evianna snapped. "A car hit her. Some stupid unsparked asshole. All right? But it's not just on him. It's on you and your father and whoever else there that chased her away... She couldn't have been thinking right. She mustn't have been paying enough attention. Too distracted worrying about whatever sent her running in the first place. So I'm asking you again— what happened there last week?"

I couldn't find my words. Celestine was dead? Dad had just gone to see her two days ago. And now...

A chill crept over me as I remembered what Ky had said about the Assembly's report, the witch and her unsparked lover. Both of them killed in supposed accidents. Maybe Dad had found out more from Celestine than he'd told me. Or maybe someone else had.

A car might have hit her, but what were the chances it had really been an accident?

CHAPTER TWENTY

Damon

*N*ormally I felt pretty good when I finished a job for Silvio. Like I'd pulled one over on the assholes in this town, all those pricks I knew looked down on me when they bothered to look at me at all. But this afternoon, as I ambled through our pathetic excuse for a downtown, my mood felt a lot like the sky overhead: hazy with shifting clouds.

My footsteps sounded too loud on the sidewalk. The muggy heat congealed against my skin, but at the same time I felt too exposed without the familiar weight of my jacket.

Silvio's guy had teased me about the lack of leather jacket when I'd shown up at the meeting spot, even though I'd have been sweating buckets if I had worn it. And he'd mentioned their "successful" rendezvous with

Derek yesterday, with a meaningful look I hadn't liked at all.

They shouldn't think it was a favor or that I owed them anything. I'd made up some story about how I'd overheard the guy talking about moving in on their territory, pretended he was one of those posher city criminals. It wasn't like Silvio's bunch minded the excuse to push around some slick Mercedes-driving dude. But my nerves still itched at the memory of Silvio's raised eyebrows and the questions Rose had asked me yesterday.

It was really too early to head home, but I didn't much feel like figuring out where Brad and George had gotten to and loitering around Main Street with them. Maybe I just needed to take my mind off all this crap. Crack open a beer, put some action flick on the TV, and see if I didn't feel better by the final explosion.

I was just changing direction when Gabriel stepped out of the town's auto service shop in front of me. He had a plastic bag that looked heavy slung over his forearm, but he carried it like it was nothing, of course. Goddamn unshakeable Gabriel.

"Hey," he said, and tipped his head toward the shop. "I had to pick up a couple parts for the garage."

"Sure," I said with a shrug, like it wasn't anything to me. Which it wasn't. "Don't let me stop you from heading back. I've got my own stuff to do." All my big plans. The fact that I didn't have any somehow made me feel more ticked off at him.

Gabriel gave me that look he'd had even when we were kids, casual but considering. Never intrusive, exactly, but a prickle ran over my skin at the thought of what he might be seeing. As if he had any right to make judgments when he'd only just gotten back in town.

I started to walk away, but Gabriel made a quick gesture with his hand, beckoning me out of the way of the shop's door, closer to the building where we weren't stopping foot traffic. My gut tensed, but I went. It *was* Gabriel. He might have something important to say, as much as I hated to admit it.

He glanced at the sidewalk and then at me, with that considering look again. His mouth slanted down. I braced myself for some kind of criticism.

"We haven't had much of a chance to catch up since I got back," he said quietly. "But I know things were tough for you even before I left. I was distracted by how things were going with my dad, and—but that's not really an excuse. I wish I'd been around to help more. It wasn't quite the same for the other guys, was it?"

For a few seconds, I could only stare at him. Was Gabriel... *apologizing* to me? I didn't even know what to say to that. Only that an uncomfortable thickness had formed in my throat. I swallowed.

"I got by," I said, aiming for nonchalant. My voice came out a bit rough anyway.

"Yeah, you did." His smile slanted too. "I know a lot has changed. I just wanted to say that, and—if you ever do want to talk with someone who maybe can understand..." He spread his hands.

"Right," I said. "I'll keep that in mind."

I said it like a dismissal, and Gabriel caught my tone. He nodded to me with a quirk of his smile and headed down the street. I pushed myself on toward home, trying to shake off the weird feeling his offer had given me. I didn't *want* to be feeling grateful toward Gabriel.

Then I forgot all about him when I turned the corner toward the house that held my basement apartment.

Two figures were standing outside the house. One of them was the broad, frowning James Cortland.

Shit. Whatever *he* was here for, it couldn't be good. I glanced for the nearest driveway to bolt up, but his head had already turned, his narrow eyes fixing on me.

What good would running do anyway? He obviously knew where I lived.

I let myself keep walking, keeping my expression bland as if I had no idea who this guy was. I didn't know how much he knew. Maybe he didn't know much at all. He sure as hell wasn't learning anything *new* from me.

The woman at Cortland's side was about half his size, middle-aged with light red hair pulled back into a bun. Her dark gaze was even sharper than his. She nodded once as I reached them, and a prickle ran down my back.

I hadn't seen her do anything magical, but I knew it. She was a witch, like Rose. And not like Rose at all.

I moved as if to walk around them, and Cortland held out a meaty hand. "Hold on a second there," he said.

The longing for the shield of my jacket rose up again, as if it could have protected me from whatever magic these two were planning. I made myself shrug and gave them a puzzled look. "What do you want?"

"I think you'll be able to tell me what happened to this," Cortland said. He pulled his phone out of his pocket. Cracks splintered the screen where I'd stomped on it before tossing it into a public trash can—because really, did this prick who'd been helping Rose's stepmom scheme against her deserve his phone back in working condition, if he'd ever managed to find it? I didn't think so.

But he had found it. And then he'd found me. I caught myself just before my gaze slid to his companion. Her magic—that must have been how.

"Well," I said, "it looks like you broke your screen. Since it's your phone, not mine, I'm not sure why you think I'd know how you managed it."

"You probably think you wiped it off," the woman said in a dry voice. "Not well enough."

I had wiped my fingerprints off it, but I guessed not well enough to evade her magic. Okay. My throat tightened, but I kept my voice steady. If I'd left some trace of skin or whatever the hell she'd used to track me down, that was all it could have been. A trace.

"I don't know what you're talking about," I said. "I saw a phone on the street the other day, picked it up to see if it belonged to one of my friends, but it didn't, so I left it. If that's the one, that's all I know about it. It wasn't even cracked when I saw it."

The pair didn't look convinced. Well, what were they going to do to me? Start throwing around magic right here in the middle of the street? A car rumbled by us. Some lady was rocking her kid back and forth in his stroller down by the corner. I knew how much Rose's people liked their secrecy.

I was about to tell them to take their suspicion and shove it up their asses when Cortland narrowed his eyes even more and said, "You're one of the boys Rosalind used to run with, aren't you?"

A jab of ice cut through my stomach. "Rosalind?" I repeated as if I didn't recognize the name, but I wasn't sure I'd managed to stop my expression from twitching.

"Rosalind Hallowell," Cortland said, slow and dark. "Or Rose, if you prefer. When was the last time you saw your old 'friend'?"

My heart had started to thud. He'd only just recognized me. He didn't know a thing. I kept my tone as even as I could. "Rose? I haven't seen her in ages. They all moved off somewhere years ago. What does she have to do with anything?"

That last question might have come out a little too aggressive. Cortland shifted a step closer. And his witch accomplice came with him. It was even harder not to eye her hands, wondering if she was going to cast some spell with them now. But *I* wasn't supposed to know anything about witches.

"Why don't you tell us what she has to do with this?" Cortland said.

"You know, this is getting a little too weird for me," I said. "I told you everything I know. Unless you're some kind of cops and you can show me your badges, I'm out of this conversation."

I moved to cut across the lawn toward the driveway, and Cortland caught me by the elbow, jerking me to a stop. I flinched and spun to face him again.

"Look here, you little piece of trash," Cortland said, his voice dropping lower. "We've got more questions, and you're going to answer them."

Every part of my body bristled at the insult. Who the hell was he to call me trash? My shoulders tensed, my hands balled into fists.

And Cortland? He fucking *laughed*.

"Do you think I'm going to be intimidated by some pathetic punk like you? I could flatten you in an instant."

Him? Not a chance. The urge to tell him exactly what I thought of him and what he'd done to Rose rushed through me. Let's see who felt so high and mighty when he realized I knew exactly what kind of scum he was.

I inhaled sharply—and a triumphant gleam flashed in Cortland's eyes. My throat closed up.

This was a fucking game to him. He was trying to rile me up so I'd say something stupid.

I almost had.

No. No way. I drew in another breath, unclenching my hands. I wasn't going to screw anything else up for Rose. Calm and careful, that was what she said she needed. So that was what I'd be for her.

I could be so much better than this asshole thought I was.

"I just want to get home and relax," I said, shaking my head. "I have no idea who you are or why you think you can talk to me like that, and I sure as hell don't feel like talking more. I'm sorry I briefly touched your phone. Maybe don't leave it lying on the sidewalk if you're going to get so worked up about things like that?"

I yanked my arm out of Cortland's grasp. He reached for me again, and I pulled my own phone out of the back of my jeans.

"Do I have to call the actual cops?" I looked from him

to his witchy friend and back. "Leave me alone. I have no idea what happened to your phone or what Rose Hallowell is up to these days, and frankly, I don't give a shit either. After what her family did to my mom, I hope I never see that bitch again."

Talking about Rose that way made me wince inwardly, but I was pretty sure it was what sold Cortland. His lips twisted as he backed up.

"Watch your mouth," he said, as if what I'd said about Rose was any worse than what he'd said about me. "And don't mess with things that aren't yours."

They walked away, Cortland muttering to his companion. My bluff had worked. I held my posture straight as I strode over to my apartment's door, but as soon as I'd shut that behind me, my shoulders sagged.

Damn. Maybe Rose had been right about the phone too. I wouldn't have taken it if I'd known he'd come chasing after me like that.

She needed to know he'd been sniffing around here. Maybe he'd try to trip her up somehow too.

I sent her a quick text—*We need to talk.*—and poked around in my fridge for an early dinner. I didn't have much of an appetite now, but the thought of trying to veg out in front of a movie was no longer appealing.

I'd given up on the fridge and was debating between ordering for pizza or Chinese when my phone's text alert went off.

What's wrong? Rose had answered.

Is it safe to go into details over the phone? I wrote back.

There was a pause. *I don't know. And you know what, it'd be good to see you anyway. I'll come to you.*

My pulse hiccupped. What if Cortland was still keeping an eye on the house—with his witchy friend who might be able to sense Rose's magical protections?

No, I wrote quickly. *I don't think you coming into town is a good idea right now.* But—shit, could I even go to her? What if that witch had cast some spell on me I hadn't noticed? *Better if I come to you. Is there any way I can make sure I haven't got some kind of tracer on me or something?*

I didn't have to explain what I meant any more than that. *I can make sure you're clear of any magic,* Rose said. *Where are you right now?*

At my apartment.

Okay. Wait a few minutes before you leave. I'll take care of it.

Just like that. My lips curled into a grin. That was my girl. *Meet you by the pond in half an hour?*

I'll be there.

She left off with a heart emoji. Damn if it didn't make my actual heart squeeze a little.

I waited a few minutes like she'd said to. Nothing changed that I could feel, but Rose knew what she was doing. Just to be cautious, I swung around back of the house, cut through someone's yard, and took a slightly roundabout route through town.

There was a good spot to hop the wall partway around the estate. I was ambling along the lonely country road, nose full of the smells of fresh grass and clover, when a pickup truck came into view up ahead with a growl of an engine. My first instinct was to dive for the brush along the shoulder and hide. Then I realized I recognized the truck.

It pulled over to the shoulder across from me, and Seth leaned out the open window. "Hey," he said. "What are you doing up this way?"

I raised my eyebrows at him. "What do you think?"

His mouth twitched. Was that a smile from the killjoy? "What are *you* doing?" I added, my gaze sliding to the back of the truck. A few boards protruded from the bed.

"Just a construction job out this way," Seth said. He hesitated. "Look, I'm sorry about the other day. The whole job thing. I still think staying mixed up with some of those guys is a bad idea, but I handled it badly."

I nodded, my jaw working. Apparently this was a day of my former friends attempting to make amends. I hadn't offered Gabriel anything in return, but maybe it was only fair that I admitted to Seth: "Yeah. Well. You might have had point. Just a bit of one."

It was Seth's turn to lift an eyebrow. I glowered at him. At the same time, I couldn't help thinking about Silvio's guy and his insinuating comments... About the look on Rose's face when she'd confronted me about how I'd set up Derek for that beating... My tongue loosened.

"I don't suppose the whole electrician assistant thing is still on offer?"

"Do you actually want to give it a shot?" Seth asked.

I looked at the ground, at my scuffed-up sneakers. It might be kind of cool, actually, learning how to channel electricity. Working with that wiring... There were a lot worse things. Was it really any *better* shifting stolen crap around for Silvio?

Didn't Rose deserve a guy with a job she could actually tell people about?

"Yeah," I said, raising my head. "Kind of stupid to pass up an opportunity like that, right?"

The smile I'd thought I'd seen before came back. "I don't think there's any good way for me to answer that. I'll talk to Mr. Lewis and let you know."

"Thanks." I shifted my weight from foot to foot. It felt right to extend a little more of a peace offering than that. "You know where I'm going... Do you want to come? I'm pretty sure she won't mind the extra, ah, company."

Seth blinked at me as if he couldn't believe I'd been that generous. Just before I started to get annoyed, his smile widened into a grin. "Sure. I think I'll do that."

* * *

Rose was waiting by the pond when we made it there, the breeze ruffling her dark hair. She turned at the rasping of our feet through the brush and let out a relieved breath, seeing me. Then her gaze found Seth. She shot me a questioning look.

"I ran into this guy on the way over," I said. "What is it Jin likes to say? The more, the merrier?"

"Fine by me," Rose said, the corners of her lips quirking up. "Hold on."

We stopped a few feet from the edge of the pond while she rotated on her feet there, weaving her hands through the air in that eerie dance that made the hairs on the back of my neck rise even as it sent a bolt of desire through me. What a fucking woman my consort was.

"All right," she said. "No one should come out this way any time soon." She stepped toward us, and I moved forward, drawn like a magnet.

She kissed me first, so long and lingering I almost forgot I did need to get some talking in before we moved on to any other activities. Then she turned to Seth. He stroked his hand over her cheek and leaned in with a tenderness that made me feel weirdly off-balance.

I should be jealous that he got to have her as much as I did. But some part of me was *glad* she had a guy who clearly worshipped her as much as I did, just in some ways I wasn't as good at yet.

She needed me, but she needed him too. She needed all of us.

She leaned into him as she looked back at me, his arm still around her. "What was it you needed to tell me?" she asked. "Why were you worried someone might be tracing your movements with magic?"

"Well, I had a little visit from Mr. Cortland today."

Rose's eyes widened as I recounted my conversation with the asshole and his accomplice, her jaw tightening when I repeated the insults he'd thrown at me. "I kept my cool," I finished up. "I think I convinced them I had nothing to do with the phone getting stolen or with you. But... I figured it didn't hurt to be careful. And I don't know how much he's keeping an eye on you too."

"Maybe more than I realized. The way you described the woman with him... That sounds like our new estate manager." Rose rubbed her mouth. "Of course, it wouldn't be *strange* for him to ask my dad for help with his missing phone, or for Dad to ask her to go do it... But yeah. I don't like it."

"What do you think our next steps should be?" Seth asked.

"For you guys? Nothing, right now," Rose said. "Keep acting as if everything's normal. But be extra cautious if you see him around. I'm... I'm going to be talking to my dad tonight. I'll know the whole truth one way or the other by then." She paused and sucked in a breath. "That's partly why I wanted to see you. I'd like to have as much power as I can stored up, in case things go wrong. If you don't mind, ah, contributing."

The reason was dire, but the understanding of what she meant stirred up that flame of desire inside me anyway. I stepped right up to her, setting my hand on her side just below Seth's arm. The warmth of her, the heat that flared in her dark green eyes, was too delicious for me to ever imagine resisting it.

This, this part I was good at.

"Take everything you need, angel," I said, and bent my head to kiss the side of her neck.

CHAPTER TWENTY-ONE

Rose

I tipped my head to the side as Damon marked a scorching path down my neck, and Seth was right there, ready to meet my mouth with his. As their heat enveloped my body, my spark shot up through my chest with a fresh rush of energy. The magic sizzled through me alongside the bronze-y scent of Seth's skin and the hum of pleasure in Damon's throat as he reached my collarbone.

He didn't stop there. In one swift movement, he yanked down the straps of my tank top and my bra, baring my breasts almost all the way to the nipples. A sigh stuttered out of me as his mouth continued downward.

Seth claimed my mouth even more deeply. As his tongue slicked over mine, the arm he'd looped around my waist slid up under my shirt. With a flick, he undid my bra completely. His other hand stroked up over my belly to tease the underside of my breast.

His thumb reached my pebbling nipple at the same time Damon's lips did on the other side. Damon grazed his teeth over the peak of that breast and Seth swiveled his thumb, and a whimper broke from my throat. Flames of pleasure washed through every nerve. I was drowning in sensation and soaring on it all at the same time.

A jolt of need that had nothing to do with my spark spiked up from my core. I ran my hand down Seth's chest to cup the bulge straining his fly. He groaned against my mouth. Then he was tearing his lips from mine to tug my top right off me. It and my bra dropped to the ground with a faint thump.

Damon captured my mouth, squeezing my nipple between his fingers at the same time. Pleasure raced through my chest. I whimpered, and he took the opportunity to tangle his tongue with mine.

Seth nibbled his way down my chest, stopping to slick his tongue over my breast. He lingered there until I moaned, lost in the pleasure the guys were provoking together. Then he continued on, down, down, his fingers hooking around the waist of my jeans and easing along the sensitive skin of my belly to the snap. Without hesitation, he popped it open and peeled them off me. He nuzzled the front of my panties, his nose brushing my clit.

"If you taste half as good as you smell, this is going to be heaven," he said in a rough voice.

"She's heaven, all right," Damon said. He played with one nipple and then the other as his other hand teased down my back to squeeze my ass. His fingers dipped between my legs from behind. I gasped as he tested the damp fabric between my legs.

"God, angel," he said with a groan. "So fucking ready."

I whimpered in agreement, pressing my lips to his again. Seth kissed me through my panties and then yanked them down to devour me skin to skin. A cry wrenched out of me as he swiped his tongue over my clit. My spark blazed and pleasure swelled, singing through my veins.

I reached for Damon to pay him back in kind. He pressed his erection against my eager hand. "That's right," he muttered. "Oh, fuck."

Every caress of Seth's mouth against my sex was building the wave of bliss inside me, but I already knew that wasn't going to be enough to satisfy me. I curled my fingers into his short, tawny waves and tugged him up for another kiss, lips to lips. Damon slid his hand around my thigh to finger my clit and then dip inside my opening. I rocked against his hand, still kissing Seth. My own hand fumbled with Damon's jeans.

He jerked them open and stepped out of them, kicking them and his boxers to the side. My fingers closed around the silky skin of his rigid cock. He made a strangled sound as I stroked him from base to tip. The head of his cock was already slick with precum.

"You want this?" he said, and plunged his fingers even deeper inside me. "You want it here?"

I whimpered in agreement and turned from Seth to

lock gazes with Damon. "As deep as you can go, as hard as you can go."

Lust flared in his eyes. "What the lady wants, the lady will get. Bend over, angel."

We ended up on the ground, on a thick patch of softly tangled grass. I tugged at Seth's jeans, and he stripped them off. "Rose?" he said.

"Sit down. I want you too."

I urged him down in front of me. Damon knelt behind me. He rubbed the head of his cock over my sex. I lowered my head over Seth's jutting erection, taking it all the way to the back of my throat. Then Damon drove into me, filling me, stretching me, so every nerve inside me quavered with bliss.

It was some kind of heaven, all right. The salty musky taste of Seth in my mouth, twitching as I swirled my tongue around his length. Damon's cock searing pleasure into me with every thrust. He gripped my hips with one hand and tucked the other around to finger my clit as he rammed into me again, as hard as I'd asked for. My spark blazed through every pore with the cresting pleasure.

Seth wove his fingers into my hair, supporting my head. His hips rocked in time with the bob of my head. His breath was ragged, his hold trembling as I sucked him harder.

I had that power. I could make this controlled, careful man come apart.

"Rose," he murmured. "I'm going to— You don't have to—"

Oh, but I wanted to. So badly. I clamped my lips even tighter around him, dragging my tongue all up his length, and his cock spasmed with a salty flood at the back of my mouth. As I swallowed, Damon gave my clit a pinch that sent an electric jolt of pleasure through my core. I shuddered, so close to my peak. So desperate for it.

Seth eased my head up to kiss me on the mouth. He stroked my breasts as Damon tweaked my clit again, thrusting even harder. I dipped lower, shifting the angle, and Damon's cock plunged against that perfect spot of pleasure.

My spark crackled like a firework. I came with a cry, toes curling and body shaking. Seth held my shoulders and Damon clutched my hips, driving even harder, even faster, sending the flames inside me searing even higher. A gasp slipped out of me, and that first orgasm tumbled into another, even stronger. Stars danced behind my eyes.

"You're the best I ever had," Damon said in a choked voice. "I could never want anyone else, not while I have you."

A groan spilled out of him, and his cock spilled after, a hot rush inside me. He rocked to a stop, bending over me. The kiss he pressed to my spine was so gentle after the furor of our coming together that it almost made me come all over again.

I rolled over to sprawl between my guys, pressing a kiss to Damon's shoulder. "Do you always get sappy when you're about to come, or is that something special just for me?"

A halting chuckle tumbled out of him. "There's never been anyone else who's made me feel sappy, angel," he said. He tilted my chin up to claim my mouth, and Seth scooted closer against my back. Magic thrummed through me as if I were made of it.

Then the clearing of a throat several feet away turned my blood to ice.

I scrambled up, instinctively grabbing my tank top. The guys leapt to their feet to shield me.

A tall figure with sandy blond hair was stepping out from behind one of the trees on the other side of the pond. My former fiancé looked us over, his eyes dark amid his fading bruises and his cheeks a little flushed. His lips pulled back in a sneer.

"So this is what all those walks in the woods were really about."

"What the hell are you doing here?" I snapped. Panic was clanging through my body. I wrenched the top over my head and groped for my panties, an unpleasant burn prickling my skin at the thought of Derek seeing me naked. At the thought that he might already have seen a whole lot more than just that. How had he gotten past the spell I'd cast?

"I thought I'd try a little walking myself. Clear my head. Then I saw you heading out here looking very purposeful, so I decided I'd see exactly what you were up to. Good thing I did." He folded his arms over his chest. "I think I've seen enough."

He turned on his heel to head back toward the house —to do what? Tell my dad? Call the Assembly? My heart lurched.

But he hadn't broken through my magic. He'd simply already been inside the area I'd closed off when I'd cast the spell. I had plenty more power at my disposal.

"Stop!" I said, with a flick of my hand. Derek's legs jarred as his feet froze in place. His head jerked around to aim a glare at me, but his expression just sent a wave of angry heat through me.

Who the hell was he to try to claim some kind of moral high ground? Who the hell was he at all?

This was done. He'd seen us. So it was time he found out exactly who *I* was.

"Rose," Damon started, his glower still fixed on my ex-fiancé.

I shook my head as I tugged on my jeans. "I'll deal with him. Everything will be just fine."

Derek laughed. "You think so? How much can your spark be lit from these clowns? They're not even witching folk, are they?"

Damon all but bared his teeth, and Seth's hands clenched. But I strode right past them, right up to Derek, stopping just a few feet away. Fury churned in my stomach. It must have shown in my gaze too, because the arrogance in Derek's expression faltered.

"Don't try me," I said, letting my magic crackle into my voice. "My *consorts* have given me more than you ever could have."

Derek's eyes widened. "Your consorts?"

"But let's not talk about that," I said. "Let's talk about you. Where should we start? Maybe with Polly? Exactly how witching is she? What did you get out of those little liaisons, other than your dick wet?"

His jaw twitched and then firmed. "I don't think you're in any position to complain when—

"Sure," I said, cutting him off. "We'll skip the 'who

betrayed who first' argument. Because I have a contract that shows it was definitely you, months before we even got to this estate. What bothers you more, Derek? The fact that you didn't get to claim my body or that you won't get to take over my magic?"

The color drained from my ex-fiancé's face behind the bruises. He didn't seem to have anything to say about that.

"Yeah," I said. "I know. And you're not getting one shred of my magic—if you still thought you had any chance of it now that Celestine is gone. Did you expect this to still somehow work out in your favor? That my dad would arrange it for you?"

I tried not to put any special emphasis on that last line, not to give away how much I still needed that confirmation, one way or the other. Derek wet his lips, his gaze darting from me to the guys who'd come up behind me and back again.

"I don't know," he said. "I was committed. I was going to see the consorting through, however it turned out."

"And what did my father think about that?"

"What would he think?" Derek shot back. "It was all Celestine. He had no idea about anything except the regular consorting."

A tight band of worry that had been wrapped around my gut released. Dad had nothing to do with it. I'd gotten worried again with Celestine's "accident," with Mrs. Gainsley going around helping Master Cortland, that he was involved somehow.

But maybe the crash *had* been an accident—or if it hadn't been, someone had pulled the strings without Dad knowing. I'd bet Master Cortland had been worried Celestine would turn him in for his assistance if she were caught. He'd already been in contact with people who'd arranged for "problems" like that to be solved in murderous fashion before. Blaming him made more sense anyway.

"Great," I said to Derek. "Then we'd better fill him in on all the details of your crimes. We can go have a word with him right now." But I couldn't let him reveal what he knew about my consorts. I had to bring that to Dad in my own time. And the last thing I wanted was anyone in the Assembly finding out.

"You won't say anything about what you saw out here, though," I added. "Nothing about my behavior or my magic or who may have kindled it."

Derek scowled. "All right," he said hesitantly.

I stepped closer. "Of course, I can't just take your word for it. So why don't you have a taste of that magic you wanted so much?" I gathered my power in my throat and poured it into my voice. "You, Derek Conwyn, will never communicate anything you saw me say or do here at the pond, or the implications of anything you saw or heard, or make any indication of those things to anyone. *Accept.*"

"I accept," he croaked, the words driven from his mouth by my magic. It hissed in the air between us and clamped around his mind, seeing my will be done.

I left him there, his feet still frozen to the ground, and turned to Seth and Damon. "You'd better leave. I'll let you know as soon as this is over."

"If there's anything we can do by staying..." Seth said.

"No. One thing at a time."

I brushed a kiss to both of their mouths. Damon held me a moment longer. "Don't give him an inch," he muttered.

"Not planning on it," I said. "You stay safe too."

As they faded back into the woods, I made a motion to release Derek's feet and bind him at a safe distance from me. He'd have to follow me to the manor, but he couldn't get close enough to hurt me.

"Let's get this over with," I said. "The moment I never have to see your face again can't come too soon."

CHAPTER TWENTY-TWO

Rose

For the first several minutes tramping back through the forest, Derek was sullen and silent. He walked slowly, with a bit of a limp. When he glanced over at me, I thought I saw him checking out my breasts. Augh. Yeah, I was definitely going to need some brain soap after today.

Insect sounds hummed around us. The light through the trees was getting thinner—it'd be almost dinner time now, but the sluggish breeze that drifted over me was still warm.

Derek stumbled a bit, skirting a log. He grimaced and looked at me again.

"You're going to turn me over to the Justice Division after this?" he said.

"I'm sure that's what my dad will think is the best decision. Don't try to tell me you don't deserve it."

"I wasn't thinking of that. I was thinking maybe you're not thinking that decision through all the way."

"What do you mean?"

He shrugged. "I understand their investigations are quite thorough."

Philomena wove through the trees to join us. "What in heaven's name is he going on about now?"

"I don't know," I said to her in my head. If there was something Derek wanted to say about my consorts or anything else he'd learned in the last hour, my magic meant he couldn't hint at that even to me. But he also couldn't say anything to the Assembly. Unless...

A chill tickled over me. "When the Assembly investigates him, they'll probably check for magic on him. They'll find my spell. Take it off him, and then he'll be able to tell them about the actual consorts I've taken." The unsparked consorts at least a few of their number were prepared to kill me and those consorts over.

Derek would go down, but so would I. Did he suspect that—that my life might be on the line? Or was he only thinking the public shame might be enough leverage?

Either way, if Dad found out about the conspiracy to enslave my magic, there was no way he'd let Derek go unpunished. No escaping the Assembly's involvement. Maybe if I'd had time to convince him of the need for secrecy... but I already knew I was going to need to ease him into the idea of my consorts. Damn.

"I see your point," I said to Derek carefully. "Maybe we should approach the situation from a different angle, then." I motioned for him to stop and looked him dead in the eyes. "I'm not marrying you. I'd rather take a newt as a husband at this point."

"Wonderful," Derek said. "The feeling is mutual."

My hackles rose, but I held my temper. "We could skip your illegal doings. Just tell my father you've been sleeping around behind my back. That you've got no interest in marrying me. That'll be enough for him to accept you leaving. And then you can just get the hell away from here. Agreed?"

A flicker of relief passed through his expression. Whatever he knew about my situation, he hadn't liked his at all. "That sounds reasonable," he said.

"Then I'll need to add to the oath you took," I said, and summoned more of my magic. "You will not speak of the contract you made with my stepmother, or any of the plans that surrounded it, or hint at them, to anyone. You *will* inform my father of your infidelity and the contempt you have for me. Accept."

"I accept," he replied, the magic twining with his words more easily this time when he wasn't resisting it.

"All right. Come on."

Philomena picked her way through the brush beside me, holding up her skirts. "So what happens after that?"

I exhaled. "I guess I come clean with Dad and hope he comes around sooner rather than later."

I let Derek do most of the talking. By the time he'd finished spilling his story—the part about Polly and his disinterest in becoming my husband, anyway—Dad's shoulders had gone completely rigid where he was standing by his desk. His jaw worked.

"You pledge yourself to my daughter, come into my home, and that's how you behave?" he said in a low, dangerous voice I'd never heard him use before.

"I would have kept my promise," Derek put in. "I still meant to marry her."

Dad looked at me. I swiped at my eyes as if fighting tears. I had started to feel truly choked up during the talk, both thinking about how long Derek had duped me and how much I wished I hadn't needed to go through this at all. If I just could have had my guys, the ones I adored who adored me, from the beginning... But I couldn't have them openly even now, unless Dad knew some loophole.

"I can't marry someone who thinks that little of me," I said in a shaky voice.

Dad's tone softened. "Of course not. Rose. We'll get this all sorted out. Can you give me a few minutes? I think I should speak to your *former* fiancé alone." His gaze sharpened again as he turned back to Derek.

My pulse hiccupped, but Derek couldn't tell Dad anything he hadn't already. My magic had seen to that. I nodded. "I'll be in my room."

"That's it," Phil murmured excitedly as I walked across the hall. "You're free of that ruffian."

"But not really free." I sank onto the edge of my bed, curling my fingers into the soft duvet. Remembering the other night here with Kyler.

Would I *ever* be able to bring the guys into my home like full partners? It didn't seem fair. To them more than anyone.

It wasn't long before Dad knocked on my door. "Can I come in, lamb?"

"Of course," I said, giving my eyes another swipe so they'd look reddened.

He eased open the door and crossed the room to stand by the bed. "Derek is leaving," he said. "As quickly as he can get his things together. You won't ever have to see him again."

I let out my breath in a rush. "Good. Thank you."

He raked his hand through his hair. "But of course now we have a difficult situation to face. Your twenty-fifth birthday is only six weeks off. I'll have to start talking to other potential consorts... You won't have as much time to get to know them beforehand as I'd have liked, but I'm sure I can find someone you'll be happy with. Or at least content, while you settle in with your powers and decide what you want to do next. Once your spark is kindled..."

"I'll be fine, even if I break the consort bond," I said. "I know. And I know it'll be okay. That's actually— I wanted to talk to you about—"

He stared to pace from one end of the room to the other, barreling on. "You don't need to worry about it at all, Rose. I should have seen the problem sooner. I take responsibility. I'll fly out tonight—you know, I might know just the fellow. We never arranged a meeting because you seemed to hit it off with Derek well, but you share a fair few interests, and he's made it known he's interested in finding a good match. Killian Sorensen. Quite the name, too." He chuckled.

I'd been about to interrupt Dad to tell him I didn't

need a consort at all. At that name, a finger of ice ran down my back. I knew it. I knew it because...

Celestine's files on possible consorts. The ideal last-minute backup guy. Killian Sorensen.

No. Derek had said Dad had no idea. It had to be just a coincidence.

"Is that one of the possible guys Celestine picked out?" I said tentatively, watching Dad's expression. "I can't help feeling—she was the one who suggested meeting with Derek—after that, and with her disappearing so suddenly..."

"Of course, of course," Dad said. His eyes were already distant, as if he were booking the plane tickets in his mind. "No, your stepmother has nothing to do with Killian at all. I'm not sure I even mentioned him to her, to be honest."

"You didn't discuss him as a possible match?"

He shook his head. "I met him in passing during some business function or another. Always thought he was a good sort, so I kept an eye on him. I can't imagine how your stepmother would have met him. She certainly never spoke about him."

My stomach twisted. He was lying, baldly. Celestine's notes had mentioned a luncheon she and Dad had arranged with Killian, and that she knew of him through one of her family friends. But of course Dad didn't have to worry about me finding that out now that Celestine was dead, did he?

He had to know about Celestine's "accident." The witching authorities would have contacted her husband as quickly as her daughters. Maybe, not realizing Evianna had harassed me about it, he wouldn't have wanted to burden me with the unsettling news right now, but I didn't see any sign that he was holding back his own grief. I couldn't see any indication that he cared at all—about anything except getting me consorted to a man of his choice as quickly as possible.

I gripped the edge of my duvet. My head was starting to spin. "Dad," I said, a little weakly, "why don't we just wait on it a day or two? Just to give me time to come to grips with what's happened. I'm not sure I want to jump right into a new engagement without a moment to breathe."

"I know, lamb," Dad said briskly. The echo of Celestine's voice rang through my mind. *He does love you, in his own way. You're his little lamb, and he wants you on a leash.* "I hate to leave you when we're going through this. But we don't have any time to spare. The last thing I want to see is you losing your magic over something like this."

Because then you won't be able to control it? I thought but couldn't say. My throat had closed up. It was hard to breathe, watching him pace and make his plans, pretending he only wanted what was best for me.

He must have orchestrated everything, all along. Did that mean he was behind Celestine's death too?

"Dad," I said, not even really knowing what I was aiming for. Just wanting to see if I could sway him even a little. "Please, can you just stay home tonight? I don't want to be alone."

He stopped in front of me, with a look so fond I thought maybe I'd gotten through to him after all. But then his gaze twitched away. He touched my shoulder, but his thoughts were somewhere else. "I'm sorry, Rose. I promise this will be for the best. You want the worthiest consort I can find for you. I have to make arrangements now."

He strode to the door. "Dad!" I called after him.

"It will all work out," he said over his shoulder. "You don't need to worry."

The door clicked shut behind him, and I was left perched on the edge of my bed, with nothing *but* worry clamped tight around my stomach.

I'd stumbled on the truth. I knew who my enemies were. It turned out they were all around me. Spark help me, where did I go from here?

CHAPTER TWENTY-THREE

Seth

"I came *so* close to telling him," Rose said, ducking her head. Under the stark lights of Jin's gallery, she looked suddenly small. "I could have ruined everything."

"You didn't," I said, sliding my arm around her. The cool air from the air conditioner tickled over my skin, and I suddenly wished we were outside in the warm glow of the sun. "You waited all this time because you weren't sure, because you wanted to be careful, and it's because of *that* you didn't tell him before you had the chance to find out the truth. You didn't do anything wrong."

"No one blames you, Rose," Jin said, looking uncharacteristically solemn. "Maybe I wasn't taking the situation seriously enough before. I tried to tell you that you could just *make* everything be okay..."

But it obviously wasn't. I'd never seen Rose this

despondent. She rubbed her eyes, the circles under them dark from lack of sleep last night. But she refused to let me take any of her weight.

"I heard your dad talking to Matt when he was getting in the car," Gabriel said. "He expected to be gone at least two days. You've got time to figure out what you need to do. What *we* need to do."

Rose glanced toward him, something hopeful lighting in her face. And Gabriel pulled back—just an inch, but I saw that hope dim in response.

What the hell was wrong with him? Couldn't he see she needed all of us now? Her whole world was falling apart.

He glanced around at the rest of us instead, like he was our leader all over again. "We have to come up with a plan of action. Quickly."

No kidding. Thankfully my brother had a way of cutting right through to the facts. "What *does* need to happen?" Kyler asked Rose. "What exactly could stop your dad from going forward with this consort plan? He still doesn't know that *you* know about the whole scheme, right?"

Rose drew in a shaky breath and stood a little taller. At her other side, Damon stood straight and fierce, looking ready to charge into battle on her behalf. Normally that sight would have irked me, but after our conversation yesterday, I felt a little more certain that he'd only go charging in where he really should.

He wanted what was best for Rose too, in his own way. Maybe we'd all been a little lost trying to figure out how we fit into her world.

No, really, we still were.

"My dad doesn't know I'm onto him," Rose said. "But as long as he still has any control over my life, he's going to be trying to marry me off. It seemed really important to him. I guess it's not just about making sure I don't use my powers in some dangerous way but also... having those powers for *him* to use however he wants? He wouldn't even listen to me when I tried to ask him for a day or two before he went running off to find someone to replace Derek."

She swiped a stray strand of her black hair back from her face. "If I displaced him, he'd have no authority over the estate at all. It'd all come to me, like it was supposed to when I was twenty-five anyway. As long as I don't give anyone reason to displace *me*. So I guess... I need to expose what he's done. While he's gone, I can go looking through his things for proof again. I found that proof with Celestine. He has to have slipped up somewhere."

"No one can cover their tracks perfectly," Ky said. "We'll find it."

"Then what?" I asked.

"The same thing I was planning to do with Celestine and Derek," she said. "I'll present the evidence to the Assembly. They'll prosecute him—at the very least he should lose any claim on the Hallowell properties in deference to me. The witching women always get priority anyway. And then... I'll wait out the time. Pretend I've decided I don't care to come into my magic. Dismiss Mrs. Gainsley and her husband from staff, have only unsparked people working at the house. I could even hire you all on, and that'll give you an excuse to be here. We'll manage."

"Is that the best you can hope for?" Gabriel said. "Living your whole life hiding what you are, what you can do?"

Rose shook her head. "I'll keep investigating the Assembly as well as I can—with you all." She shot a smile at Ky. "If it's just a small group within the witching government that's so against unsparked relations, maybe there's something I can do to change that. But I don't know how long it'll take. Or if it'll happen at all."

"I don't want you to have to live like that," Ky said. "If I can find anything... I'll go back to Seattle, and maybe together we could find ways around their security..." He paused. "When I was looking before, I saw a reference to a different sort of consorting. A soul-bound ceremony? It sounded like it's more serious—if it's something more we could do to give ourselves over, to give you more power—"

"*No*," Rose said, so sharply my brother's mouth snapped shut. Her jaw tightened. "Hardly anyone does the soul-binding consorting anymore. I doubt they ever did. It does mean sharing more energy, faster, but it's also unbreakable. Until death. And if one partner dies, the other does too."

"I'd be willing to take that chance," Damon said.

"You don't have to." Rose glanced around our group. "I have all the magic I could ever want, with all of you." Her gaze lingered for just a second on Gabriel. When their gazes met, his twitched away. I frowned.

"We're here for you," Jin said, echoing Damon's

earlier comment. He stepped forward and wrapped his arms around her in a hug. She hugged him back tightly. As Ky and Damon converged around them, Gabriel drew back a step. I followed him, motioning him toward the far corner.

"What the hell are you doing?" I said under my breath when he turned to face me there. "Can't you see she's looking to you for support too? Why are you acting so cagey?" I didn't for a second believe it was lack of interest.

Gabriel played it casual, shaking his head with a flash of his dark red hair as if in disbelief. "She has my support."

"Not totally," I said. "And she can obviously tell."

"I'm here," Gabriel said, and smiled. "This is why it's a good thing she's had you. I can see the way you've been holding everyone together, providing that voice of reason."

The compliment should have warmed me, but it niggled at me instead. He meant it, I believed that, but he was also trying to deflect me with it.

"She needs all of us," I said. "She needs *you*."

Something flashed deep in Gabriel's eyes. "I'm the last thing she needs," he murmured.

In the past, I'd always trusted Gabriel to find the right path, to steer the rest of us right. Now, for the first time in my life, I found myself wanting to shake him. But Rose was stepping out of the ring the other guys had formed around her, glancing toward us. So I settled for saying, "Don't you think deciding that should be up to her?"

"Is everything okay?" Rose asked. Again, her gaze lingered a little longer on Gabriel.

"Nothing to worry about, Sprout," he said in that easy tone that right now rubbed me completely the wrong way. "No more than you already know about, at least. Which of us do you think should head back to the manor first?"

She'd been looking for something in him that she hadn't gotten. Disappointment flickered across her face. It made my gut clench. And I found myself saying, without having planned to, "You should go on ahead. There's something I want to show Rose."

"Oh, really?" Jin said, with a raise of his eyebrows.

I rolled my eyes at him. "Not like that." I turned to Rose. "If you don't mind...? I think it should be for your eyes only at this point."

Everyone was looking at me curiously now. Rose slipped her fingers around my hand. "All right."

My truck was parked over by my dad's hardware store. Rose didn't speak as we headed over, but she kept her hand wrapped around mine. "Is this okay?" I said, squeezing her fingers. "If someone sees..."

"They won't," she said, sounding a little sad. "They won't see me at all. I'm a figment of your imagination right now." Her lips quirked upward, but even that smile looked bittersweet.

So I guessed to anyone watching, our drive out to the house was no different from all my earlier ones: just me in the truck with some equipment as if headed out to a job. As we got closer, my heart started to sink.

What if I'd gone too far? What if this put *more*

pressure on Rose instead of taking some off her? It had seemed like a good idea at the time... I'd loved working on the place more than any actual job I'd taken on. But I wasn't all that sure of my instincts these days, not when it came to all things witching.

"Are you going to tell me where we're going?" Rose asked lightly, peering out the windshield and the side window.

"You'll see," I said.

Her expression turned more serious as she watched the fields fly by. "Seth," she said, "what would you be doing right now if I hadn't come back? What did you want to be doing, in a perfect world?"

"I don't think it could be perfect without you in it," I said a little teasingly, and she shot me a look. Lord, how to answer that. I tipped my head, considering.

"I don't know. More than just doing repairs and building sheds or what have you with my dad, that's for sure."

"What kind of more?"

"Well, I guess..." A twinge rippled through my chest. Maybe this wasn't that hard a question after all. "I've always wanted to give something back to the town. To feel like I'm helping build *it* up, not just little pieces of people's private property. Sometimes I've thought about donating time and supplies to fix up that old playground in Westfield Park. Things like that."

"That's lovely," Rose said. "You *should* do that. What we have... it doesn't have to stop you. You know that, right?"

"Of course," I said. The truth was, I wasn't even sure

why I hadn't done more than think about it yet. I'd had this idea that I needed to establish myself in the business more, prove myself in my own right as more than just "that handy son of Mr. Lennox's," but I knew what I was doing already. My most recent project had proven that.

The farmhouse loomed in the distance, the For Sale sign gone, the yard neatly trimmed. I'd ended up having to rebuild the porch pretty much from scratch, but now it was completely solid. I'd painted the boards a soft yellow that looked the way that rush of magic I'd felt when I'd sworn myself as Rose's consort had felt to me. The glass in all the broken windows had been replaced. The rest of the exterior needed painting, and the roof could use some new shingles, but it didn't look like a wreck anymore, at least.

Rose's expression turned more puzzled when I pulled up the drive and parked by the garage. "Are we coming to meet someone? What's this about, Seth?"

I got out and came around to the passenger side to offer her a hand out. "I want you to meet this house," I said. "My first contribution to building something real."

I fished the key out of my pocket as we walked up to the front door. Everything—the savings account I'd nearly drained, the hours of work squeezed in around my regular jobs, the aches and the splinters—was worth it for the awe that lit her face as we stepped inside.

I'd nearly finished the interior. Every wall had been repainted: the same soft yellow here, a baby blue there, ivory in the hall. With the windows unboarded, sunlight spilled all through the wide doorways of the first-floor rooms. The hardwood floors were a little scratched up but gleaming with a fresh layer of polish. Now that I'd aired the place out, it smelled of the late spring wildflowers blooming in the field out back.

"There are five bedrooms upstairs and another in the attic," I said. "One for each of us, and you if you ever stay over."

"One for each of—" Rose spun to face me. "You and the other guys. You're going to *live* here?"

I rubbed the back of my neck. "I haven't exactly talked to them about it yet. But that was the general idea when I bought the place. I thought, with it being so close to the estate, it'd make it a lot easier for slipping in and out without anyone in or around town noticing... One step closer to actually living together, until we can do that. Because I know someday we'll figure out a way."

Rose was outright glowing now. She grasped the front of my shirt and pulled me into a kiss. As I kissed her back, relief and a stirring hunger rising through me, her fingers teased up the back of my neck into my hair. Suddenly that hunger was everything.

"Seth," she murmured. "It's beautiful. It's the best thing I've ever seen. Thank you." She blinked hard, as if trying not to cry.

Shit. That wasn't the reaction I wanted, even if they were at least partly happy tears. I kissed the corner of one eye and then the other. Then I leaned in to capture her mouth again, stroking my hand up her side.

"There's one thing it's missing," I said by her ear.

"Oh yeah? What's that?"

"It hasn't been properly christened yet."

Her lips curled into a proper smile, nothing but joy in

it just for this moment. "Hmm. I think that has to be because you've never brought me out here before. But we can fix that oversight right now."

She caught my mouth, her hands gliding up under my shirt spreading heat in their wake, and I gave myself over to the woman I couldn't imagine loving more.

CHAPTER TWENTY-FOUR

Rose

"When is that woman going to *leave?*" Philomena muttered. "Surely she has something to occupy herself with that will take her out of that office?"

"I can't imagine she'll stay in there all day," I said, snuggling deeper into the firm cushions of one of the armchairs in the manor's library. I was flipping through an old witching text and listening to the sounds that traveled through the open door at the same time.

The estate manager's office was just across the hall. Mrs. Gainsley had been rustling around in there for the last hour.

"Can't you just whisk yourself into your father's office with that magic of yours?" Phil asked, swishing her skirts as she paced the library floor. "Why, I'd be off to

Paris and, my, even the Orient in a flash if I had that kind of power."

I gave her a wry look. "I *don't* have quite that kind of power. Teleportation takes a lot out of you. If I tried to get to Paris I'd probably end up somewhere in Idaho. Anyway, Dad had Mrs. Gainsley put some kind of magical lock on the room to make sure no one went in. I'm not sure if jumping in there might trigger it. I need her gone so I can fiddle with the spell more carefully. And I want to look in her office too."

My last search of Dad's office hadn't turned up anything, after all. But this time I knew he'd be gone at least a couple days, and he'd left his computer behind. That was enough time for me to secret it away to Kyler for a proper analysis, in case he'd hidden incriminating material on there.

And if Mrs. Gainsley was helping Dad—she must be, she was the one meant to conduct my consort ceremony now—as well as Master Cortland and who knew who else, searching her work materials seemed like a good idea too. If I could ever get access to them.

Her footsteps tapped out into the hall. My heart leapt. I tensed in the chair, waiting and listening...

A door clicked shut. A few moments later, the pipes in the walls hummed. The bathroom. When the door squeaked open again, the estate manager headed straight back to her office. I suppressed a groan and tipped my head back in my chair.

There had to be something else I could do in the meantime. This might be the only day I got without Dad here. I couldn't count on him staying away longer. I'd asked Gabriel to tell me as soon as the call came into the garage for one of the drivers to pick him up at the airport...

The cars. Dad had gotten Matt to take him out in the Bentley last night. He always took that car, whether he was driving or being driven, whenever he went out. Maybe he'd left something in it. It couldn't hurt to check.

"Come on," I said to Phil. "We're going down to the garage."

"Oooh!" Phil said, producing her fan out of thin air and peeking at me coyly over the top. "To visit that new young man of yours?"

"No, to search Dad's car." Although if I happened to see Gabriel, that wouldn't exactly be a bad thing. "And I don't think I can call that young man 'mine.'"

"No? I've seen the way he looks at you," Phil said as she trailed after me to the stairs.

"So have I," I said. "But... We kissed and he took off on me. He said he couldn't do it." My throat tightened at the memory. "He's helping every way he can. But expecting him to get that wrapped up in my life... It's obviously too much. I can't blame him. I don't *want* him putting his life at risk like that."

He couldn't have been clearer in the last couple days that while he still intended to help, that was as far as it went. I could practically feel the wall he'd build around himself, keeping me at a distance. Which he had every right to.

I darted across the drive and slipped into the garage's

dim, narrow hall. The place still felt like a stable, even though it had been converted almost a century ago. The door by the Bentley's "stall" was down at the far end.

When I eased out beside the car, in the empty spot where Celestine's Jaguar used to be parked, darkness settled around me with the damp smell of concrete and motor oil. I left the door slightly ajar to let in a thin streak of light. It took only a snap of my fingers to unlock the Bentley's driver-side door.

I started there, conjuring a tiny beam to act as a magical flashlight. My search under the seat turned up nothing. I moved to the passenger side, checking between the seats, in the change holder, and opening up the glove compartment. Nothing waited in there but the manual and car registration as well as a small package of those licorice candies Dad loved.

The tickle of their smell in my nose, mingling with the warm woody smell of his cologne that clung to the seats, made my heart ache. How could he be the same father who'd cuddled with me and read stories to me and snuck downstairs with me for midnight snacks? How could that man be plotting to marry me away as some kind of slave?

I wasn't sure I'd ever be able to ask him. I wasn't sure I wanted to hear his answer.

I scanned the trunk and then climbed into the back seat in a last ditch effort to turn up something, anything.

As I bent over to check the floor, footsteps rasped in the garage hall. I ducked down, my pulse skipping, peering between the seats. When a familiar chiseled face framed by dark red hair peered past the doorway, I exhaled in relief. Straightening up, I nudged open the car door. "It's just me."

Gabriel came out into the car bay, cocking his head. "Did you need a drive somewhere?" he said with a teasing note in his voice. "You're more likely to get it if you come tell someone first."

I mock-glared at him. "I was checking the car to see if my dad left anything here. Seems like no. But I can't get into his office while Mrs. Gainsley is hanging around up there."

"I would have thought you could find some way around that, Miss Witch." He dropped onto the seat next to me and glanced into the storage nook on the door.

"Not so easy when the person I'm trying to get around is also a witch who isn't supposed to know I've got magic yet," I muttered. "I can't cast anything on or around her."

"I've worked on a couple cars where the owners wanted to keep certain cargo... discreet. Let's check the usual suspects." He prodded the base of the seat, I guessed to check whether it would open. When nothing happened, he moved to the padding at the back.

I watched him for a moment, torn between the tug I felt with him so near me and the distance I could still feel in his demeanor. We were friends, that tone, that smile, said. Nothing more. I got the sense he was going out of his way to make that clear. My throat tightened.

"I'm sorry about the other day," I said.

Gabriel's head jerked up. "What?"

"In my room, when I—" I gestured vaguely, my cheeks flushing. "I wasn't trying to push you into anything. I wouldn't want to. I guess I just misunderstood."

Gabriel just looked at me for a moment, his expression unreadable. "It's okay," he said, not confirming or denying. "You don't have to worry about that."

"So we're good?"

He gave me that characteristic grin. "We're always good, Sprout."

I wasn't sure I totally believed that, but the tension inside me eased off a little. I shifted over so he could check the middle section of the seat. His hands moved with practiced certainty.

"Is this what you'd want to keep doing?" I found myself asking. "Here, or in town, after this mess is over—working on cars? In between all those trips you're still planning, of course."

Gabriel chuckled. "I think so, as long as I can find the work. It doesn't seem as if people are going to stop driving cars any time soon. And I like working with the internal systems, figuring out how to boost their performance, taking care of them when they're running down. Everything connects to everything else in a clear sequence. You can always see what needs doing, if you bother to pay attention."

And Gabriel always did. There'd never been much that escaped his notice.

"Switch?" he said, and I scooted past him, holding my breath at the brush of his body past mine, so he could check the other side. More safe conversation topics—that was what I needed.

"Where *are* you thinking you'd want to get to now that you've been all over South America and wherever?" I said.

"Hard to say where I'd go first. I'd like to see more of the really big cities here—get out to New York, for example. And Alaska, maybe—it must be pretty amazing to experience the kind of stark wilderness you can get up there."

"A pretty far cry from Argentina, I bet," I said.

"Sure," he said, glancing up with a twinkle in his eye. "But that's the whole point. I want to experience at least a little bit of everything while I'm here on this planet." He patted the seat. "I think we're all clear as far as secret compartments go—"

One of the garage doors started to rumble open at the other end of the building. Gabriel stiffened.

"Get down," he whispered. I was already flattening myself to the seat, snuffing my magical light with a flick of my fingers. He dove past me to tug the door shut with a soft thump and lay down next to me. I wasn't sure which was more responsible for the pounding of my heart—the thought that I might be caught or the heat of Gabriel's well-muscled body aligning with mine.

A voice carried down the bay. Tyler's reedy tenor. "Where are you taking it?"

Matt's lower, gruffer voice answered. "Just out to Farmington. Got to drop off some business contracts for the boss."

Just the regular staff, not Mrs. Gainsley or anyone

witching. It probably wouldn't have mattered if they'd seen us by the car. Now that we were hiding together inside it, though, we couldn't exactly casually climb out without raising a few questions.

I breathed in and out slowly as Matt started the engine on whichever car he was taking. Gabriel shifted his weight, staying on his side as much as he could so he didn't squash me into the seat. His chest was pressed against my breasts, his thigh between mine. That slight movement sent a quiver of desire up from my core.

His breath spilled over the side of my face, slightly ragged. I swallowed hard, trying to focus on the sounds of the car, on what Matt had said, on anything over than the guy lying over me—

An idea sparked in my head. Farmington. Down the road that went past Master Cortland's house. It seemed like Master Cortland was turning to Mrs. Gainsley as his go-to witch when he needed magical help. Celestine had used him to get at me... Maybe I could use him too.

"Sorry," I whispered. I eased my hand away from my side and turned my head to concentrate on its movements. Gabriel adjusted his weight to accommodate me. The friction between our bodies sent a fresh wave of heat through me. I narrowed all of my attention away from that onto my hand.

I moved it in a slow circle, swiveling at the elbow. A seeking spell, a reaching spell. It sent my magic spiraling out across the countryside toward Master Cortland's house and settled around the familiar bulk of his presence.

Yes, he was home. Just outside the house. Perfect. I'd rather do this outside with more room to work with.

I clenched my hand and then released my fingers, twitching them as they unfurled. Casting my magic out, out, across that distance with a flare of my spark in my chest.

Out there in his yard where Master Cortland stood, wavering lights with the impression of faces would have shot up around him. Eerie and vague but clearly magical. I made them sway with my fingers for several seconds to make sure I'd have caught his attention. Then I balled my hand into a fist, snuffing them out. Sucking all that magic back to me so there'd be no trace for Mrs. Gainsley to test.

I sagged back against the seat. The magicking had left me a little breathless. Or maybe that was because of Gabriel, braced against me still. The car Matt had taken had rumbled off, but Tyler was still puttering around the garage. A faint squeak suggested he was polishing one of the other cars.

"What did you do?" Gabriel asked under his breath. His face was so close to mine I could feel the movement of his lips in the jitter of breath against my cheek. Every inch of my skin screamed for me to move, to increase the friction, to pull him closer, but I clamped down on that urge.

"I think I sent a red herring for Mrs. Gainsley to go investigate," I said. "We'll see if it works. If I ever get to leave this car."

He chuckled softly. "I can try and lower myself onto the floor."

I touched his side before he could move. "No. It's okay. The last thing we want is Tyler noticing us like this. His shift is almost over anyway." I hesitated. Gabriel's heart was thumping in his chest almost as hard as mine. "Unless you're uncomfortable. I'm not going to try to— I meant what I said. Whatever you feel—or don't feel— toward me, it's totally fine. I never expected anything."

Then I shut up before I babbled into even more awkward territory.

Gabriel bowed his head. His forehead touched mine. "I know. It's not that, Rose. You didn't do anything wrong, I swear it. You have no idea..."

I waited a moment after he trailed off. A quiver ran through my nerves. *It's not that*, he'd said. Not that he didn't have those kind of feelings for me? I couldn't hold back the words.

"Why don't you tell me? Seeing as we don't have a whole lot else to occupy us at the moment."

He adjusted his weight again, tension coiled through his muscles, and his thigh slid deeper between my legs. I bit my lip against a gasp of pleasure.

He was turned on too, I realized all at once. It wasn't discomfort making his heart thump. Not if that hard length resting against *my* thigh told me anything.

Gabriel drew in a ragged breath. "You've got no idea how hard it is to be this close to you and not make a move," he said thickly. "Maybe the rest doesn't matter. What do you want, Rose?"

"Right now?" He did want me. I was starting to feel dizzy with desire. It caught hold of my tongue. "I'd pretty much die for you to move your leg just a little closer."

His breath stuttered. Then, slowly and deliberately, he shifted his thigh so it pressed right against my clit through our jeans. "Like this?"

I swallowed a whimper. My hips flexed against him before I could stop them. A bolt of pleasure shot up from my core. My spark didn't brighten, because its connection was only to my consorts now, but the rest of me all but blazed.

My hand fisted around the side of his shirt, as if that could hold me in check. "Gabriel," I murmured.

"Rose." His head dipped beside mine, burying his face in my hair. He rocked against me at the same time as he kissed the crook of my jaw.

A whimper slipped out of me, too desperate to contain. I clamped my lips shut.

"You like that?" he whispered, his lips skimming my skin.

"So much. Please."

I didn't even know what I was begging him for, but somehow he did. He adjusted himself again, lifting away from me for one brief but painful second, and then he was settling himself flush between my thighs, his rigid erection against my sex. A strained sound worked its way out of his throat. As he stroked against me, a moan traveled up mine. Before it could break from my lips, I clutched his hair and dragged his mouth to mine.

We kissed, hot and messy, as we arched against each other. I didn't know what we were doing, but it felt so good I didn't give a shit.

My teeth grazed his lip. He kissed me harder, his hand shoving up under my shirt. His thumb teased over the peak of my breast so gently I almost lost it just like that.

My fingers traveled down his side to grip his hips. Pulling him to me, like I'd wanted to so badly earlier. Like I'd thought *he* wouldn't want. But there was no denying the hunger in his mouth as it devoured mine and the rocking of his hips and—

The garage door down the bay grated shut with a thump and a cutting off of the light. Gabriel startled. He pushed off me into a kneeling position, peering through the window. I knew with the silence that had fallen that Tyler was gone. It was just us and our heaving breaths in the tight space of the car.

I couldn't see Gabriel's expression in the darkness, but I felt his body tighten. "Shit," he muttered. "I didn't mean to—" He eased farther back, reaching for the car door. "You should go. See if that plan of yours worked."

His voice was strained but firm. I peeled myself off the seat, every nerve trembling. When I touched Gabriel's arm, he flinched. *Flinched.* My heart dropped to my gut.

"I want you," I said. "I want you with me, in case I wasn't clear enough about that before. What you do with that information is totally up to you, but you have to know that much."

"You don't know me, Rose," he said. "Not any more. Not really. The guy you want, he doesn't exist. It's been at least ten years since he did."

He clambered out of the car and held the door for me to follow him. I scooted across the seat. My mouth had gone dry. "What makes you think I wouldn't want the guy you are?"

He gave a rough laugh. "It's better for both of us if we don't go there, I think. I'll help you. I'll be here for you. But I shouldn't have crossed that line. It won't happen again, I promise."

CHAPTER TWENTY-FIVE

Rose

It wasn't hard to look as if I barely noticed or cared about Mrs. Gainsley bustling to the manor's front door. I was still dazed from that... whatever that had been with Gabriel. I don't think the estate manager even noticed *me*, perched there on the sitting room sofa, willing my stirred-up hormones to settle down.

It won't happen again, he'd promised. But, snuff my spark, I couldn't think of much I wanted more than another interlude like that, only more of it. I'd felt the desire radiating through him.

But desire wasn't enough. He didn't want *me*, not completely. Only enough to give in to an urge when it was almost unavoidable.

The front door clicked shut behind Mrs. Gainsley. I pushed myself off the sofa. I had bigger concerns anyway.

Four consorts who had dedicated themselves to me in every way that I had to protect. A life to claim for myself.

I headed up the stairs and stopped on the upper landing, where I could see through the large triangular window that loomed over the door. Mrs. Gainsley crossed the drive to the garage. A few minutes later, her Lincoln pulled up to the front gate. Beyond the wall, it turned left, the right direction to head to Master Cortland's house.

My ploy had worked. He'd seen the magic and called on her to investigate.

Now I needed to do my own investigating.

When Meredith had been our estate manager, I'd never found her office locked with anything other than a regular key. Today, I could feel a tremor of magic as I reached my hand toward the office door. It wasn't just Dad's office Mrs. Gainsley had secured. She wasn't taking any chances. Other than assuming there was no way anyone else in the house could work around her magic, that was.

It was only about a five-minute drive out to Master Cortland's house. I didn't know how long she'd spend there looking around, so I'd have to make this as fast as possible.

When I'd broken into Celestine's private magicking room a few weeks ago, I'd had to strain myself to shift her spell. But that had been with an unkindled spark, only faintly lit by a guy I wasn't yet consorted to. Now, with the passion of four consorts behind me, I found I could ease the protective spell on Mrs. Gainsley's office door to the side with just a swift swipe of my hand. I didn't disturb it, only moved it. It would feel exactly the same to her when she got back.

I eased open the door and slipped inside.

The space should have felt familiar. I'd been in here so many times when it had belonged to Meredith. The desk and the filing cabinets stood where they always had. But Meredith's soft amber perfume had vanished, replaced by a sharper, citrusy scent. The old leather desk chair had been swapped out for a straight-backed wooden one, the only padding a thin velvet cushion inlaid in the seat. A small brass clock sat at the back corner of the desk, its faint ticking reminding me of the seconds speeding away until the time Mrs. Gainsley might return.

I yanked open the filing cabinet drawers one by one, with a twist of my fingers when I found one locked. A lot of the documents inside were left over from Meredith's time, nothing Mrs. Gainsley had anything to do with. I knew for sure Meredith hadn't been part of Dad and Celestine's plotting. I'd practically told *her* outright what I'd suspected, and she hadn't shown a hint that she was worried I'd uncover a real plot, only confusion.

If only she were still here. I didn't even know where she and her husband would have left for. They'd lived on the estate since before I was born.

I shook that painful thought aside and kept digging. In the lowest drawer, I found some files Mrs. Gainsley had clearly put together. Some new vendor forms to do with the wedding. The reschedulings she'd started working on this morning, not cancelling but postponing. So Dad was smart enough to realize he wasn't going to convince me to take a new husband in just two weeks' time. He still expected it to happen in five. One week's buffer before my twenty-fifth birthday...

What did he plan to do if I outright refused Killian? *Could* a consorting work without both consorts' agreement? Surely the Spark would know what was in a witch's heart and refuse to form the connection if she were coerced...?

But Dad believed he had enough sway over me, I guessed. His little lamb. I'd always followed his guidance before now, hadn't I?

How surprised he'd have been if he'd known how much I'd done in the last few weeks behind his back.

Nothing about those records was at all incriminating, though. I moved to the other cabinet, tuning out the *tick tick tick* of the clock as well as I could. Meal plans, notes on the gardening schedule for the summer, interviews arranged with a few possible temporary employees for when one of the kitchen staff was off on maternity leave... Everything neat and precise as the woman herself. Not at all what I needed from her.

My teeth gritted. Well, what did I expect? Mrs. Gainsley was the underling in this scheme. Dad had been so careful to keep himself out of the actual arrangements... He must have had Celestine handle everything even with Derek, so he couldn't be implicated if Derek lost his nerve. He'd had Celestine so cowed...

A shiver ran through me as I tugged Mrs. Gainsley's lock back into place. *Had* Dad arranged Celestine's "accident"? As much as I'd disliked the woman, the idea made me feel sick. But what better way to ensure that she never revealed what sort of man he was to anyone else?

Who else would have had anywhere near as much reason to kill her?

She'd looked so scared at the thought of him learning of her failure the last time I'd spoken to her.

My teeth worried at my lower lip as I darted down the hall to Dad's office. He'd been in such a rush when he'd left. I could hope he'd been a little bit careless, couldn't I? By all that was lit and warm, please, let him have slipped up somewhere.

The spell Mrs. Gainsley had placed on his door was essentially the same. All it required was a slide to the right of the knob so it no longer affected the lock. I paused and cast a quick tendril of magic to search all around the doorframe.

It was a good thing I hadn't assumed she'd taken the *exact* same precautions. There was another spell embedded in the floor on the threshold. If I'd just walked in without catching it, I wasn't sure what it'd have done. The energy in it felt prickling hot.

I wove a sort of basket of magic with my hands, encasing the second spell. Then I shifted it too, over into the wall. Letting out my breath, I hurried inside.

The growl of a car engine outside made me jump. I sprang to the window. Relief washed through me when I saw it was just an old clunker sputtering on past the estate. I still had at least a little time.

I'd already searched the shelves, the books. I pulled open the desk drawers again, just for good measure. Nothing relating to my impending consorting jumped out at me.

A tremor passed through me as I popped open the

laptop, sitting down in Dad's leather chair. The smell of those licorice candies hanging in the air no longer felt remotely comforting. What if he kept all his secrets locked inside his head where I could never prove they existed.

Shoving aside my doubts, I peered at the computer screen. If I could find something without having to take the laptop out of the house, that would be even better, even if I doubted my chances. First to deal with the password... I'd never learned any forms for interacting with computers, but it was a matter of sorting, and fitting into place, and opening. I'd learned plenty of gestures that captured the right sensations.

I focused on the password box and arched my arms in the air. My hands bent and flexed as I shaped the magic around the computer. Release. Let me in. Just one more nudge...

A cool sweat had broken out on my forehead, but the screen jittered and switched to a loading symbol. I let out my breath in a rush. It had worked.

The files readily at hand all appeared to have to do with Dad's business. This deal and that one, various financing collaborations he set up between witching businesses across the world. His most recent opens were all from that Cairo project he'd spent so long working on.

I opened up his email and skimmed through that too. Cairo this and Cairo that. There was one of the company presidents urging him to put together some sort of celebration around the sealing of the deal, like Dad had said. Dad's response, begging off because of my wedding —so much for that. I searched for anything to do with

Celestine, or with me or my consorting, and came up empty.

Maybe there was nothing to do now except bring it to Kyler and hope he could work his own brand of magic on it.

I was just opening a few last applications at random when an alert popped up on the corner of the screen. Dad had his text messages connected to his laptop. He hadn't thought to turn that function off—why would he, when no one should be on this computer other than him.

The message was from Mrs. Gainsley, replying to something Dad must have sent her. *I can get the contract drawn up as soon as Mr. Sorensen is on board. Just say the word.*

My pulse thumped. Mr. Sorensen—my supposed new consort. Of course. He would need to give his magical signature just as Derek had on his contract with Celestine.

And he'd have to give Dad the final authority over what he did with me. Celestine wasn't here anymore to be that buffer. I just had to wait until they'd signed the contract and then steal it out from under them like I had the old one.

Once I turned that contract over to the Assembly, we'd be safe. The estate would be mine. Everything else —who lived where, how I hid my magic—I could figure out later.

But that was still counting on me being able to find that contract in time. If text messages came into the computer, maybe there was some way of seeing old ones?

The sound of another engine filtered through the

window. My head jerked up. This time it was Mrs. Gainsley's Lincoln, cruising along the road to the gate.

I scooped the computer under my arm and ran for the door. As the gate hissed open, I pulled Mrs. Gainsley's security spells back into place. Then I ran for my room to dig out my old backpack.

I was going for a little hike this evening. But it wasn't going to be in the woods.

CHAPTER TWENTY-SIX

Kyler

*R*ose had only been in my apartment once before, but somehow it had never felt quite as much like a home until now, with her stepping back inside. The place in my chest where the magic of the consort ceremony had wound through me filled with a glow where it had been empty a moment ago.

What would it be like to live with her someday? To *see* her every day, morning through night?

The thought turned the glow into an ache. We still didn't know if we could ever have that kind of closeness, even though we were already bound together more closely than most people who were married. It might even be better for her if we never did.

"Sorry about the rush," Rose said, setting her canvas backpack down on my coffee table. "I know you might not be able to do a completely thorough search just tonight. But Dad called and confirmed he'll be back tomorrow, so we don't have much time."

"It's fine," I said. "I can do a lot with just a few hours, believe me."

Rose had looked steady enough when we'd all met up this morning, but her father's betrayal was obviously weighing on her. Her smile was a little tight, her posture tensed. When I touched her arm and drew her closer to me, she relaxed a little, but not completely.

Well, why should she? The other guys and I were as much a part of the problem as part of the solution, weren't we?

Rose tucked her head under my chin, snuggling closer for a second, and I let myself set aside those worries, just reveling in the soft warmth of her, breathing in the faintly sweet lilac scent of her hair. I kissed her forehead. "If there's anything we can use on that computer, I'll dig it out. You can be sure about that."

"I know," she said, and hugged me tighter. "My knight with shining code."

I laughed. "No one's ever put it that way before. I'll try to live up to the title."

Rose curled up on the couch next to me as I opened up her dad's laptop. "I magicked my way through the password," she said. "I'm not totally sure how to reactivate it so he doesn't realize something's wrong."

"That's fine. It should be easy enough to restore. You've just saved me one step." I opened up a new window and started delving into the computer's inner workings. Lines and lines of code, and not particularly shiny either. After a few minutes of running a baseline set of tests, I glanced over at Rose. "This could take a while, and it's not going to look very exciting. If you wanted to just leave me to it, I'll text you if I find anything."

She gave me a look as if I'd made the most absurd suggestion in the world. "And go where? Back to the house with Mrs. Gainsley lurking around? No, thank you. Some unexciting time sounds good to me right now. Especially if I can spend it sitting here with you."

She tipped her head against my shoulder and let her hand rest on my thigh where it wouldn't get in the way of my typing. Her fingers didn't fall too close to any, ah, sensitive areas, but suddenly it was a little harder to drag my attention back to the computer.

This wasn't a good time to be getting horny. I was supposed to be saving all of our lives here.

And I could still feel the tension in her body even as she leaned into me. She knew how much depended on our success even better than I did.

I ran a deeper search, and my heart leapt. "Here's some messages about your marriage... These ones are just him passing on word that the original reception date has been cancelled. Apologies and all that. Lots of condolences in return."

Rose laughed, but the sound had an edge to it. "Imagine the condolences if they knew the truth."

About her real consorts? My gut clenched.

I made myself go on, sorting through more emails and

text messages along the same lines, but my uneasiness didn't fade.

Fuck it. I should just say something. Last time I'd gotten all twisted up thinking I knew how Rose felt, it'd turned out I was totally wrong. We were partners now. I had to trust her, not jump to conclusions.

"Rose," I said tentatively, "have you been having any... regrets about the consorting?"

She turned her head to look at me, her expression puzzled. "The consorting? You mean with you and the other guys?"

"Yeah," I said. "I mean, just that—it got you out of the ceremony your stepmother was planning, but now you could be in even worse trouble. You could end up having to hide your magic for the rest of your life. If you've been thinking that maybe it would be better to sever the bonds, now that your spark is kindled, so you can look for a guy your people wouldn't, you know, kill you over, I think we'd all understand."

Rose's eyes widened. "Kyler," she said, sounding pained. She slid her fingers up my jaw and kissed me, so achingly sweet I didn't know how to take it, only that I wished we didn't have to stop. I pushed the computer onto the couch beside me and turned to face her. She ducked her head, her hand running down my chest.

"Why would you ask me that?" she said thickly.

"I don't know," I said. "Common sense? I can already see how hard it is for you. And—when I brought up that other ceremony, the soul-bound one, the idea that it would be permanent seemed to really bother you."

She shook her head, raising it again. Tears glinted in

her eyes. "Ky, I haven't regretted committing myself to the four of you for a single second, not for what it's meant for me. If we ever dissolve the consorting, it'll be because you want your freedom back. I sprang it on you all so fast, and you hardly had time to really think about it, and now your lives are on the line... The last thing I'd want is for you to be tied to me even more than that."

"*Oh.*" Her hesitation wasn't for her sake, but for ours. The ache of my worries fell away. I pulled her to me, kissing her hard. At the pleased hum that crept from her throat, it took all my self-control not to tip her over on the couch and forget about the damned computer and all the rest.

I pulled back just far enough to speak, my face still close to hers. "I haven't regretted it for one second either. This is exactly where I want to be, Rose. There's no risk that wouldn't be worth it."

Her mouth twisted into a bittersweet smile. "Are you sure? This can't be the kind of life you were expecting. What future were you imagining for yourself before I came along?"

"Nothing I can't do now that you're here," I said. "You know what I'm into. I figured I'd keep doing my work and gaming and reading up on new things. Do you have any idea how much new research you've inspired?"

A laugh burst out of her at that. "Were you really in danger of running out?"

"You never know," I said. "And—you know, I've always kind of dreamed about coming up with really useful code of my own. Programs that will help people in ways no one has thought of yet. And you, and the magic, and this whole world I'm aware of now... It's opening up totally new ways of thinking that could take me way farther than I'd have gotten otherwise. I couldn't have gotten *that* inspiration anywhere else."

"I'm sure you'd have come up with something brilliant anyway," Rose said, but her voice had softened. "But what about when you're not working? You must have thought you'd find a girlfriend—a wife—you could actually go out in public with, share a house with... All that usual stuff."

I touched my forehead to hers. "Rose," I said, "I spend at least half of my social life online, talking to people I've never even *seen* in real life. The only long-term girlfriend I've ever had, I never got to touch, never heard her voice except through the computer speakers. I don't really do 'usual.' I didn't dream about having what I have with you right now because I never would have thought I'd get this lucky, not because it's less than what I'd want."

"Oh." A brighter smile crossed her face. "Well, all right then. When everything with my dad is over, we'll see how good a dream we can make it."

I kissed her one more time, offering up every ounce of feeling in me before I got back to work. "Let's get this part over with as quickly as possible, then."

I grabbed the computer and dove back in. I had to live up to the love Rose was offering me. Had to prove myself worthy of it.

Maybe the estate manager would give us the key. If Rose's dad had texted Mrs. Gainsley about the contract, he might have mentioned other aspects of the plan to her in the past.

I scraped through the computer's history, the files and history her dad probably felt had vanished into the ether. But very few things are ever fully deleted once you've brought them onto your computer, not unless you *really* know what you're doing. And if Mr. Hallowell was lax enough to let his text messages sync to his laptop, I could tell right off the bat he wasn't a tech security expert.

The name Gainsley came up in a discarded message from last week. I pulled up that thread and started to skim it.

"What's that?" Rose asked.

"Your dad was discussing hiring Mrs. Gainsley with some other guy... That name looks familiar. Hold on."

I snatched up my own computer and checked the notes I'd made in Seattle. Rose peered at the messages. She said what I was just confirming. "Frankford. I know him. He's with the Assembly. The head of one of the divisions—Education, I think. Dad's always been very careful to stay on his good side." Her wry smile slanted. "I wouldn't have thought he'd be checking with that guy about our estate manager, though."

"It looks like Frankford was recommending Mrs. Gainsley to him. Look at this. *You need someone with the proper discretion and the skill required, of course.*"

I paused. Discretion and skill were reasonable things to want in an estate manager in general, I guessed. But something about the phrasing sent a chill through me. I dug farther back into the thread of communication between the two men. Then my hand stilled. My stomach dropped as I read an earlier exchange.

Integrating a binding into the ceremony? Frankford had written. *I'll be interested to hear of your success with that.*

My wife is investigating the details, Mr. Hallowell replied. *There has to be a subtler way than the current methods of control.*

And then, most damning, Frankford's response: *We'll all be grateful for your efforts if you succeed.*

Rose had been reading alongside me. Her hand tightened around my arm. "He was talking to Frankford about it. *Openly.* And Frankford..."

"He approved of it," I filled in. My heart had started to thud. No, this wasn't how our investigations had been supposed to go.

"Not just him," Rose said quietly. "'We all.' How many witching folk know about this?" Her voice started to rise. "And what does he mean about 'the current methods.' How many other witches have they done something to, to control their magic? Spark help me... How many people in the *Assembly* are part of it?"

"You could still take whatever evidence we can find to the Justice Division, right?" I said, but my voice sounded weak to my own ears.

"The Justice Division that has a secret department for killing off any witches who step out of line in a way they decide is intolerable?" She buried her face in her hands. "I should have known. The Spark only knows how many other secrets they're keeping. If it's my dad's doing that Celestine is dead, he wouldn't even have needed to make up a story. They were covering up their own tracks too."

"We don't know that for sure."

"No," Rose said. "But we know enough. I'm not getting any help from the Assembly. Not when it comes to my freedom."

CHAPTER TWENTY-SEVEN

Rose

The last time we'd all gathered by the old stone towers it'd been an exhilarating celebration of love. Coming here now, with so much gloom hanging over me, felt almost wrong. But with Derek gone and Dad away, the estate seemed like the safest place for a group meeting. I'd made sure no one was nearby this time before I'd cast a wide rebuffing ring around our meeting spot.

I stepped into a pool of early morning sunlight that streaked between the branches overhead. The day was already warm, but even that glowing beam couldn't quite shake the chill that had gripped me since the discovery Kyler and I had made last night. The lush scents of the vines and the foliage around us tasted too tart as I inhaled.

Everywhere I looked, everything I touched, I seemed

to find sharp edges.

Jin sat down on a rock near the edge of the clearing. He held a stick braced against the ground as if he meant to sketch in the dirt with it, but his hand stayed in place, his gaze fixed on me. Damon stood near him, his arms folded over his chest and his expression even darker than usual. The twins had arrived together, but Seth had hung back as if to keep an eye on the whole group while Kyler had walked right up to me, taking my hand in his with a squeeze of support.

And Gabriel. Gabriel, who was one of my guys but not, leaned against one of the towers in a stance that looked relaxed, but his gaze never quite met mine. I could kind of understand that. Every time I looked his way I remembered the feeling of his body pressed against mine in the dark car yesterday morning.

After I'd sent out the group message last night, I'd texted him separately. *You don't have to come. If you'd rather sit this one out, it's fine.*

Don't be silly, he'd written back. *I want to be there. That hasn't changed.*

Right now, it felt as if an awful lot had changed. The awkwardness after our first kiss had expanded at least tenfold. But I wasn't going to confront him in front of the other guys. Especially not when we had so much else to worry about.

"The group has assembled," he said now in his usual easy voice. "What do you need from us, Sprout?"

My lips twitched at that old nickname, wanting to smile but not quite making it. "I'm... not completely sure. There might not be anything else we can do now. But I was hoping if we talked it through together, we'd figure out any possibilities we do have."

"What's the picture right now?" Jin asked. "What are the pieces we do have?"

I sucked in a breath. "Well, there are clearly people in the ruling body of witches who support the kind of scheme my dad was orchestrating. It sounds like there are other witches who've been trapped in similar ways. So if I report him to them, there's as much chance they'll help him finish the job as bring him to justice."

"Let's get down to the foundations, then," Seth said. "What needs to happen so you can be safe?"

"It sounds simple," I said. "It's the same thing I needed before. I need my dad off the estate, stripped of any authority over the property or me... and I need it before he tries to see this new consorting through. I just don't know how I could justify it if I can't point to his crime."

Damon cocked his head, his dark eyes flashing. "You can't point to *that* as his crime. If you want someone out of the way, you just have to find *something* to pin on them. It doesn't even have to be something they actually did, right?"

Gabriel straightened up. "That's a good point. If they won't care about his real crime, frame him for something they will care about." His gaze came back to me, settling somewhere in the vicinity of my cheeks rather than directly looking me in the eyes. "What do you think your Assembly would get worked up about?"

I blinked. I hadn't thought about that. "I'd still need proof of whatever it was. But I guess there'd be all the same sorts of things regular law enforcement cares about."

Kyler nodded, his hand tightening around mine. "So, theft, assault, murder..."

"I can't set him up to have *killed* someone," I said. My stomach turned.

"They're very concerned about how you all use your magic, aren't they?" Gabriel said. "Keeping it a secret. Not mingling with the 'unsparked.' If he exposed that part of your society somehow..."

"*He* doesn't have any magic himself," I said. "I can't pin anything magical on him."

Seth frowned. "Is there any way he could do something with magic without it being magic he cast himself?"

Jin tipped his head toward me. "You cast that spell on the necklace I made for you. I take it it's possible for magic to stay in objects. Are you the only one who can use something you worked on?"

I hesitated, my hand rising to the lump of the pendant under my shirt. I'd kept wearing it even though Derek was gone. It still made me feel safer, as false a feeling as that might be.

"No," I said. "Anyone could use the power that's been put into an object." That was what my stepsister had accused me of doing, wasn't it? Hurting Celestine with some sort of enchanted tool. I hadn't. But Dad could hurt someone that way. Or at least, could look like he had...

"We'd need an object. And witnesses, so it wasn't just my word. Enough witnesses that the Assembly couldn't ignore it." My pulse skipped a beat. "His Cairo deal. It's the most important thing he's worked on all year. They only just finalized it—some of his colleagues have been encouraging him to host a celebratory party."

Gabriel snapped his fingers. "Yes. I've heard him talking about that on the phone out by the garage. More than once. He was putting them off because of your wedding coming so soon..."

"But my wedding isn't happening anymore. At least not that soon, as far as he knows." The tendrils of an idea started to twine together in my head. I slipped back through my memories to that first day when Dad had returned, when everything was different. The fancy case he'd shown me, the artifact he hadn't dared let the unsparked staff handle. All the power it had once contained. "I think that's it. At least, it's the start of a plan."

Gabriel grinned. "All right. Then all we need to do is work out the details."

* * *

Dad had said he'd call around noon to update me on progress with my potential consort. It was half past twelve, and I was so wound up at the thought of the conversation ahead that I startled whenever a door squeaked in the house.

"I think you'd better send one of the cleaning staff around with some oil for those hinges," Philomena said, with an arch look.

"It's an old house," I said. "Things squeak." I paced

from one end of my room to the other and then sat on the bed. "Come here?"

She sat down next to me. It used to be that Phil was so real to me, so solid in my imagination, that I could all but feel the layers of her dress as they fell against my leg, smell the powdery floral perfume she wore. Now, she was so far from the life I was living and all the dangers that had come with it, she'd gone almost filmy.

But it still was a comfort having her here next to me.

My phone trilled. I jumped again, and then I pawed for it. Dad's number showed on the screen.

"Dad," I said, hoping I sounded reasonably normal. "Hi. How's it going over there?"

"Oh, very well," he said in his warm baritone. He did sound happy. Killian must be getting on board. "I'm taking my time to do my due diligence, but I do think my instincts were right. There's a good partner for you here."

"I guess it'll be easier to tell when I actually meet him," I said.

"Well, yes."

"Dad," I dove in. "I had an idea—not to do with the consorting. Well, sort of. I thought it would be a good way to take my mind off of everything that happened with Derek. And your mind off Celestine's leaving. I know how hard that was for you."

"I've made my peace with that," Dad said.

He didn't take the bait. Didn't mention her death. Trying not to distract *me* from my consorting? How long did he think he could hide that information?

Then again, Evianna hadn't bothered me again. Maybe he had reason to believe no one would ever mention it in my presence. I knew how much one spell could control what people said.

I restrained a shiver. "I know," I said. "But still…"

"Why don't you just tell me about this plan?" Dad said. He sounded curious, not suspicious. That was good. "What are you up to, Rose?"

"Well, that Cairo deal was so important for you, and I feel bad that you couldn't properly celebrate it because of all the wedding plans—but now that those have been postponed, I thought we could host a party at the manor this weekend. You won't have to do anything other than invite the right people. I'll take care of getting the house ready. It'll give me something to do. So it'd be for you and for me. What do you think?"

Dad was quiet for a moment. "Are you sure, lamb?" he said. "Having a bunch of my business associates in the house, when you're dealing with so much?"

He made it sound like he cared. He made it sound like my well-being meant something to him. My fingernails dug into my palm. I forced myself to smile, as if he'd be able to hear my expression over the phone.

"I really think putting this together will help me deal. Wipe all that pain out of my mind. Let me start over with a clean slate."

"Well, I suppose I could start getting in touch with people… And at least you would have some company. It might take some pressure off, early on."

My smile faltered. "What do you mean?"

"I'm arranging with Killian for him to come by for an initial visit this weekend," Dad said. "If all goes well, that'll be your first meeting with the man you'll marry."

CHAPTER TWENTY-EIGHT

Jin

"It should be fine," Rose said, but from the set of her mouth, she was trying to convince herself as much as me. "It's not as if he's going to throw me into a consort ceremony with some new guy the second he sets foot on the estate. It doesn't have to affect our plan at all."

She was perched on a stool in my studio, ankles hooked around the wooden legs as she sketched the light impression of one of her magical glyphs on a square of wood about the size of her palm. I was holding and painting another of those squares, the plastic-y tang of acrylics in my nose. Not my favorite medium, but we needed something that would dry quickly. The brush whispered over the faintly textured surface, tracing the lines of the glyph and blending them into the broader pattern of colors.

"*Could* he force it on you?" I asked. "If it's even possible for you to take another consort now."

"I don't know." She frowned at her drawing. "If he's got the power of the Assembly behind him... I don't know what anyone's capable of anymore. I thought it was just my stepmother and some twisted sense of jealousy. But it goes so much deeper..."

"Hey." I finished one last brushstroke and set the piece down in the trough of my easel. With a swipe of my hands against my painting jeans, I went to Rose's side and slid my arm around her. "We're getting everything in place. They have no idea how deep *your* powers go now that you're awake, Briar Rose."

She twirled the pencil between her fingers. "If this even works."

"Well, I can't comment on that, since I'm not the one with decades of magical study behind me. But *you* are."

"I just never learned how to use my magic but keep it hidden at the same time." She dragged in a breath and recovered her smile, even if it was a small one. Tipping back her head, she gave me a quick kiss. "How's the painting coming along?"

I showed her the fifth one, which I'd just finished. She hummed approvingly. "It's perfect. You can't make out the glyph at all. But it'll still hold a magicking like my pendant."

"And these are just meant to amplify the main attraction?" I said.

She nodded. "I can put these around the table—I'm thinking as coasters under the vases. I won't put any magic in them yet. If the larger spell doesn't have as much impact as I intended, I can call on those to enhance it without having to do a casting overt enough to be noticed."

"And then you cow all those assholes who were trying to put you in your place."

She laughed, a little roughly. "Or I get us all killed. I know the situation is what it is and I have to make the best of it, but it seems so unfair sometimes, you know? They've done so much wrong, but if I make one small slip any of the gazillion places I could misstep, I'll get all the blame. Just for trying to own my life."

"There are always people trying to squash those who are more powerful than them," I said. "Out of fear or jealousy... I saw enough history traveling around with my dad to have figured that out. You're part of a grand tradition."

"Lucky me," she said, but I saw a glint of genuine amusement in her eyes. She added one final touch to her drawing and handed the wooden square to me. "What were your favorite places overseas? What made a city—or some other place—a Jin kind of spot?"

I heard the plea underneath the question. *Take me away from this town, just for a few minutes.* My throat tightened. I'd imagined having Rose here in my studio, lighting up inspiration inside me, but I'd hoped the first time would be a happier occasion.

That was all I'd ever wanted, wasn't it? For her to be happy. To bring happiness to her while the other guys carried on all doom and gloom. But maybe they'd been what she actually needed right now. Reveling in her power didn't do her any good if it was going to get her killed.

So I was doing the best I could now. Contributing something concrete, something to help her survive. I could focus on ways to light up her life after we were sure of her keeping that life.

"It's hard to pick," I said, picking up my paintbrush again as I thought about my tour across Europe and Asia with Dad and the band he'd been subbing for. "Sometimes it felt as if every place I went changed me a little, made me want different things. I don't know how many I could go back to and still feel the same way. But where I had the most fun at the time... Probably Berlin and Shanghai."

"Interesting combination," Rose said.

I chuckled. "I'm not sure I'd want to do them back to back. But they're both so vibrant, so much energy and so much enthusiasm, in the architecture and the events and the people. I'm not going to lie: As much as I enjoy checking out some history, it's the modern cities that really get my engine going. Present and future over the past."

"All right." Rose's lips curled into a sly grin. "Tell me your craziest story from each."

My eyebrows leapt up. I swirled paint over the wood, thinking back. Probably best to edit out the bits that had involved other girls. Rose knew I'd gotten around, but there was no need to rub it in.

"Hard to pick," I said. "There was a lot of craziness. In Berlin... There was this one club I went to, in the middle of the dancing they turned on black lights and handed out neon paint, and we all just threw it at the walls, the floor, each other." I grinned at the memory. "And then we danced some more, smearing it around, just this vast sea of glowing chaos. That was pretty epic."

"Wow." Rose's expression had gone distant and dreamy. "I'd have liked to see that."

"Maybe we'll go find that place again sometime," I said, and she turned those dreamy eyes on me. The affection on her face sent a flicker of warmth and a strange ache through me at the same time.

I was giving her a temporary escape. She'd turned to me for that. But it wasn't enough. I wished I could paint her way right out of this situation, into a world where she could really live with her magic, with people who wouldn't care how she'd gotten it.

Since I couldn't, I rambled on about other adventures as I finished the last few paintings. Rose asked a few questions here and there, but mostly she just listened and sketched her glyphs. When I'd set down the final one, she came over to the easel and wrapped her arms around me, ducking her head against my shoulder.

"Thank you," she said. I didn't think she meant just the paintings. The ache in my chest grew.

Someday she'd have more to thank me for.

I traced my fingers along her jaw and leaned in for a kiss. Rose kissed me back with an eager murmur that sent an ache to completely different parts of my body. Damn, the hunger this woman stirred in me. What I'd be thankful for was a day when I could have her in my bed every night and every morning. If the other guys joined us, that would be fine too. As long as I had her.

"You're going to need all the magic you can possibly get for this weekend, right?" I said teasingly, my hands coming to rest on her waist.

A giggle escaped her. "What could you possibly be suggesting, Mr. Lyang?"

"Well, that last piece is going to take at least a half hour to dry. We might as well spend that time... productively." I eased my fingers up under her shirt.

She swayed into my touch, kissing me again, harder as I reached her breasts. Then she pulled back from me with a hitch of breath. Her hand rose to my cheek.

"You know being with you is about so much more than that, don't you?" she said, searching my eyes. "I've got so much magic in me I don't know how I'll ever use it all. I just want you. I love how you make me feel. I love being with you. I don't want you, or any of the guys, to ever think—"

"Hey." I nuzzled the side of her face. "I know. You don't have to say it. Believe me, the last thing I feel is used."

When we returned from my bedroom flushed and temporarily sated, I checked the paintings and stacked them in a small box. Rose stole one last kiss before we headed down to the car she'd brought outside.

The afternoon was getting late. Our shadows stretched long across the sidewalk. A few other boxes with supplies for her dad's party were already stacked in the car's back seat. I added mine to the lot.

"You're not worried about your estate manager seeing them?" I asked, brushing my hands together.

Rose shook her head. "There's nothing to see until I work the magic on them. I guess I'd better head back."

"Yeah," I said, fighting the urge to touch her again, even briefly. Out here on the street, even with whatever magical precautions she'd taken, it didn't feel safe.

Especially not when a slightly scruffy looking old man was striding down the street toward us, already glaring... at me?

No, at Rose. His eyes narrowed further as he came up on us. I'd seen him before, hadn't I? At the town museum that one time. He'd left the archive room right when we'd come down to meet Rose. He'd looked pretty grouchy then too, but I'd assumed it was because of the room getting crowded. Maybe not.

He stopped on the sidewalk near us. "What are you doing out here again?" he demanded. "Don't you have enough to keep you busy out there in your fancy estate?"

Rose gave him a quick, tight smile. "There are a lot of things in town I can't get at the manor," she said, keeping her voice gentle.

The old man huffed as if she'd insulted him. "Well maybe you should see about changing that. We don't need your types intruding on this place. It belongs to *us*, not you."

I thought I saw Rose suppress a wince. "I'm sorry you feel that way."

My hands clenched. She was trying to diffuse the situation, keep everyone happy—and another time, maybe I'd have joined in. But this jerk didn't deserve to be coddled at her expense, when she had so much else weighing on her. A sharper anger than I'd ever felt before flared inside me.

"A lot of us feel that way," the man started in again.

"That's enough," I said, stepping forward so he had to back up, away from Rose. His gaze shifted to me, his face flushing. I barreled on before he could try to say anything. "You don't know this woman at all. I do. And I promise you this town is better for every minute she's in it. From the way you're ranting, I don't think anyone could say the same about *you*."

The old man sputtered, but my words seemed to have deflated his bravado. His shoulders hunched. "I was just saying my piece," he muttered, and hurried away.

When I turned back to Rose, she blinked at me. "Wow," she said. "I don't think I've ever seen a fierce Jin before. Not that I mind."

My face heated a little, but inside I felt more sure, more settled, than I had in days. "I guess I'm trying out lots of new approaches these days," I said with a wink. And then, more seriously, "I mean it, you know. *I'm* better, every moment you're in my life. I want to be everything I can be for you."

Even though we were standing there in the middle of the sidewalk, Rose reached out and grasped my hand, just for a second. Emotion shimmered in her eyes. "You're already everything I could ask for, Jin," she said softly.

I might have done just about anything then. Might even, while there was no one else in sight, have dared to lean in for another kiss. But Rose's phone buzzed in her pocket. Her brow knit as she pulled it out. When she saw the message on the screen, any remaining flush drained from her face.

"I've got to get back to the house," she said. "Dad's home early."

CHAPTER TWENTY-NINE

Rose

My hands gripped the steering wheel of the old Buick tightly. The car was the least fancy one in our garage, but that was why I'd picked it. I'd gotten my license while we were living in Portland, but I hadn't had a whole lot of opportunities for driving practice. I didn't want to be maneuvering a car I was afraid to dent along the roads.

Of course, it wasn't the thought of denting this car that had my body tensed. It was knowing Dad was waiting for me on the other side of that stone wall coming into view up ahead.

I willed my fingers to relax and reached up to hit the control for the gate. The wrought-iron bars hummed open. I pulled the car through the second I could and drove right up by the front steps to make it easier for the porters to carry in my purchases.

Mrs. Gainsley appeared in the doorway right behind the porter who hustled out. A prickle ran down my back. I'd told Jin I wasn't worried about her seeing the art I'd had him make, but I couldn't say I was really keen on the idea of her inspecting it either.

My instinct was to grab that box and carry it up to my room myself. But that would only make her curious what I'd gotten that I was being so protective of. I dragged in a breath and smiled at the porter.

"You can put most of these in the corner of the dining room for now. This one should go up to my room. Thank you!"

He bobbed his head and hefted the first two.

"You've done a lot of shopping," Mrs. Gainsley observed in her dry voice. "The manor is quite well-stocked already, from what I've seen."

I shrugged as if I hadn't thought all that much about the matter. "This is the first party we've hosted here in more than a decade. I figured a little updating for the occasion couldn't hurt. With Dad's business partners coming, I want everything to look as good as it can."

"I suppose that's an admirable sentiment." She smiled at me, no cruelty in it. What was I to her—just a job?

I lingered by the car as Gabriel ambled over from the garage to collect it, even though I could have just left the keys in the ignition. I wanted to see with my own eyes when the porter took that last box. As he tugged it out, I handed the key ring over to Gabriel, giving him a smile I hoped looked suitably employer-ly. "I managed not to do any permanent damage—to or with her."

Gabriel shot me a grin, but his eyes stayed a little more serious for the instant before they slid away from mine. "Never worried you would, Miss Hallowell."

I couldn't say anything more to him with Mrs. Gainsley watching. I hurried up the steps as he ducked into the driver's seat. "My father is here?" I said to the estate manager. "He texted me saying he was almost at the house."

Before she could answer, Dad's voice rang down the front hall. "There she is. Come on, Rose. I've got lots to show you."

He beckoned me into the parlor he'd just emerged from.

I pasted a smile on my face and went to join him. The savory smells of a pork roast and baked apples were drifting from the kitchen. Mrs. Gainsley had the staff putting together Dad's favorite dinner. As if the trip he'd just been on had been his victory more than for my sake.

Of course, that was actually true.

Dad had already retrieved his laptop from his office. The laptop I'd spirited off to Kyler's apartment just last night. I glanced from him to it as I sat down on the stiff Victorian sofa next to him, but he didn't look as if he'd noticed anything off. Ky's password reactivation must have worked fine.

"First off," Dad said, "Killian sent back a quick message given that he can't arrive in person for another few days." He brought up a video on his phone and handed it to me.

A slim guy with sleek chestnut hair smiled at me from the screen. "Rose," he said when I started the video playing. "I'm sorry we'll be meeting under these circumstances, but I'm very much looking forward to getting to know you and seeing how things, should we say, 'spark' between us."

His light voice sounded smooth enough, but I thought I caught a desperate gleam in his eyes. What was it Celestine had written about him? He'd want to use my power to reclaim his family's estate. From its rightful owner, presumably. I passed the phone back to Dad, my smile getting stiffer.

What promises had my father made about how Killian could use my magic once he had me like a puppet on a string?

"Killian's actually quite a crafty sort," Dad said eagerly, shifting his attention to his laptop. "I hadn't realized. He makes tools by hand for witching use— wands and ceremonial bowls and daggers and the like."

I managed not to stiffen at the word 'dagger.' The spell that would have bound my magic to my consort's will involved a dagger, to invoke a stabbing pain if I tried to resist his demands. Did Dad even know that, or had he simply passed on Celestine's notes, wherever she'd kept them, to Mrs. Gainsley for her to sort out?

He entered a password and brought up a website that displayed some of what I guessed were Killian's goods. They were well-crafted, the etchings of the glyphs precise, the designs elegant. If I hadn't already known what lengths Killian was apparently willing to go to for magic of his own, I might have seen that as a good sign.

"They're lovely," I said with as much enthusiasm as I could fake.

"He's done quite a bit of studying in the historical records and lore so he can bring that knowledge to the work," Dad said. "So you two should have quite a bit to talk about there."

Spark help me, when was the last time I'd had space to even think about my job digitizing historical documents? I hadn't even written a word in my compilation of modern witching history since my confrontation with Celestine.

It was awfully hard to see much point in adding to it when there was so much I clearly hadn't even suspected... so much that I couldn't expose without putting everyone I loved in danger.

My heart squeezed at that thought. I looked at Dad, who was talking about some other theoretically wonderful thing about my theoretical new consort-to-be —at the light in his hazel eyes and the warmth of his smile and all those familiar things that were part of the father I'd used to love.

No, that I still loved. You couldn't break a lifelong bond so easily. I hated what he planned to do, what he was already doing, trying to bring the scheme together... But that couldn't totally erase all those fond childhood memories. The thought of what I meant to do to him brought a sharper ache into my chest.

That father had loved me too. Surely he had. Where had that man gone? *Why* was he doing this?

"Dad," I heard myself asking when he paused. "If you had magic, the way I—the way I will, what would you use it for?"

Dad blinked at me. A shadow darted through his

gaze, so briefly I almost missed it. But it had been there. Some darker intention my question had roused.

He had an answer. And that was *my* answer, maybe. There was something he wanted to use my magic for, something he knew he could never have simply asked of me.

"I've never really thought about it," he said, lying as easily as breathing. "I've been more interested in seeing what you'll do with yours when your spark is kindled."

"Really?" I said, letting my brow knit. "You've never considered it at all?"

He smiled, the corners of his eyes crinkling. "That isn't a witching man's place, is it?"

The reply was so absurd in the context of everything I knew that it sent a flare of anger through me. I couldn't help saying, a little pointedly, "I suppose. But you know if there was ever anything you needed, once I have my magic, you'd only have to ask."

His eyes twitched, just slightly. A tiny hint of guilt. The twist of my gut wasn't really triumphant.

"I appreciate the sentiment, lamb," Dad said, glancing away. "Now why don't you tell me all about this party you've been planning?"

All the parts he was allowed to know about, I'd be happy to ramble on about. "I came up with the menu and Mrs. Gainsley put out the order for the groceries we'll need. Lots of hors d'oeuvres to start, and then for the big dinner I decided on goose, just to make it extra special. I arranged for a band to come for a little live entertainment, and..."

I went on for a few minutes about my various plans,

which I *had* put a fair bit of thought into. When I started to wind down, Dad brought his hands together in a brief round of applause.

"I didn't know you had that kind of event planning aptitude in you," he said playfully. "You seem awfully keen on celebrating this deal of mine. You hardly know what it's about."

I shrugged. "I know it's something that'll bring more money into the witching community, to make it easier for us to survive without relying on the unsparked. And I know it meant a lot to you. That's enough."

He studied me a little longer than I really liked. I jumped to a change of subject. Something I was going to have to bring up eventually anyway. "I was thinking... We could show off that artifact you brought back. Use it as a centerpiece on the dining table. If that's all right with you? I'd make sure none of the unsparked staff handled it —I'll set it out myself."

"I like that," Dad said with a nod. "I picked it up on my way out of the city. None of the others have seen it yet."

"Are many of your colleagues going to be able to make it?" I asked. "I know it's short notice..."

I held my breath waiting for his answer. He smiled again. "Most of them were more than happy to make the trip, considering they've been hassling me to do something like this for days."

"Anyone I've met?"

"Oh, I'm sure you've met most of them at one time or another. The Wilkinsons, the Hardings, the Frankfords, Evelyn Kingsley..."

He kept going, but my mind caught on that one name. Frankford. The man who'd advised Dad on hiring Mrs. Gainsley, who'd been eagerly looking forward to the results of the bastardized consort ceremony, would be here in this house in just a few days.

My jaw set. He'd get a show all right. They all would. Just not the one they'd been imagining.

"That's great," I said when Dad finished. "I'm preparing for lots of guests. Invite as many more as you'd like."

The more witnesses, the faster he'd fall—and the sooner my consorts and I would be safe.

CHAPTER THIRTY

Rose

The rumble of a car engine reached my ears all the way in the dining room where I was laying out the decorations. My pulse skipped. I slipped down the hall to the sitting room to look out the front window.

A sleek silver sedan had just pulled past the gate. Another car, longer and even more stately, drew up beside it. The passengers, one couple that looked around Dad's age and another older, stepped out.

Dad came into the front hall. "Did you tell people to arrive this early?" I asked him. It was only mid-afternoon. I'd been working around a supposed six o'clock cocktail hour start.

He shot me a smile. "They're not your responsibility yet, Rose. Don't worry. A few of my closer associates are coming a little early so we can discuss other business before we begin our celebrating."

That was just like Dad. Squeezing work into every spare minute he could. Proper etiquette dictated that I should stick around and say my hellos before they all holed away in Dad's office.

Mrs. Gainsley appeared, moving past Dad to open the front doors, which was somehow more dignified than him doing it himself. The two couples came up the front steps, murmuring in quiet conversation with each other. The younger couple both had gray sprinkled in their light brown hair, the man's tousled and ash-brown, the woman's a cinnamon-brown bob brushing her jaw. The man in the older couple had gone completely slate-gray, the woman's hair ivory-white and cropped close to her head. His eyes were a paler gray. Something about them and his thin, angular face struck a chord of recognition in me.

"Rose," Dad said with a sweep of his arm, "Diana and Renato Almeida all the way from Lisbon. And I'm sure you've met Helen and Charles Frankford at least a few times. Ladies and gentlemen, my daughter Rose."

"A pleasure to meet you, dear," Mrs. Almeida said. She shook my hand, and then the others in turn. My skin crawled as Mr. Frankford's cool, dry grip closed around mine. I smiled at him as well as I could manage.

Here was the man who'd encouraged my father to enslave me. My gaze slid to his wife, her faintly lined face nearly as pale as her ivory hair. Did *her* smile look a little stiff as she accepted my hand? Had he harnessed her magic to his will somehow—or his daughters, if he had them? Nausea crept through my belly at the thought.

"Lovely to meet you too," I said on autopilot. "I'm so

glad you could make it. I know what a great win this deal was for everyone who was working with Dad."

"An even more delightful young lady every time I see her," Frankford said, slapping Dad on the back. I wanted to vomit.

Another engine sounded outside. I stayed where I was, greeting and offering compliments and thanks, ignoring my queasiness as another couple, then a solitary witch and an unpartnered man, arrived in quick succession. They all smiled and complimented me, our house, and the idea of this party in return. My quick searches of their expressions gave me nothing to go on. How many of them knew what my dad intended to do to me? How many of them encouraged it?

Could *all* of them know? These were his closest associates, he'd said. Perhaps in more ways than one.

When they went up to Dad's office as I'd expected, I drifted back into the dining room. Almost everything there was already in order. Dark blue silk table cloth, candles in silver holders waiting to be lit, white roses spaced down the length of the long table and on the side tables around the room. Jin's little artworks lay under them, the hidden glyphs ready to help channel any magic I cast their way.

The space in the middle of the dining table, in front of the seat reserved for Dad, was lacking its centerpiece. I'd taken the Egyptian wand from Dad this morning for my preparations, but it was still in my room. Waiting to have its magic cast on it.

I'd better get that done before the real party kicked off. Dad might be the host in name, but I needed him to feel totally confident in the arrangements I'd made and my ability to keep things running smoothly—so that he wouldn't feel the slightest doubt about how the night was going before the grand finale.

And Killian would be here not long after the party started. I'd be expected to entertain him and pretend I found him entertaining.

"What a beautiful spread," Philomena said, shimmering into being beside me. She clapped her hands. "I wish it were a better occasion."

"No kidding," I said, moving away from the table. "I wish I'd planned dinner first instead of three hours in. Then we could get everything over with."

"Oh, but half of the impact is in the build-up," Phil said sagely. "I can't imagine I ever would have frightened off that rival of mine—Claudette, like to put wagtails to shame—if we hadn't had the most luxurious picnic before the bees."

I raised my eyebrows at her, but my stomach balled as I headed up the stairs to my room. "Your bees didn't even sting anyone. This... is going to be a little more dramatic than that."

I closed the bedroom door and locked it. Before anything else, I dug out my secret phone and sent a quick text to the guys. *All's well so far. One more piece to put in place.*

Make them wish they never messed with you, Damon wrote back, with a devilish emoji.

We're standing by if you need us, Seth added. I could picture him side-eyeing Damon's enthusiasm.

They were standing by, but this part only I could do.

I went to my desk where I'd left the gilded case. My breath came a little shaky as I popped it open. I didn't want any magic lingering on the case itself where one of the witches present might sense it. That power had to stay completely contained until Dad opened the case to show off his prize.

The polished wood felt warm, the edges of the inlaid gems almost gritty, as I eased the wand out. I set it on the floor in the middle of the room.

It would have been better if I could have worked in the magicking room—the public one or even the private one that had been Celestine's but should by all rights now be mine. But that would look far too suspicious, so I'd have to make do in here.

I shut the curtain, cutting off all but a faint glow of sunlight. Then I pulled out the tools I had secreted out of the magicking room yesterday. A dagger, a length of fine silver chain, and a sprig of dried belladonna. In theory, any spell could be cast with just one's mind and one's magic, but with a larger magicking, it was much easier to focus your energy when you had tools to direct it.

"I trust you're not actually planning to unleash a dramatic storm of stinging bees," Phil said, plopping down on my bed.

I had to laugh. "No. It's more complicated than that too. I need it to... to hurt some of the guests, and to affect Dad's behavior so it looks like he's doing it on purpose. But nothing so powerful it can't be subdued." A tricky balance.

Breathing slow and even, I laid the chain in a circle around me and the wand. Then I grasped the hilt of the dagger in one hand and the belladonna sprig in the other. First... first I would need an urge to dig into my father.

I swiveled on my feet and looped my arms through the motions I'd charted out over the last few days, piecing together fragments from my years of learning with lore gleaned from the old texts to weave a spell completely my own. My spark flared brighter in my chest. Its warmth bled from my muscles and spilled from my skin. Magic coalesced around the wand by my feet.

Yes, grip him. Grip him and control him the way he'd planned to do to me. At least he'd get to shake off that spell after a few minutes. I wasn't going to enslave him for a lifetime.

My fingers tightened around my tools. I dipped low and stretched my arms high. A fancy illusion to begin with, as if he only meant to entertain. Ease them into it. Phil was right. The more build-up, the deeper the shock.

I cut the dagger through the air. Deeper, sharper, the urge turning angry. Vision twisting, seeing more than what was there. And then a burst of violence, turning it out on them. All of them—smiling Frankford, cool Mrs. Gainsley, every other person at that table who'd have happily seen *me* in magical chains or dead alongside my consorts.

A jolt of my own anger shot through me. For an instant, I pictured writhing figures, expressions contorted with pain, and my spark danced higher with a heady wave of satisfaction. All the ways I could bend them to my will, punish them for all the crimes they'd already committed...

I started to whip the dagger faster through the air,

and caught myself at the last second. A trickle of cold ran through my body, momentarily dampening my energy.

What was I doing? *That* wasn't the plan. I wanted just enough damage for them to think Dad was a true threat. Nothing permanent. No long-term damage.

And yet some part of me was disappointed, knowing that.

I swallowed hard and refocused on the spell. With a twist of my fingers, the belladonna caught fire. I trailed its pungent smoke through the air. Clouding the mind more, adding an extra edge to the punch of aggressive magic, and then burning it all away.

I was breathing hard when I eased to a stop, hunched over the wand. My nose prickled with the thin smoke and sweat dripped from my forehead. But it was done. When I brushed my fingers over the wand, it thrummed with contained power.

A knock thumped on the door. I startled, the last shreds of the belladonna sprig falling from my hand.

"Rosalind?" Mrs. Gainsley said. Snuff my spark, if she smelled that smoke—if she saw any hint of my magicking—

I scrambled to my feet. "Yes?" I said. A quick kick sent the chain sliding under my bed. I thrust the dagger under my pillow.

"I wanted to go over a few last minute meal considerations," she said. "May I come in?"

I could practically feel her already reaching for the door knob. How suspicious would she be to find it locked?

My hands darted in opposite directions. One

whisked a breeze through the room and back out the opposite window. The other released the lock. I snatched up the wand and tucked it back into its case, just as the knob turned behind me.

"All right," I said, turning around with a quick swipe at my forehead. "I was just deciding what to wear."

Mrs. Gainsley stepped into the room, leaving the door open behind her. She cocked her head. "I'm surprised you didn't choose your dress days ago."

Had her eyes narrowed a little, taking in the room? I pushed a giggle from my throat. "Oh, I had, but now I'm rethinking it. So hard to decide."

The estate manager's lips curled with a hint of amusement. Yes, let her think I was being a ditzy, nervous girl. She wouldn't look for a powerful witch there.

"It turns out we're short on radish," she said, glancing over a slip of paper she was holding. "The chef wanted to know if you're all right with substituting red onion— that's his recommendation. And he wondered if you had any preference which of the hors d'oeuvres went around first."

Was that all? I could have really laughed. "Red onion is fine. And he can use his own judgment for the order— whatever's the easiest sequence to prepare them in, I suppose."

"Good. Thank you." The estate manager gave me another sharp look. "You'd better get on with that dress-choosing. Your potential consort will be here in just a couple hours, along with the less important guests."

She hustled away, leaving me with an uncomfortable prickling in my chest. I waited until she'd descended the stairs, and then I tucked the wand's case into the box with Jin's art and followed.

The staff had strict instructions not to enter the dining room until after Dad and I had admitted our guests. And the initial magic on the case should only work on Dad. But my lungs still constricted a little as I laid out the last pieces of my plan.

It wasn't all an unpleasant sensation. I imagined Killian's slick figure sitting at Dad's left, facing the first blow of magic, and that satisfied heat flickered inside me again. He'd deserve it. So many of them deserved more than I was doing—

I halted, bracing my arms against the back of one of the chairs and leaning my face into my hands. No. That wasn't how I wanted to think. That wasn't how I wanted my magic to make me feel.

It was a dark spell I'd cast. There was no escaping that. How much of that darkness had crept into me during the magicking?

How much had already been there?

The power of my spark stirred in my chest. I could bring this whole house down in an instant if I wanted to. I knew it, as surely as I could count the staccato beats of my heart. That was exactly why Dad and Celestine and whoever else had wanted to constrain my power. But I *would* never do anything that destructive, lose control over good sense and decency... Would I?

My gaze came to rest on the gilded wand case, and a fresh tendril of nausea coiled around my stomach.

Spark help me, what if I already had?

CHAPTER THIRTY-ONE

Gabriel

I gave one more swipe with the rag to the freshly waxed side of Mr. Hallowell's Bentley, my eyes on my work but my attention on the gate. Most of his guests—and Rose's—weren't supposed to be arriving for a while yet, but I couldn't help listening for the sound of a car.

The car in front of me was a fine one. I always thought it was kind of a shame when total jackasses owned nice vehicles. His car deserved better.

And let's not even get into what his daughter deserved.

To check the task sheet Matt had pinned to the board just inside the garage hall, I took the long way around—skirting the front of the garage and coming around to the side door so I could casually glance toward the manor. The old house with its weathered stone and spiking turrets looked no more ominous than usual, but that was still pretty ominous.

This was the only view I was going to get of the party. The knowledge that Rose was taking such an immense risk all on her own itched at me, but I couldn't think of a single excuse that would get me in there for more than a minute or two. And making that intrusion would catch her dad's attention.

No, it was better for her that I laid low and stayed out of the way. Better for her if she didn't even need to think about me. I'd already jerked her around enough. I'd be keeping watch out here from my apartment, and if something went wrong, if she needed me...

My jaw clenched. Who was I kidding? We'd been there before, in the line of fire, when her stepmother had dragged her away, and I hadn't been able to do a single thing to help her then.

I peered at the task list for several seconds before my brain caught up and recognized that in my furor of keeping my mind off the impending party, I'd finished every single job. Matt's voice from earlier that afternoon came back to me. *Take it easy, kid. You know they will be. No one's going to be making any urgent trips tonight.*

Damn, I couldn't sit in the apartment for the next two hours just waiting for the real waiting to start. I paced back and forth in the hall, willing Matt to appear and give me something to do, but then I remembered he'd headed for home. He wasn't usually here on the weekend at all— it'd been a short shift preparing for the party. Tyler wasn't around at all. It was just me and the cars.

I stepped out into the yard, thinking I'd give the

hubcaps an extra polish or something, and just then the front door of the manor opened. Rose slipped out, clutching her purse at her side. She glanced straight at the garage, as if that had already been her destination.

Maybe it had been. When I hesitated, she tipped her chin up with a flick of her gaze toward the apartment. She didn't need to do anything more than that.

I hurried up the steps, my heart thumping faster. Had something gone wrong? A sudden vision darted through my mind of plunking her on the back of my motorcycle and ripping the hell out of here to who knew where.

And what, leave the other guys behind? That wasn't happening. If she got the hell out of here, it'd be with them, not me. As it should be.

I left the apartment door unlocked. Stalking through the living room, I jerked the curtains shut. Grabbed the worn shirt I'd left on the armchair and tossed it in the bedroom laundry basket. I was just re-emerging when Rose ducked in.

She turned the deadbolt with a thud. Then she stood there in the momentary silence, her fingers tight around her purse straps, looking as if she wasn't completely sure how she'd ended up there.

I stayed on the opposite side of the room. Easier to keep my impulses under control that way. "Rose?"

She let out a shaky breath. With a few quick gestures, she cast some sort of spell—maybe to make sure her presence wouldn't be noticed from outside. Then she turned to me. "I'm sorry. I know you don't want to get too involved. I just... You're the only one who's *here*."

You don't want to get too involved. Was that the

impression I'd left her with? I guessed it made sense she'd have interpreted my actions that way after I'd pushed her away, even if I'd tried to tell her differently.

"It's fine, Rose," I said. "But if you want me to reach out to the other guys—"

She shook her head, cutting me off. "No. I didn't mean, exactly— I *want* to talk to you. You'll be honest with me. Won't you?" Her gaze held mine, those dark green irises turned liquid with worry. Her distress made my chest ache. I had to step a little closer.

"Always, Rose. What's going on? What's the matter?"

"I just..." She looked at her purse with an expression as if she were afraid to put it down and yet hated having it near her at the same time. Carefully, she slid the strap off her shoulder and set it on the floor beside the door. "Everything's ready," she said, straightening up. "I cast the last spell. That wand my dad brought back from Cairo is in there." She motioned to the purse.

"Did the magic work the way you wanted?"

"I'm pretty sure it did. It feels right. Well, it feels like I did it right. The other kind of right... That's why I'm here." She looked down at her hands.

I motioned her over to the sofa. "Sit down. Gather yourself. I don't have any place else to be."

Her lips twitched with a hint of a smile, but it faded quickly. She clasped her hands together on her lap as she sat down. Her gaze darted back to her purse.

"It'll hurt people," she said as I sat down across from her.

"That was the idea, wasn't it?" I said. "Just enough to scare them?"

"Yeah. And I thought I was okay with that. But—" She met my eyes again. "Some part of me wants to do more than that, Gabriel. Some part of me wants to *really* hurt them for what they were willing to do to me. For what they would do to the guys if they found out I'd consorted with them."

The ache in my chest expanded. Oh, Sprout. She'd never had to think about really hurting anyone before, had she?

"I think that's understandable," I said. "Hell, *all* of me wants to mess them up for messing with you."

"But you wouldn't."

"Because I know it'd be more trouble than it's worth. But you're doing this so you and the guys can be free of your dad."

"I know. I just..." She rubbed her mouth. "I feel like maybe I'm proving them right somehow—my dad and Celestine and whoever else. They thought my power was dangerous, and now I'm going to show just how dangerous I can be. I'm acting *like* them—lying, manipulating people to get my way. If I stoop to their level, what does that say about *me*?"

"Rose," I said firmly, "they were scheming—still are scheming—to trap you in a loveless marriage where your husband and your father control every spell you cast. Where they can torture you if you try to go against them, for the rest of your life. Nothing you're thinking of can be half as bad as that. Besides, it's not the same. If you caught a fox in a snare and it bit you, is that stooping to your level or just fighting to survive?"

"I had other options, though," she said. "I could have

just run, like I was thinking. Hidden out somewhere until after my birthday, when Dad couldn't go through with the plan anyway."

"But you don't know that he wouldn't have found you before then, and then you'd have been in even more trouble," I pointed out. "And even if you'd managed to stay away for long enough, the second he found out about the guys, you'd have been screwed. You stayed here for a reason."

"That's the other thing. It's not just me. If I make a mistake here, they're all going to have to live with the consequences—or die with them—too."

I clenched my hand against the urge to reach out to her. "We all know you're doing the best you can."

She shook her head. "I shouldn't even be here now. That's why you've been keeping your distance—so I don't get you too tangled up, so it's not your life on the line too —and here I am—"

She pushed to her feet, spinning toward the door, and then I had to move. I sprang off the sofa and grasped her arm before she could take more than a step. With a gentle tug, I turned her to face me. "What are you talking about, Rose? I'm here for you. I *want* to be here for you."

"But not too close," she said, looking up at me, her voice raw. "You said you'd tell me the truth, Gabriel. You don't really trust me either, do you?"

I stared at her. Fucking hell. I'd thought I was doing what was best for her, and somehow I hadn't realized just how much it was hurting her.

Maybe it didn't matter whether I was the kind of man

she needed right now. Maybe what she needed was just to know how much she had me.

"Rose," I said. "I promise you, it's not that. It's not— You're everything I could have wanted. Hell, I'd share you with four other guys in a heartbeat, take whatever time you could give me. I just don't want to screw up *your* life."

A startled laugh burst out of her. "How could you possibly screw up my life more than it already is?"

"I already did once, didn't I?" I said, waving my other hand. "I pulled you in with us, I encouraged you to run around with us when we were kids, and then your stepmother came down on you and I couldn't do shit. I *promised* you we'd be there for you and it happened anyway. They dragged you away from your home. Maybe your dad wouldn't even have felt he needed to do this crazy magical binding if it wasn't for us—for me."

"Gabriel." Rose caught my hand and brought it between us, wrapping her fingers around mine. The warmth of her touch sent a shiver of desire through me even through all the other emotions churning inside me. "It was my choice to hang out with you guys. I knew even when I was seven years old that I was breaking the rules. You didn't force me into anything. And if *I* couldn't do anything about my stepmother, how could you possibly have changed her mind?"

"I don't know," I said. My pulse stuttered at the words I was about to say. I forced myself to hold her gaze. "But it's not just you. Everyone in my life—I couldn't save my dad. This job was his life after my mom left, you know, and then he lost that, because of me. I know he never forgave me. And I could never make it up to him."

"Gabriel," Rose said again, softly, but I didn't let her stop me.

"I went looking for my mom after he died, you know. Tracked down her new family out in Nevada. She acted like she didn't even know me. Like I had to be some kind of crazy person. The last time she'd seen me I was five years old, and she couldn't even—"

I caught myself just before my voice broke. With a ragged breath, I finished. "I break things. I break people. There's obviously just something about me... So it's better if I don't stick around anywhere too long. I don't want to get close to you because I don't want to get close to anyone, because something always goes wrong."

As the last words spilled out of me, I felt wrung out. Drained. I'd never admitted that all out loud to anyone before. I wasn't sure I'd even admitted it to myself all at once.

Rose was silent for a long moment. Her hand squeezed tighter around mine. "So this whole time you've been pushing me away out of some idea you were protecting me from *you*?"

"I guess you could put it that way."

"Well, you're wrong," she said. "For starters, you never broke me. I was fine. I missed home and I missed you and the other guys, but look at me. I survived. I'm stronger now than I ever was. And that's the other way you're wrong. You're not going to break me now. There's nothing you could do that could hurt me more than I've already been hurt by people who owed me more, and I'm still standing."

"That doesn't change—"

She raised her hand from my hand to my chest, resting her fingers lightly there. "If you really don't think there'd be anything wrong with me lashing out at my dad and the people working with him, then how can you think there's anything wrong with you? Haven't you always done everything you could to help me, to help everyone you care about? If it counts for me, it should count for you too."

I didn't know how to answer that. My heart beat beneath her hand and the ache inside me seemed to bleed right out to the edges of my skin, but the pain of it was almost pleasant now, like the hot glow of the sun when you've come out of somewhere cold.

Tentatively, I eased my arms around her. I gathered her against me, tucking her head under my chin, feeling her soft warmth all along my body, the rise and fall of her breath.

This was Rose. *My* Rose. She would let me call her that. She'd already told me, more than once, how much she wanted me. And here she still was, in spite of everything.

This was what it felt like to hold her in my arms. She didn't feel at all fragile now. Strength was coiled through those muscles, and power I couldn't even imagine simmered deep inside her.

I let my head dip, just a little. Just enough to brush my lips against her temple. Her breath caught. I kissed a little lower, and lower still, charting a slow path across the curve of her cheek. Her fingers curled into the fabric of my shirt. I had just enough self-control left to murmur, by the corner of her mouth, "If you need to get back to the house—"

"Not yet," she said. "But the Spark help me, Gabriel, if you back away again—"

I captured her mouth with mine, cutting off her words. Letting my kiss be my answer. She melted into me, one hand trailing up over the back of my neck, sending tingles down my spine. Her lips parted under my mouth, offering me entrance, and I had to take it, teasing my tongue over hers, tasting how sweet she was all the way through. She made a hungry sound and pulled me even closer.

I traced her sides down to the hem of her shirt. Hell, yes, that was coming off of her. I tugged, and she eased back half a step to let me pull it up over her head. For a second, I just stood there gazing at the slim curves of her breasts in the black bra that was as glossy as her hair.

She made a twitching motion with her hand, and the back unclasped itself. The bra tumbled to the floor, leaving her completely on display for my approval. In an instant, I was rock hard.

"Fuck *me*," I muttered to myself.

She laughed, mischief dancing in her eyes. "That's the general idea."

I caught her waist and pulled her back to me, kissing her shoulder, her collarbone, the top of her breasts. Rose's chest hitched with desire. But just before I reached those perfect pink tips, she touched the side of my face and drew me back up.

"You know it's not just tonight I want," she said, her gaze searching mine. "I want to belong to you and I want you to belong to me—all of us, together. It's never going to feel totally right without you, Gabriel. But only if that's what you want too. If you're not sure—you don't have to decide right away—I just don't want you to think this is only messing around. I want all of you, even the parts you're scared of."

I swallowed hard, tenderness and lust singing in harmony through my veins. "And I want all of you, Rose. Every fucking day I can have you. Even the parts *you're* scared of. I think maybe those are the parts I love the most."

A shimmer filled her eyes, but any tears there were happy ones. The smile that split her face had nothing but joy in it. She bobbed up on her toes to press her mouth to mine.

"I won't let you down," she murmured against my lips. "I won't let any of you down. I swear it."

"You could *never* let me down," I said. Then I was kissing her again, my thumbs stroking over her breasts. A whimper crept from her throat as I brushed my knuckles over her nipples.

I cupped my hand under one and brought my mouth to it. She moaned breathlessly, gripping my hair as I swirled my tongue over that stiffened peak. Her hips canted toward me, and even more heat gathered at the base of my cock.

We were doing this. She was mine. I was hers. Maybe it had always been as simple as that.

I moved to her other breast, grazing my teeth over her

nipple until she cried out with need. She wrenched at my shirt, and I tugged it off. I swept her off her feet in one smooth movement, gathering her against me, chest to bare chest, to carry her into my bedroom. Her arm slid behind my neck, and she drew me into another kiss.

We fell onto the bed together, a jumble of limbs and desperate mouths. I peeled her jeans off her and kicked mine off when she grasped the waist. Then we were close, so close, my erection sliding against her core with only two thin layers of silky fabric between us. She arched up to meet me. We ground together, kissing hard and hot, an even headier friction than what we'd had the other day in the car.

I wanted her. I *needed* her. She knew every part of me so well, and now I'd know her from the inside out. I tugged her panties off her, and she fumbled with my boxers. Then her hand was gliding up over my cock, her thumb slicking over the moisture already beading at the tip. I groaned.

"Rose." Was I going to be this honest? Yes, she deserved that. She'd laid bare every fear she had to me without hesitation. I kissed her again and leaned my head close hers, our noses touching. "I haven't actually done this before. Everything but, yeah"—hands and mouths, giving and receiving—"but going all the way... just never felt exactly right with anyone." Too close. Too dangerous. Too much of a connection.

Rose's eyes widened. "Gabriel," she said, sounding awed. "And you're sure you want it to be me, like this?"

A strained chuckle spilled out of me. "I've been sure of that since pretty much the first moment I saw you, sweetheart," I said. "I just don't know how long I'm going to last."

"I'll take whatever you can give me," she murmured, tipping her mouth up to meet mine.

I slid inside her with that kiss. Pleasure shot through me as the hot slick center of her closed around me. She raised her legs, urging me even deeper, and I accepted that invitation with a groan. Oh, God, all the times I'd passed up the chance at this sensation—but it wouldn't have felt quite like this. Not with anyone but her.

I didn't have a single regret about that choice.

"You feel so good," Rose said, clutching me. The words and the tightening of her sex around me sent a fresh wave of bliss through me. I pulled back and plunged in again, finding a rhythm that was already spiraling me toward release.

"You too," I mumbled. "So fucking good. There couldn't have been anyone better. Never."

She clenched around me again at those words, and I was lost. A stuttered cry broke from her lips. My balls clenched and my cock jerked inside her. I kept thrusting, spilling myself into her. My hand dropped to finger her clit, to draw out her pleasure, and her eyes rolled back.

"Gabriel," she gasped. Her body shuddered around me, and I knew I'd brought her to her peak too.

I eased out and sprawled down on the bed beside her. She snuggled close, hooking her leg over my thigh so we aligned perfectly.

"I don't want to go back," she said. "I want it to all be over already. I want to just get on with my life with the five of you. Why does it have to matter to anyone else?"

"Because people are assholes?" I suggested.

"An awful lot of them, yeah." She cupped my cheek and kissed me again. "But I'm ready for them now. Thank you."

I gave her a confused look. "Did you get more magic from that—when I'm not—?"

She touched my lips to stop me. "No, but that's not what I meant anyway. Thank you... for believing I won't be broken."

I hugged her to me, wishing I didn't have to let her go either. Wishing I didn't still feel as if I were already broken. But it didn't matter if I was. I'd shown her those cracks, and she'd wanted me anyway.

"You'll break *them*," I said. "And I'll be watching from the wings to cheer you on."

CHAPTER THIRTY-TWO

Rose

*a*t eight-thirty, the party was going full speed ahead. Dozens of witching folk in trim suits and elegant dresses meandered through the manor's front rooms, plucking up hors d'oeuvres that a couple of the kitchen staff were carrying around and drinking fine champagne and wine. The scents of thick and spicy sauces inspired by Egyptian cuisine drifted down the hall. In the great room where most of us had assembled, the trio of classical musicians I'd hired were keeping up a lively tune on their instruments.

"Quite a turn-out," Philomena said at my side. "You've pulled off a dashing success."

"Sure, if all I was trying to pull off was a happening party," I said to her in my head. The more important part of the evening we had yet to reach. But despite the worries humming through my nerves, I was looking forward to getting it over with. Not least because of the guy at my other side.

Killian Sorensen had insisted on clamping one cool hand around my forearm about an hour ago, and he hadn't let go since. I'd opted not to make any kind of scene, but my skin was crawling more with every passing minute. He smiled at me now—a bright but thin smile that brought a gleam to his eyes I couldn't help seeing as predatory.

"Did you want some more wine?" he asked, leaning closer than he really needed to in order to be heard over the music and chatter.

I forced myself to smile back. "No, I think I'll wait for dinner." The truth was I'd poured most of my first glass into one of the potted plants when no one was looking. I needed a clear head tonight.

Killian didn't look all that concerned by my refusal. Why should he? As far as he knew, I was a jilted young witch desperate for a consort, any consort.

Thank the Spark I'd only have to keep playing that role for another hour.

We took a turn around the room, greeting a few late arrivals to the party. I stopped by a small group of Dad's colleagues I recognized from gatherings in Portland. I did still have some groundwork to continue laying.

"Rose!" one of the witches said. "You must be so proud of your father, my dear."

"Oh, yes," I said. "It's wonderful to see him getting the chance to relax and celebrate. Especially after the stress he's been under lately with his work. He deserves a reward like this."

Just as I'd seen in conversations like this earlier, every set of eyes abruptly focused more sharply on me at my comment about stress. No one had mentioned Celestine's death so far, so I had to assume her "accident" had been kept as quiet as possible, but Dad's colleagues must have at least known she'd left. Now I could add a new dimension to their thoughts.

"Has he been pursuing a new project that's been giving him some difficulty?" the witch's husband asked.

"I'm not even sure," I said with a wave of my hand and a laugh—a laugh I let sound a tiny bit forced. "He's been holed up in his rooms so much in the last couple weeks, so dedicated to whatever he's doing. I'm sure having all this company will do him some good. But it's been ages since I talked to you. How is your daughter doing in her new job?"

Just like that, I changed the subject—but I could see their gazes linger a little longer than usual, speculatively, when Dad entered the room. They wouldn't say anything outright to him, of course. But I'd planted a few more seeds of doubt about his mental well-being.

That knowledge made me feel powerful and slimy all at once. I closed my eyes for a second, reminding myself of Gabriel's comment about the fox in a snare. I was biting my way out the only way I knew how, to free myself and my consorts. My guys were here with me even if they couldn't be in the manor.

A bell rang to summon us for dinner. My pulse kicked up a notch. "Tell me more about your research into traditional wand-making," I said to Killian as we moved toward the hall, to distract myself from my nerves

—and to set the stage even more. "I've been even more curious about how methods have changed since seeing that artifact my dad brought back from Cairo. Are there a lot of differences across witching communities in different cultures?"

Killian started rambling on about the contrast between Eastern and Western magical tools, and I watched the party-goers around us. In the dining room, everything was laid out as I'd placed it before the party. The wand case sat in front of Dad's chair. I took my seat at his right, Killian finally letting go of my arm. My heart thumped even harder as Dad settled into his chair. His eyes flickered toward the wand case, pulled away, and flickered back again.

My magic was working, drawing him in.

Our guests gathered all around the huge table. The servers swept around them, setting down plates of the appetizer. The tart and savory smell made my mouth water even though my stomach was too twisted up for me to look forward to eating.

Well, I wasn't going to be doing much eating tonight anyway. It was kind of a shame, all that good food that was going to go to waste.

I almost laughed—possibly hysterically—at that thought. My fingers clenched together in my lap. Then I made myself tap Dad's elbow.

I'd done everything I could to prepare. It was time to see this plan through.

"You should give a little speech," I said. "Now that we've got everyone in the same room. A toast or whatever."

"Of course," Dad said, patting my hand. "You think of everything, don't you?"

He stood up, and the chatter around the table quieted. Everyone looked to him.

"Friends and colleagues," Dad said. "I'm honored to have you here today, and to have orchestrated the deal we're all celebrating, which will bring even more security and prosperity into our community. I have to of course give thanks to my two long-time associates who helped broker that deal..."

As he went on giving credit where due and telling a couple of amusing stories about the trip to Cairo to make his audience laugh, I curled my fingers in a quick form under the table. A tiny jolt of magic to fully activate the energy with which I'd imbued the wand. I didn't even look at the case, just kept my gaze on Dad with an encouraging smile, as if I had no idea what was coming.

The servers brought another set of plates out, and Dad reached for the wand's case. "It's also my pleasure," he said, an eager glint lighting in his eyes, "to share with you an artifact I brought back from my travels there. I've never seen anything quite like this rare piece before. It cost me a small fortune to obtain it, but well worth it to own an ancient part of our history."

My breath caught as he popped open the case. He lifted out the wand with a grin that was maybe over-wide now. The gems embedded in the wood flashed with more than just the reflection from the crystal chandelier overhead.

An awed murmur passed through the crowd of guests. Killian leaned close. "That *is* a spectacular piece.

Your father didn't mention he'd obtained something like that."

Because he'd been too busy selling me into magical slavery, presumably. I shot my supposed consort-to-be a quick smile, honestly grateful for the opportunity to add to my groundwork. "You'll have to ask him to let you have a closer look later. Although he hasn't let *anyone* touch it since he brought it home." I let out a giggle intended to sound a little nervous. "He snapped at me when I picked it up in his office right after he got back."

The last word was only just dropping from my lips when other breaths caught all around the table. The second part of my spell was bearing fruit.

In a literal sense. As Dad held up the wand, a glimmering image of a tree sprouted up from its tip. It grew up toward the high ceiling and out. The filmy, glowing branches arched over the dining table, glittering apples and pears forming at their tips, as if beckoning the guests to take them. Eddies of wild magic whirled around the room, tracing spirals of sparkles in the air.

The server who'd just walked back in dropped his plate with a crash. He stood stock still, staring. The guests near him jerked around. A few people gasped. One man leapt to his feet.

"Maxim, that's enough. Think of the *company*."

He jerked his gaze toward that server and the other who was gaping motionless on the other side of the room.

But Dad's face was lit with a hungry glow. *More*, my spell would be whispering to him on a level below sound, below thought. *Look what you've created. You have to see more. Can't they all see how beautiful this is?*

"Dad," I said, as if to try to stop him myself. Mr. Frankford, at his other side, sprang up and grasped his hand.

Physical contact was the trigger for my spell to shift again. Anger contorted Dad's face as his friend tried to wrench the wand away from him.

"No!" he shouted. "It's mine. You will all bow down!"

He lashed his arm, and the tree's branches fragmented into blazing vines. They streaked through the air, darting in every direction, searing lines of fire rippling all down their lengths and casting a wavering reddish glow over the room. With a hiss and a crackle, the vines smacked into the witching folk who'd started to get up all around the table, into Frankford and his wife, knocking them to the floor.

I hadn't realized just how terrifying the scene would be in real life. A shriek I didn't have to force burst from my throat as I ducked beside the table. Never mind Jin's artworks—the spell I'd cast already was plenty powerful on its own.

Heat filled the air. A sweat that was both temperature and fear broke over my skin. Frankford was lying on the floor by Dad's other side, clutching at his neck. One of the flaming vines had wrapped around his throat, searing the skin with a burning-flesh smell that made my stomach turn. The veins stood out in his temples as he thrashed.

All that power was mine. And I'd thought I was holding back.

Someone cried out on the other side of the table. There was a thump and the crackle of smashing glass.

The remaining vines whipped through the air overhead, seeking more targets.

Over it all Dad was still hollering in a now-ragged voice. "You think you can hurt me? I'll show you what you get for that. Don't you dare try to cut me down!"

The words barely made sense. But his magic- and fury-addled mind would be seeing the figures around the table lunging at him with spells and weapons. My spell would be telling him he was only defending himself in the moment.

Someone had to stop him. Please, soon. This was enough. But I couldn't be the one to end the spell.

I flinched as a vine blazed past me, even though I knew they were magicked to avoid hurting me. Then a voice charged with power rang out from the end of the room.

"That's enough!"

A wave of magic swept over us, crashing through the vines and throwing me against the floor. My tailbone jarred. In the wake of the new spell, everything was silent except Dad's frantic babbling.

"No. No. It's gone. It can't be gone. I swear, you come into my home and you—"

Hands clapped together. His mouth clamped shut. I peeked out from under the table, my legs shaky, to see one of the older witches standing at the far end of the table. Her power radiated off her as she stared down my dad.

"Someone call the Assembly," she said. "And anyone who can, help me see to the wounded. And get the staff out of here!"

Dad dropped down in his chair, his arms stiff at his sides, his expression rigid. She'd cast another spell on him, one meant to hold him in place, clearly.

Despite everything, my heart wrenched as I got to my feet, taking a step back from him at the same time.

The magic I'd cast would be crumbling away like that burnt belladonna. In a matter of seconds, no shred would remain but the memories that would seem perfectly real in his mind and the actually real memories of all these witnesses. I'd left no chance for anyone to realize that his breakdown had been provoked by an external source. Even the wand, still clutched in his hand, was completely hollow of power now.

Voices carried all around me. People hustled past me to see to Frankford and his wife, the other fallen witching folk with their burns and bruises. Someone—probably Killian—let out a groan of pain behind me. I could only look at Dad.

Check mate, I thought. *I've won.* But the sense of victory came with a discomfort like a thorn digging into my chest.

If there'd been any other way to save my guys, I'd have taken it.

CHAPTER THIRTY-THREE

Rose

I took a sip of my tea as if to compose myself. The honey-laced jasmine flavor did actually settle my racing pulse a little. I brought the cup back to the saucer on my lap and gave the Assembly investigator who'd arrived a half hour ago a pained smile.

"I'm sorry there isn't more I can tell you. Even though he seemed so worked up about his 'artifact' when he got back from Cairo, and even more distracted than usual, I thought it was just excitement about the deal. I never would have thought he'd *hurt* anyone."

It wasn't hard to work a wobble into my voice. I really hadn't thought Dad could be that cruel, not up until the moment when he'd lied so blatantly to my face about his hopes for my consorting.

"Thank you for speaking with me all the same," the woman said, brushing her fawn-brown hair back behind her ear as she considered her notebook. "You've been able to shed some light on his behavior leading up to this incident, at least. I'm sure it's quite a shock, especially when coupled with your— Well, with everything else you've been facing."

My broken engagement, she meant. I bowed my head. Or maybe that was two broken engagements now. Killian had been tended to by a witching doctor and then hightailed it out of my life, thank all that was lit and warm. Enslaving an innocent witch, no problem. Tying himself to a potentially crazed father in law, no thank you. I guessed he had his priorities straight, anyway.

"It's been a difficult few weeks," I said. "What's going to happen to Dad now?"

"We have to wrap up the investigation, and then we'll continue to examine him. There will be reparations to be made, restrictions placed. I expect it'll be some time before we feel he's safe to return to regular society." Her mouth twisted sympathetically. "It's unlikely he'll return home until at least a few months have passed. You'd be best off not waiting for him, Miss Hallowell. While he's in Assembly custody, this estate is under your authority. You should go on with your life as well as you can."

"I'll try," I said. But as I walked her to the front door, a glow was already spreading through my chest. She got into her car and drove off down the road. The sun beamed down over the front gardens, warm and bright. The breeze was rustling through the gardens.

I had no one and nothing to answer to, at least for a short while. I'd even dismissed Mrs. Gainsley this morning. I'd acted distraught, told her I blamed her for not noticing that my father was up to something sinister. It had felt pretty good to say a few cutting things to her even if they weren't exactly the most accurate cutting things. She'd protested, but, like the investigator had said, my word was the law here now.

It didn't even matter if the Assembly decided Dad was ready to come home in just a few months. I'd be twenty-five then. As the only living female Hallowell, now of age, all the family properties would officially belong to me. I'd still have to keep my magic hidden from him, but I could send him off to Portland or wherever else, and there'd be nothing he could do to challenge me.

I was free. For the first time in who knew how long, I was really and truly free.

A smile stretched across my face as I leaned into the sunlight. Then Gabriel came out of the garage, and my lips curved even higher.

I came down the steps to meet him. With Mrs. Gainsley and her husband gone, no staff here on Sunday except a couple of security guards and the woman who handled our weekend cooking and cleaning, there was no reason I couldn't reach out and take his hand.

He ran his thumb over my knuckles with a gentle pressure that sent a pleasant shiver over my skin. "Miss Hallowell," he said in a teasing voice. "I thought I'd see if you'd be interested in taking a drive."

"You know," I said, "that sounds lovely. I know just the place."

I got into the front seat of the Buick next to him, because why not? We weren't likely to pass anyone on the way, and if we did, it wouldn't look all that strange. At least, from what they could see from outside the car. After Gabriel turned onto the road outside, he let his hand drop from the steering wheel to rest on my leg. The warmth of his hand bled through the thin silk of my dress, and heat spiked up my thigh.

The old farmhouse looked different from even when Seth had shown it to me just last week. For one thing, it looked even less old. The clapboard slats had been painted a pale yellow like the porch, a hue that matched the sun's glow. A porch swing hung on gleaming chains beside the front door. And a tall hedge had been planted in a wide rectangle around the back of the house. Voices carried over it as we got out of the car.

A wooden door opened in the hedge and Seth's head poked out. His expression brightened when he saw us. "You made it quickly. Come on back. It's probably about time we took a break."

"You wouldn't be giving us a break if Rose wasn't here," Damon muttered as we slipped into the yard. He stood up from the bed of flowers he'd been planting and wiped his dirt streaked hands on his jeans. "This guy is a slave-driver, just so you know," he said to me, but there was a playful gleam in his dark eyes.

It did look like the bunch of them had been working hard. Kyler set down the bag of mulch he'd been laying along the base of the hedge and grinned, swiping at the sweat-damp curls sticking to his forehead. Jin had been trimming a lilac tree near a wrought-iron bench with a sheen of sweat on his bare shoulders. Seth knelt down to finish assembling the matching chairs. The whole yard smelled like freshly turned earth, the prickly evergreen of the hedge, and the musk of my guys at work.

"Looking at this place, I'm starting to think I'll have to give up that garage apartment after all," Gabriel said. "Good call on the hedges. Tall enough for *lots* of privacy." He tipped his head toward the wall of dense, dark leaves beside us and slung his arm around my waist. Casually, but I felt all four of my consorts mark the gesture in an instant.

"So you finally decided you're joining us, huh?" Damon said, not exactly friendly but not exactly not either.

"If there's room for one more in this group," Gabriel said, holding Damon's gaze. He offered the words like a question.

"As far as I'm concerned, you never left," Jin said as he straightened up. He ran a hand through his blue-streaked hair and shot us a smile.

"I think we all figured it was just a matter of time," Seth added. He tugged the last screw tight with his wrench and set the chair upright.

"Yeah," Kyler said, with an arch of his eyebrows and a wider grin. "What took you so long anyway?"

Gabriel spread his free hand, his mouth curling sheepishly. "I just needed to be sure I was making the right choice—for everyone." His gaze came back to Damon.

Damon ambled up to us with his usual cocky stride. "As long as you remember who was here from the start," he said. He set his hand on my waist just below Gabriel's arm and leaned in for a kiss. I felt Gabriel tense slightly behind me, but then, as Damon angled his head to deepen the kiss, he bent to press a kiss of his own to the back of my neck. Desire unfurled inside me.

Damon stepped back, looking satisfied. Gabriel tucked his head over my shoulder. "Whatever you need, whenever you want me," he said. "This ceremony we need to do—"

I put my hand over his, squeezing his fingers to stop his words.

"We've got time. There's no need for you to rush into it. I wish none of us had needed to rush. As well as that's worked out after all." I beamed at my guys. "And now we're free. I can come see you here every day—spend nights here—you can come to the house. I'll have to figure out the best timing so that it's not noticeable enough for gossip to start in town, but... there'll be no more fiancés. No more estate managers to dodge. No schemes hanging over me. Just us."

"And we're going to be amazing," Jin said. A desire that matched mine colored his voice. He came over to take my other hand.

I tugged him into an embrace, breathing in the lingering scent of paint that always clung to him. When he stepped back, Kyler and Seth had joined the small circle around me. The slimmer twin touched my cheek and kissed me so hard I was breathless when he eased back. Then Seth stepped forward, brushing a strand of hair back from my face, gazing at me so fondly my heart swelled in my chest. It felt ready to burst with all the love I wanted to offer, all the love they were offering me.

"I want to spend as much time as I can with all of

you," I said. I reached to grip Seth's hand. "We'll go out to that old playground and I'll help with the restoration—and then we'll find something new to build for the town."

I looked to Kyler next. "We'll curl up on the sofa and you'll tell me all about your latest discoveries—or the amazing programs *you're* building."

My gaze slid to Jin. "We'll go walking through the estate to find new pockets of inspiration for your art."

I turned to Damon. "We'll steal apples from the orchard and go skinny-dipping in the pond and not care what anyone thinks, like we're kids all over again."

Then I hugged Gabriel's arm, still wrapped around my waist. "We'll race off on your motorcycle to all the places where no one knows where I am and see what new experiences we can dive into, with home always right here to come back to."

"Sounds like nirvana to me," Jin said. "But you know, I think right now we should be celebrating *your* accomplishments." He teased his fingers down my side, and a fresh quiver of desire ran through me. "From what I've heard, there are a whole lot of beds in that house that need breaking in."

"I'll second that motion," Ky said. He eased past Jin to kiss me again. Then he pulled back far enough to murmur, "There is something I was thinking it'd be fun to try the next time at least a couple of us were together."

I had to laugh. "Have you been researching again?"

His grin turned wicked.

Seth cleared his throat. "Well," he said, "I happen to know that the room with the biggest bed is the one in the attic, which technically is Rose's." His lips twitched upward as he met my eyes. "It's also soundproofed."

A flush washed over me. "All right," I said. "You thought of everything, didn't you?"

"Sounds good to me," Damon said, nudging me toward the house, his eyes dark with hunger. "Let's give the new boy a taste of what he's in for."

"You make it sound like a bad thing," I said.

He chuckled. "Not at all. It's just a matter of whether he can keep up." He aimed a challenging look at Gabriel.

"I'm looking forward to trying," Gabriel said, sounding amused.

Seth led the way into the house and up the stairs. When we reached the attic with its vaulted roof, I sucked in a breath. He hadn't done much decorating yet, but there was a big oak bed with a king-sized mattress, a little reading nook by the dormer window with an armchair, and a low bookcase just begging for me to add some of my books to it. It already felt like home.

Seth smiled at me a little shyly. I pulled him to me and kissed him with all the love and gratitude I had in me. His hands smoothed over the sides of my dress, and others joined them. Damon stroked my hip as he leaned in to kiss the crook of my jaw. Jin grazed the swell of my breast as he nibbled my earlobe. The rising flood of sensation made my head spin.

Damon eased my dress up, sliding it over my head, and Kyler knelt to press his lips to the sensitive skin at the back of my knee. Gabriel claimed my mouth next, cupping my breast through my bra. Jin slid his hand down to the front of my panties. I moaned, rocking into his touch, alight with pleasure.

"What was your big idea, Ky?" Seth asked, his voice thick.

"Mmm. Maximum pleasure for our consort," Ky said. He stood up, his gray-green eyes gone languid in an unexpectedly seductive way. "C'mere, Rose."

The other guys drifted around us as he led me to the bed. My skin tingled with anticipation. "I don't think we want any of this in the way," he said, unclasping my bra. Jin moved to slide down my panties without waiting for instruction. There was the rasp of a zipper as Ky kicked off his own pants. "Stay right there, Jin. We're going to give her everything, inside and out."

Jin's eyes lit with delight. He kissed my thigh, easing his mouth up my leg as Kyler dipped his hand to my sex. I hummed encouragingly. Ky explored the slickness of my folds with a groan.

"Lean over a little—hold on to the bed post?" he murmured. I did, my fingers curling around the polished wood, my feet edging apart instinctively. He rubbed his rigid cock over the curve of my ass and then down to my core.

"Fuck," he muttered. Then he was sliding inside me with an eager thrust that sent a jolt of bliss through me. I gasped and moaned.

Jin took that as his cue. He set his mouth over the front of my sex and flicked his tongue against my clit. I cried out louder as ecstasy spiked through my nerves. My spark shot higher, blazing through my nerves.

"Oh, God," Ky said, thrusting slow and steady. "I

love being inside you." He pushed himself in all the way to the hilt, sending pleasure shuddering through me.

Damon came up beside me. He kissed me on the mouth, swallowing my next moan, and then sat on the edge of the bed where he was the perfect height to test his teeth against my nipples. Another cry broke from my throat. Jin swiped his tongue over my clit, the rhythm of Kyler inside me pressing me harder against the other guy's mouth, and it was a wonder I didn't explode right then.

Through the haze of bliss, I raised my head. My gaze locked with Gabriel's, watching where he stood by the bed. His face was flushed and his eyes bright, but he was holding back as if he wasn't quite sure how he fit in. The bulge of his cock strained against the fly of his jeans. Spark help me, I wanted him too. Wanted him to know how much he was a part of this crazy wonderful love we were making.

I motioned to him and to the bed with my free hand. He climbed onto the mattress, coming to a stop on his knees a foot away from me. He bent down to kiss me, and I hooked my fingers over the waist of his jeans. Closer. Off.

He sucked in a breath as I slid his cock free from his boxers. I swiveled my tongue around the head, and he groaned. "Rose," he said, sounding almost incredulous. Incredulous but happy.

Seth clambered onto the bed too, sprawling with his back against the pillows. I glanced at him as I stroked Gabriel's cock. Seth shook his head with a smile that looked totally relaxed and freed his own cock from his slacks.

"You and I got first shot christening this place," he said. "I'm happy to watch—and I've got a great view right here."

He rubbed his hand up and down his erection. The sight of him touching himself turned me on even more, another burst of pleasure rushing through me alongside the heady burn inside me and the quivering of my nerves around my clit and my nipples.

I lowered my mouth to Gabriel's cock, letting the rocking of my body guide it to the back of my throat. His hand fisted my hair. "Oh, yeah. Just like that. You're amazing, Rose."

Damon bit down on one nipple. I gasped and sucked Gabriel down even deeper. Ky picked up the pace of his thrusts, and my legs started to wobble. Pleasure surged up through me, my spark searing higher with it, building and building, and Jin scraped his teeth over my clit and—

Fireworks burst behind my eyes as that immense wave of bliss crashed over me. I moaned, my mouth clamping around Gabriel's cock.

"So good," Ky said, his thrusts becoming erratic. "Rose." His hips stuttered with a hot spurt. I sucked Gabriel hard, riding out the wave, and he came too with a salty gush. Then he was pulling me up to kiss me on the mouth.

The moment he let me go, Damon hooked an arm around my waist and tipped over with me onto the bed. He kissed me hard and murmured by my ear, "Ready for round two, angel?"

"Fuck, yes," I managed to mumble. The aftershock of my first orgasm was still ringing in my veins, but a fresh wave of desire coursed through me.

Damon slid into me with one quick thrust, and I nearly tipped over the edge again just like that. Jin was scooting onto the bed next to us. I reached to grip his cock, and he groaned. I stroked him in time with Damon's already shaky thrusts inside me.

"Tell me you're almost there," Damon said. "Let me take you all the way."

"Please," I said around a whimper, arching my hips to meet him. He plunged into me even harder, and I lost it again, every nerve singing with the flood of ecstasy.

Jin braced his hand over mine, and we finished him off together. My head rolled back just in time to see Seth coming with us, his gaze fixed on me.

I flopped back on the bed, boneless and sated. The guys snuggled around me, an arm looping over me here, a face nestling against me there. I sighed and wriggled deeper into their combined embrace.

For a while we just floated on the afterglow. But as I came down, a totally different—maybe even silly—but no less potent desire rose up inside me.

"You know what?" I said.

"What, Rose?" Gabriel said, kissing my hip.

I ran my hand over his soft hair. "I want to do something totally, amazingly normal with all of you. Let's... let's go make lunch. And watch TV. And argue about who's going to take out the garbage."

"That would be Seth!" Damon announced. "He cares the most."

Seth laughed.

I made a face. "Okay, maybe we can skip the arguing part. But you know what I mean."

"Yeah," Kyler said. "I think we do."

We peeled ourselves off the bed and managed to reconstruct our clothing into some semblance of neatness. In the big, sunny kitchen on the first floor, I found Seth was one step ahead of me there. A fresh loaf of bread I was going to bet his and Kyler's mom had baked sat on the counter. There were cold cuts and cheese in the fridge.

I grabbed them. Jin started slicing the bread. Damon brandished a knife with the mayo. Gabriel searched through the cupboards until he found some plates, and Ky studied the offerings with a thoughtful eye.

"The best combination of flavors would definitely have to be pastrami and Swiss," he said. "But turkey and Havarti can give it a run for its money."

"We're making sandwiches, not science experiments," Damon said.

Ky shrugged with a brilliant smile. "Same difference."

"From an artistic standpoint," Jin put in, "we could really use some pickles. That splash of green will tie it all together."

"Add it to the list," Seth said, jabbing his thumb toward a magnetic pad on the fridge.

Gabriel chuckled, shaking his head, and went to write it on. I looked around at all of them—my guys, together the way we should be—and a lump of emotion filled my throat.

Here we were. One big, weird, spectacular family. I didn't care if I never got to show another person outside this house my magic. I had everything I could have wanted from my life right here.

"Turkey for me, please," I said, leaning across the counter to grab it. My fingers had just closed around the package when the front door slammed open.

"Stay where you are!" a sharp female voice rang out. "Hands up and still."

My heart lurched. We all froze. Damon's fingers tightened around his knife as several sets of footsteps thumped into the house behind me.

"I said hands *up*," the woman snapped. "Rose Hallowell, and possibly present company as well, you're being taken into custody by the order of the Assembly."

ABOUT THE AUTHOR

Eva Chase lives in Canada with her family. She loves stories both swoony and supernatural, and strong women and the men who appreciate them. Along with the Witch's Consorts series, she is the author of the Dragon Shifter's Mates series, Demons of Fame Romance series, the Legends Reborn trilogy, and the Alpha Project Psychic Romance series.

Connect with Eva online:
www.evachase.com
eva@evachase.com

Made in the USA
Las Vegas, NV
17 February 2023

67697903R00187